The Truth Behind the SHADOW

ELENA MARICA

First published in Great Britain by Elena Marica

Copyright © Elena Marica 2015

The rights of Elena Marica to be identified as author of this work has been asserted in accordance with section 77 and 78 of the Copyright, Design and Patent Act 1988.

All rights reserved

No part of this publication may be reproduced, stored in a retrieval system, or transmitted in any form or by any means (electronic, mechanical, photocopying, recording or otherwise), without the prior written permission of the copyright owner.

A CIP catalogue record for this book is available from the British Library.

ISBN: 978 - 0-9934402-1-2

This book is a work of fiction. Names, characters, places and incidents are either a product of the author's imagination or are used fictitiously. Any resemblance to actual people, living or dead, events or locales, is entirely coincidental.

To all those who still believe in true love

Prologue

Julia Belmonte, a top model, is drawn to a crazy passion where her successful career takes second place for a short space of time. The intricate love story with the American billionaire, the passionate sex and higher state of love, would make Julia the queen of this story.

Chapter One

Alejandro Quintana's private jet touched down in Milan in the early evening. During the flight from New York, the skies had been clear and time was on their side, but now the clouds tinged pink as the sun slipped over the horizon. As the jet taxied to a halt, Alejandro glanced across the aisle at Jack Walker, his chief financial officer.

Together, they made a formidable partnership in the luxury yacht business. The two men disembarked in companionable silence, each thinking through his part in the deal they hoped to close tomorrow.

As they exited the terminal, the sleek black sedan that Alejandro preferred to use in Milan pulled up to the curb.

"Nice timing, buddy," Jack said.

"Nothing but the best," Alejandro said, smiling. "I promised myself that once I made The Signature

Quintana number-one in the industry, I would never wait at the airport again."

Jack raised his eyebrows and Alejandro added, "There's too much work to be done to spend my time on the sidewalk."

Jack laughed, and the two men got into the car as the driver loaded their bags into the trunk. Alejandro smiled grimly and reached for his phone. As much as he enjoyed traveling to Italy, feeling an ancestral connection to the country, this deal was crucial and his focus had to be on tomorrow's meeting.

"We're on our way to the hotel, Nino," he said over the phone, keeping his voice low. "Make sure everything is ready for the meeting with the Russian clients tomorrow. And call the Genovese Port Authority and check that the yachts are in good condition after transport."

"Everything is okay." Nino Rondine's voice was brisk; the sign of a man who knew his boss needed facts, not reassurance. "I've already checked. The new transportation company we hired is very professional and the yachts have arrived with no damage."

"Good." Alejandro caught Jack's eye and nodded before turning back to the call. "Those yachts cost me a fortune, and the Russians put down a big deposit. I don't want any surprises tomorrow."

"No problem," Nino assured him.

"See you tomorrow then." Alejandro disconnected and tucked his phone into the breast pocket of his well-cut suit.

"I'm beginning to think you don't trust my skills anymore." Jack's voice was light, but Alejandro recognized the concern underneath. Jack Walker was one of the best numbers men in the business, but his newly-finalized divorce had shaken Jack's confidence. *Hopefully he'll recover soon;* thought Alejandro—they couldn't afford any distractions until this deal was signed and delivered.

"Of course I do," Alejandro said. "I just want to make sure everything is perfect. And speaking of the meeting, are all the papers ready and the contract prepared?"

"Chill, Alejandro, that's my job," Jack said. "Try to relax. There's a big fashion show on tonight, a great opportunity for you to unwind."

"I'm not sure about going out tonight," Alejandro said his mind still full of foreign exchange numbers and docking charges.

The car pulled up at the The Exclusive Hotel before Jack could protest, and a smartly dressed doorman opened the door and ushered the two men into the lobby. Alejandro smiled at Jack's awe. They were both self-made men, but Alejandro's parents had brought Italian culture and an appreciation for fine living with them when they immigrated to New York. Jack's Midwestern upbringing had been loving, but lacking in material comforts. His mouth still gaped in awe whenever they found themselves in luxurious surroundings, and even Alejandro found himself gazing with appreciation at The Exclusive's blend of historic architecture and contemporary Italian design.

"It's the best place to stay. We're right in the heart of Milan, near the Opera and the Cathedral." Alejandro loved Milan. The elegant lifestyle, designer boutiques, fines dining, and the amazing museums and cathedrals. He was glad to share his beloved city with his friend.

When they reached the penthouse floor Alejandro said, "I'm tired. I'll take a shower while you check over the papers. Maybe we should both turn in early."

The valet opened the main door of his suite and Alejandro stepped in, looking appreciatively at the lush surroundings and remembering the marbles soaking tub from his last stay here. His mesmerized eyes glimmered at the gilded trimmings, plush curtains, and innumerable decorative silk pillows which hinted at regal and timeless opulence. It never failed to amaze him. He walked across the carpeted floor and twirled the shining faucet.

"Maybe a bath."

"Someone's getting too old to party?" Jack shot him a grin and followed Alejandro into his room. "The runway starts at eight, and we're on the list for Ruben's after party. Tonight's our night to have some fun!"

After setting Alejandro's leather case on the luggage rack, the valet accepted a generous tip and left with Jack's luggage, bound for the other suite.

Alejandro turned to Jack.

"Why it is so important for us to go to this fashion show?"

"Because Ruben is my best friend from high school, and has beautiful models working for him," Jack replied. "I remind you, we are in the capital of the fashion world. The most gorgeous women from everywhere come here to be discovered. And I feel like doing some discovery tonight."

"I'm beginning to think you are addicted to women," Alejandro said.

"Oh please." Jack waved a dismissive hand. "What do you expect me to do? Wait for Cindy to come back?"

"That might not be such a bad idea." Alejandro smiled, but he hoped Jack would never take back the woman who had cheated on him more than once, before she'd found a richer man. Still, waiting instead of diving into a new relationship couldn't hurt. Jack needed to bide some time to absorb some of the lessons from his previous relationship. He'd been much older than Cindy and no one had expected the marriage to last. Alejandro had hated hearing the gossip about his friend, but also knew the truth—*she had* married Jack for his money, Jack *had* been sucked in by her spell binding vile ways, and he had also been relieved of a large chunk of his fortune very quickly.

"I can't believe she left me after everything I did for her." Jack stared out the window, a disgruntled expression crossing his face.

Alejandro couldn't help pointing out the obvious. "Her current man is a billionaire."

"Yeah," Jack snapped irritably. "I guess that's moving on up. Anyway, she's beautiful and she seemed like fun, but as a wife I can assure you she turned out to be a big waste of time. Not interested in the bedroom. All she wanted to do was shop and get Botox."

"Don't say I didn't warn you about marrying a woman twenty years your junior," Alejandro said.

"I admit it—you were right. Forget about Cindy. Let's enjoy. I think we should go to this show and look at babes."

"I gave up those kinds of things a long time ago," Alejandro replied, as he took his jacket off and placed it on the elegant suede leather sofa.

"Right," Jack said. "And that's exactly why you're

still single at thirty-four."

"Agreed." Alejandro shot him a grin. "Success is a lonely and difficult path."

"Thank you for that sage advice," Jack said, punching Alejandro lightly in the shoulder. "You need to loosen up. Maybe it's your lucky night. The woman of your dreams has to be out there somewhere, and you're not going to meet her in a hotel room."

"Oh thanks," Alejandro said. "Advice from a man who's so good at love."

"That's funny, coming from you!" Jack said. "We're in Milan. You told me Milan was, and I quote, 'INCREDIBLE.' Is spending the night in a hotel room the experience you had in mind?"

"You're not going to give up, are you? Go get settled in your room and unpack. I'll meet you downstairs in the bar—have a drink; I may be a few minutes late."

Alejandro headed for the bathroom, not sure if he really needed a night out, and at a fashion show, no less. There was work to be done. Anything else can surely wait.

Chapter Two

Alejandro couldn't complain about the view—they'd been ushered to seats in the front row, the girl with the clipboard finding Jack's name on the list as a personal friend of Ruben's. But watching the girls parading the catwalk in extravagant clothes left him cold. *Nothing interesting here*, he thought. This wasn't his kind of night. In fact, he was getting bored.

A burst of applause yanked him from his thoughts and he looked up curiously. A woman appeared at the far end of the runway, and as she posed, the music changed to a deeper house beat, the colored lights flashing in sync with the music. She began to walk, and unlike the hard, stomping strides of the other models, this woman moved sinuously with panther-like grace, her perfect body clad in a short, sophisticated white dress. Part of him knew it was the magic of the moment, the sounds and the setting, but still, she oozed confidence and strength, and it appeared the world was at her feet.

Alejandro put a finger to his mouth, leaned back and appraised her, trying to catalogue what it was that made her such a standout—just as he did with the lines of his beautiful boats. She was tall, her long legs toned and the muscles sculpted softly, as though she worked out. Her long black hair fell like silk to her shoulders, and her tanned olive skin contrasted with the deep, red lipstick she wore. *Irresistible.* Alejandro found himself mesmerized, caught in the spell of her emerald-green eyes. This was the type of woman he dreamed of, the type of woman he'd thought was a futile dream.

He turned to Jack. "God, that woman takes my breath away. I've met some beautiful women in my life, but she is intoxicating me with her beauty."

"Julia Belmonte. She's twenty-four, been on Ruben's list for seven years, since she started working," Jack said.

"Do you believe in love at first sight?" Alejandro shook his head as he stared at her—at *Julia*—on the catwalk. "Somehow, one day, this woman is going to be my wife."

"You sure know how to pick." Jack followed Alejandro's gaze as the model hit the other end of the catwalk and was bathed in an explosion of flashbulbs and pulsating lights.

Julia turned and walked smoothly back up the runway. As she passed the two men, Alejandro found himself willing her. *Look at me, look at me.* As if his thoughts had been shouted aloud, she turned her head a fraction and smiled slightly, showing pearly white teeth.

Alejandro couldn't take his eyes from her. *How could this be possible?*

"This girl has something special, am I right?" Jack nudged him and Alejandro turned to his CFO.

"I have to meet her. Tonight. Will she be at Ruben's after party?"

"I can ask." Jack looked at Alejandro, smirking.

"What's so funny?"

"Success is a lonely and difficult path, right?"

"I changed my mind. As you said, tonight's our night, so let's enjoy it."

"Sure," Jack said. "I just don't want to see you disappointed. Julia's—well; she's not like any woman you've ever known. And she's not easy to impress."

"Are you saying she is too good for me?" Alejandro frowned.

"I'm just saying the Alejandro I know is too smart to fall for a girl you've never even talked to."

"Maybe you have forgotten a small detail about me," Alejandro said. "When I want something, I always get it."

Jack stared back at him seriously. "I know. Everyone knows that about you. But women like Julia are sought after by many men. You're not the only one who'll fall for her. Ruben says she's pretty quiet about her personal life—maybe she's not even single."

"I'm Alejandro Quintana and I do not compare myself with others."

"You're a grown man and I sure can't stop you from whatever dumbass plan you have."

Alejandro frowned again. "It was your idea to come to this fashion show, but now I have the impression that you are not so pleased."

Jack gave him a wicked smile. "I just want to warn you, women like Julia will always take full advantage."

"I'll keep that in mind." Impatience surged through Alejandro. He and Jack were good friends, but after Jack's last experience, what business did he have giving advice on love? "What the hell is your problem? Find your friend Ruben, and find out where they're going after the show."

Julia's dresser helped her remove the sexy black evening number she'd worn to close the show, and passed her a short silk robe before leaving to hang up the couture gown. Julia removed the dramatic makeup she'd worn for the runway with two quick swipes of a cleansing cloth, and began to apply the simpler look she preferred for going out. Her olive skin needed no foundation. She framed her clear emerald eyes with only a thick coat of mascara and a hint of eyeliner. She saw a figure advancing in the mirror and turned as Ruben came in and stood beside her.

"You were beautiful tonight! Once again, the audience was crazy for you. I think the designer is a little jealous, but your picture in his dress will hit so many covers, he would be a fool to complain."

"In this world you need to always be at the top." Julia winked at her agent as she applied lip gloss.

"Right on." Ruben nodded in agreement. "Sometimes I wonder how you manage to keep all those people loving you so much."

"That's my job. On time, happy face, pretty poses. A face is nothing without hard work and a professional attitude."

"Well you certainly do it well. Most models are basket cases. Am I fat, am I pretty, and does anyone like me? I have never seen a woman as secure in herself as you are."

"You have helped me find that security, my friend." Julia had fought for success and grasped every opportunity, ever since she'd done her first shoot at sixteen. Now she was finally famous, and she had her enough money to do whatever she wanted. She loved job, loved knowing how to turn and look, how to make the heads turn, and make the most of what God and her magnificent genes had given her, loved that she could control every movement and create perfection—or as close as any human woman could get.

Ruben watched Julia brush her hair, the long, lush mass she'd refused to cut, no matter the dictates of fashion. "I still can't believe that a beautiful woman like you is still single."

Thoughts flew through Julia's mind. In her time as a model, she'd had to be strong and she'd had to sacrifice, and she was never going to give it up. Not until she aged out, and definitely not for a man. She hesitated for a second before responding.

"I want to concentrate on my career, especially now. This is my best moment and I want to live it while it lasts. And anyway, I haven't met Mr. Perfect yet and I don't want to settle for Mr. Good Enough." Thinking about giving up her job—the thing she loved most in the world — made her uncomfortable and she changed the subject. "I thought we could go for that dinner tonight? Before the party?"

"Of course. Let's celebrate our success. By the way, some friends of mine from America are coming with us," Ruben added.

Julia wasn't surprised. Ruben always invited his friends for dinner after the fashion show. Some of them mooned around her like lovesick calves, some of them tried to play it cool, but all of them were—eventually—boring. She'd be polite and let them dominate the conversation, extending an impression that she was awed by their charm, while she relaxed and enjoyed fine wine and delicious food. Over the years, she'd mastered this skill, and somehow she enjoyed it. Every time she was introduced with yet another complicated personality which failed to impress her. Yes, Julia was looking forward to a night out. *Let's see what's in the box this time.*

Chapter Three

Alejandro Quintana was proud of his success. Born in Italy, he'd grown up in New York when his parents immigrated to the United States to give him a better life. Nothing had been handed to him. He mused as he waited for Jack. He had worked for everything he'd gotten, and he'd finally bought the company where his father had worked for more than twenty-five years, ushering it to heights beyond expectations.

Alejandro's management degree and natural skills had built the company up quickly, and it wasn't long before The Signature Quintana had become well-known and respected and started billing millions of dollars each year. It had been Jack's suggestion to open more branches. On their list of places full of fashionable people with disposable wealth, Italy had called...and here Alejandro was.

Jack met him on the sidewalk outside the palazzo that had held the fashion show. "Ruben's asked us to join him for dinner."

"And?" asked Alejandro.

"And meet Julia Belmonte."

Alejandro smiled. Back in the country he loved, and about to meet the woman of his dreams.

At the table in the small *restaurant*, Ruben introduced Jack and Alejandro as his American friends, "But it's been quite a long time since we caught up." Ruben turned to Jack. "When you called me from New York, I couldn't believe you still had my number."

"When I called you I wasn't sure you'd still have the same number!" Jack laughed. "It's been more than two years since I've seen you."

"The agency keeps me busy," Ruben said. "Tell me, how is your beautiful young wife—Cindy?"

"Okay—well, we're divorced," Jack muttered.

Alejandro noticed Jack's embarrassment and picked up his glass. "I think we should drink to the beautiful models here tonight."

He glanced up as Julia crossed the restaurant from the ladies room.

"I see you have noticed our beautiful angel." Ruben moved his chair to make space for Julia to sit down, across from Alejandro. His eyes twinkled, and Alejandro knew Jack must have said something. They all clinked glasses, and Jack and Ruben smiled knowingly at each other.

"I've been meaning to ask you," Alejandro said. "Where do you find such beautiful models?"

"All over the world." Ruben smiled. "But Julia is my favorite; she is from Argentina."

"You are very lucky," Alejandro stared at Julia hungrily. *One day she will be mine.*

"Yes, I am very lucky indeed." Ruben said. "She bills more hours than any of my other girls."

Jack caught Alejandro's eye and gave a wide grin. Alejandro leaned closer.

Jack whispered, "This is a challenge you're not going to win, buddy."

Alejandro frowned. This was an unfamiliar feeling. He was not used to losing control. True, Julia Belmonte was one of the most beautiful women he had ever seen, but this was more than just her beauty; there was something that pulled him to her. An irresistible force he couldn't explain. As she talked in her amiable voice, he wanted her to keep talking. A curious paradox shadowed his mind. He wanted her to talk to him, but at the same time he was devoid of any conversational skills.

Across the table Julia was checking her phone. She

seemed unaware of Alejandro's presence—certainly, she wasn't paying him any attention—but Alejandro couldn't take his eyes off her.

"Do you enjoy doing shows in Milan?" he finally asked.

Julia made a noncommittal noise, still typing on her phone. Alejandro's interest was fired even more—he was not used to being ignored. By anyone. *Is she playing hard to get?*

Conviction filled him. *Jack must be finding it hilarious.* He would not give up easily, no matter what Jack thought. The moment Alejandro had seen Julia smile at him before she left the catwalk; a tremble had run through him. *Anticipation.* He would have this woman. He would win her.

Jack looked from tycoon to supermodel, still smiling. Alejandro beckoned Jack to lean closer and spoke in a low voice.

"I will not leave the city until she is in my bed."

"Whatever you say, Alejandro. She doesn't seem to care about anything but herself," Jack said. "I think you're wasting your time. Give up."

"Soon she will care about someone else." Alejandro didn't care what Jack thought. Julia was the woman he had always pictured for himself and nothing could stop him from this radical pursuit.

Ruben interrupted them. "So, Alejandro, did you enjoy the fashion show?"

"Yes I did. It was a very nice collection, indeed. I was very pleased to be there tonight." Alejandro didn't take his eyes from Julia as he spoke. Julia didn't take her eyes from her phone either.

"She's toying with you." Jack whispered. "She doesn't care about men."

"That's what they all say," Alejandro murmured. "But I know better." He watched as Julia wiped a napkin across her lips and continued to ignore him. As he watched, she checked the time and stood, turning to Ruben.

"It is past midnight. It's time for me to leave."

"Why so early?" Jack teased. *You're not Cinderella.*

"Because it's past midnight, and it's time for me to be in my bed." Julia laughed delightfully and impacted at Alejandro's heart, shattering it to a thousand pieces as if it didn't had room for anymore bliss. *She had such a pretty laugh.*

"Are you sure?" Ruben asked. Jack knew his friend loved playing Cupid. Despite his warnings, he hoped Ruben would be able to entice her to stay.

Julia raised an eyebrow. "Yes, I am sure."

"I'll take you home." Ruben stood, shrugging his

shoulders at the other two men.

"It's not necessary; the taxi driver is waiting for me downstairs." Julia kissed Ruben on both cheeks and turned to leave, still totally ignoring Alejandro and Jack.

"I'll see you tomorrow. Take care," Ruben said, sitting back down and picking up his glass.

Alejandro was dismayed. His dream woman was leaving and he hadn't exchanged ten words with her. *What am I supposed to do now, run behind her and tell her I am crazy about her?* No, he needed to keep cool.

Jack placed a hand on his shoulder.

"Not much luck there, my friend."

"I can assure you, one day this woman is going to fall for me." Alejandro was suddenly, irrationally irritated. Jack had put his fear into words.

"Well, so far she doesn't seem to have any interest in you," Jack replied.

Alejandro threw him a look. "You certainly know how to put me off, don't you? Maybe we should get back to the hotel."

"That might be a good idea." Jack shot him another grin. "There's no action here anymore."

Chapter Four

The sun pouring through the window woke Julia late the next morning. It was in the middle of March, but Milan was graced with a beautiful sunny day, as if spring was around the corner. As she brewed her coffee, her thoughts returned to the strange night she'd had. Her phone chimed, and she rooted it out of her handbag.

Remember lunch!

Samantha knew her only too well. They'd been firm friends since meeting four years ago, when Samantha had been dating Julia's friend Roberto Benetti. Julia had been struck by Samantha's absolute confidence, and her striking eyes, which held many shades of brown, like the amber of the sun setting behind the mountains, had made an immediate impression. Julia had never seen such strange eyes before. Samantha's red, curly hair brushed her shoulders, and she was pretty and smart enough to have caught Julia's attention. They'd become close friends, and since Julia had made her home base in Milan, where Samantha's law firm was based, the two women met as often as the long hours of their high-powered careers allowed. Julia knew Samantha sometimes envied the high-fashion life—last week, she'd said, "I wish I was like you, Julia." Julia had only shrugged and asked, "Why?"

Julia finished her coffee and dressed, selecting an aqua-green top that showed off her olive skin and gave her a chic, romantic look, a pair of skinny trousers, nude heels and a stylish light jacket. By the time she reached the restaurant, the always-prompt Samantha was waiting for her at a table on the terrace. They kissed each other's cheeks.

Now her friend greeted her. "You don't give a damn if someone is waiting hours for you." Samantha waved the waiter over and ordered champagne.

"People have to wait for me if they need me," Julia replied. "That's my motto and I'll stick with it." *Maybe that's why Samantha admires me. My self-confidence.*

"So why are you late today?" Samantha asked.

Julia slowly lowered her glamorous sunglasses and looked over them. "I woke up late; I had a mental night!"

"That's always your excuse," Samantha pointed out.

"Not this time. I really did have a crazy night. Jesus, you wouldn't believe it." Julia smiled at Samantha, knowing her friend couldn't resist the bait. And she wanted to tell someone about Alejandro. *She needed to.*

Samantha grinned at her.

"Okay, okay, let's hear what happened this time."

"You think I am inventing some excuse?" Julia raised a sarcastic eyebrow.

The waiter suddenly appeared to pour glasses of champagne, and Julia checked him out. Her gaze flustered him and he barely stopped himself from spilling the sparkling wine, his hands shaking. When he left, they burst out laughing together.

"He came out from nowhere," Julia said.

"Don't you worry about him. Carry on, what happened last night? How was the show?"

"The show was fine—but last night, after, Ruben took me for dinner with the other models and some of his friends. There was this man…he watched me the entire night. On the catwalk and then afterward at the restaurant."

"That's interesting! A man was staring at you. As per usual. Carry on!"

Julia looked at her friend, amused; she knew Samantha was always up for listening when it came to men. Julia sipped her champagne, drawing out the moment.

Sure enough, Samantha asked, "Was he good looking?"

"I couldn't see him very well because I was concentrating on avoiding his gaze. He didn't take his eyes off me all night!"

"What do you mean; you didn't see him very well? He was sitting at the same table!"

"He made me nervous. I pretended to look at my phone the whole time, and whenever I tried to look up, he was staring at me. I had to keep looking away. All I saw was dark hair, intensely blue eyes…and his elegant and stylish suit. That I could look at and it didn't stare back."

"So this blue-eyed, well-dressed friend of Ruben's was interested in you, and you didn't even give him a chance to speak?"

Julia bit her lip, unsure for once. "I know. I was kind of scared. He unsettled me. He didn't take his eyes off me the whole night, not once. Like I told you, it made me nervous, and I was upset with Ruben, too—I don't know why he invites people to our table! Then this morning, on my way here, Ruben called. He told me that this man is a very important person in America and has a huge company in New York. He comes to Milan often for business."

"Well, nothing out of the ordinary!" Samantha exclaimed louder than she realized. "He's just a rich man—you've been chased by plenty of those!" The couple at the next table turned around and Samantha gave them a sharp look.

"Samantha—" Julia replied quietly, because the last thing she needed was to attract attention off the catwalk, on her own time, "—what do you mean by that?"

"You should talk to him. Get his number from Ruben." As Samantha spoke, Julia could see her calculating. "He's rich and important, you're a famous model. That's a good match."

"I don't think you get the point. I am an independent woman and I won't choose a man just because he is rich. Money is not everything, you know that!"

"Oh, come on Julia, without money we go nowhere in life! Lucky us, we have our careers; we can take care of our own lifestyle. But having more money won't kill anyone," Samantha added with a grin. "And you know what? You should start to live your life. You're twenty-four years old, for God's sake! You've been single for more than a year! After you broke up with your last boyfriend it seemed like you lost interest in all men. It's not natural."

"Maybe you are right," Julia said. "But I don't want to take that risk. To fall for someone and go through that hurt again."

"Life is just one shot, darling, so enjoy it! And who said you needed to fall in love?"

"Oh come on, Samantha. We are not here to discuss my future. First of all, I don't need a man in my life now, and second, I am very happy with my life the way it is."

"No doubt about that." Samantha picked up her glass of champagne and looked over the rim at Julia. "You've made it perfectly clear. I can see the happiness."

"Very amusing," Julia said.

"Well, I'm not as lucky as you, with all the men you get," Samantha replied.

"Your life is much more interesting than mine. All those clients you fuck around with when they are 'in crisis'?"

Samantha extended a sultry smile. "It helps them get over their divorces."

Julia couldn't help laughing.

Samantha drained her glass and set it down with a click. "Oh, great! Now it's you laughing at me." She summoned the waiter with a graceful gesture. "Anyway, we'd better wrap up—I have a deposition in half an hour."

"What's it about?" Julia asked.

Samantha leaned in and lowered her voice. "Can you imagine, my client embezzled a few millions from his own company, claims his ex-wife did it, and now he's suing her to get the money back. They're both completely bonkers."

"You are the best with the bonkers cases."

"If I win this case it's not going to reflect well on my career. I'm hoping they'll agree to mediation. Meanwhile, Mr. Bonkers and I are having a lovely time. He's…luscious."

"Always a new conquest." Julia smiled at her friend, and then sighed. For Samantha, a man was fun while the affair lasted, then she moved on to the next one as efficiently as closing a case.

Samantha pushed back her chair, then stood up and put her jacket on. "Call me later; I want to find out more about this mysterious stranger."

"I'm not going to call Ruben up and ask him. I don't want to chase after a man, no matter how intriguing."

Samantha gave her a long look. "Have I ever told you you're a stubborn woman?"

Julia smiled back at her. "Only a thousand times maybe?" But that's fine I still like you, you are my best friend."

It was the right thing to say. Samantha gave her a

penetrating gaze like an attorney summing up a witness, then softened and leaned in for a hug. "You always know the right thing to say." They smiled at each other, savoring the moment. Men might come and go, but they would always be best friends. That was the most important thing.

Julia waved as Samantha crossed the piazza, and then turned toward the side street where she'd parked. She felt switched on. *No, she wasn't going to chase after a man. But maybe he'd cross her path again.*

By the time she'd navigated the horrendous Milanese traffic in her brand-new red sport Songentti S90—a treat she'd bought herself to celebrate last year's September cover—Julia had forgotten about the night before and the man who'd stared at her.

She spent the afternoon updating her social media, enjoying seeing the #belmonte hashtag hovering in the top ten, then practiced yoga and ate a light dinner. *Early to bed for me*, she thought, after last night's late night. Last night—better not to think about last night.

But she couldn't sleep. Julia put on the TV, hoping it would lull her brain into relaxation. Flipping channels, she came to a Christmas-themed romantic comedy. She watched for a little while, but it made her sad. *Why put on this kind of movie on in March? No-one should watch this stuff alone.*

The last few years had been very good—certainly, there were ups and downs, but Julia had grasped every opportunity that came her way.

After her first season in Milan, everything had changed. Her face defined the new look. Her confidence made her irresistible to the best designers. Everyone wanted her to wear their clothes, on the catwalk and at red-carpet galas and celebrity-studded parties. She'd signed a fabulous contract with Ruben&Fashion and her life had switched gears faster than she'd dared to imagine. But Julia's inner instincts had kept her safe—she'd made sensible choices with her eyes open, sticking to only the best editorial work and making sure Ruben demanded top dollar for her runway appearances. She'd known from the beginning, as a successful model working only with the best designers, she would make enough money to set up her own business. Her dream—the one she told to no-one—was to open a resort near the sea, perhaps later expanding to build a small hotel in the mountains.

Mountains—that made her think of home. It had been a while since she'd called her mother in Argentina. She pictured her mother sitting by the window overlooking a vast patch of green land. She wondered how much had changed since she left. She reached for the telephone.

"Hi Mamá!"

"Hello my dear! What a pleasant surprise. I was thinking of you the other day."

"I'm sorry. I've been busy at work. How's everything going at home?"

"Here is all good, your sisters and I miss you so much. It's been two years since we've seen you!"

"I know. Tell me about it," Julia sighed. "I miss you all, too. Time goes so fast, but you know I hope I can come soon and we can spend some time together."

"Your sisters will be very happy to see you. And so will I."

"It will be great when we get together again."

"You should not let another Christmas go by!" The voice on the other side trembled a little. Homesickness rushed through Julia.

"I can't wait to enjoy your coffee and fresh biscuits again." She closed her eyes and thought of the small kitchen of her childhood home. She tried to re-embrace the aroma of her Mama's delicacies, but nothing came. Mama loved to cook and every Christmas Eve she spent all day in the kitchen, making a glorious feast.

Minutes later, Julia could almost smell the cinnamon and sweet spices.

She brought her mother up to date on her latest shows. She remembered the time when she could talk for hours with her and the topics hurled like a cyclone, but something felt out of place now. An awkward silence followed every now and then, and Julia had to make an effort to think of a new topic of conversation whenever she felt the current topic was coming to an end. A last, she reassured her that she was safe, and agreed that she shouldn't focus on her career so much that she never saw her family.

"But Mamá, I want to take care of you and the girls. Especially since Papa…"

"We won't talk about that."

Julia turned the conversation to more pleasant things. After she ended the call, she leaned back on the sofa and relaxed, sweet memories lulling her to sleep.

Chapter Five

Alejandro Quintana knew that the Russian investors would not be easy to deal with, but according to Jack they were ready to close the deal today. He was already ready to move on—he wanted to finalize this deal, as he had another meeting lined up with potential investors later in the day.

As Jack and the Russians discussed the contract, Alejandro browsed through the folder of specifications and deck plans and let his thoughts wander. As a boy, his father had often brought him to the dockyard; it kept him out of his mother's hair. He remembered his father's callused hands shaping the boat, the perspiration running down his tired face. He'd tentatively asked, "Papa? Do you think one day I could buy one of these boats?"

"That's my dream for you, Son. To buy and sell these boats instead of sanding and painting."

Alejandro looked at him with admiring eyes. His

father had a gift. He somehow knew the exact spot to put his feet in. He could sense troubled water from a distance and never stepped into a venture of which he was not so sure of.

Alejandro had run his small hand along the smooth wood of the side of the boat—he had already learned that customers who bought a yacht valued quality and design. He'd reached for a towel and wiped his father's brow, promising himself that he would one day make his father proud.

His father's labor had sent him to the best schools, and he'd studied hard to win a scholarship to university, where he finished his degree in Business Administration. He'd secured an entry-level sales position where his sharp eye and easy manner with even the wealthiest patrons had impressed his bosses. He'd paid attention, cultivated relationships, and invested wisely. Eventually he'd been in a position to buy the now-struggling company where his father had worked. With hard work, long hours and skillful handling, Alejandro had transformed it into the most successful custom yacht builder on the East Coast. Each 'The Signature Quintana' yacht was a vessel his father could be proud of.

The boardroom conversation washed over him. Jack was going over wire transfer schedules and delivery dates. Alejandro glanced at Nino Rondine, who also looked bored by the long negotiations. Nino thrived on rainmaking, but once the customers committed to purchase, his job was nearly done. He leaned toward Alejandro, keeping his voice soft.

"I am going to a party next Saturday in Lake Como," Nino said quietly. "You should come with me. Lots of big celebrities. I heard that Ruben is coming, too, and bringing some of his beautiful models."

Alejandro's interest was piqued. His eyes beamed with a distinct vibrancy. "That would be a pleasure."

"We must always appreciate beautiful women," Nino said.

"Maybe, but I am interested in just one," Alejandro replied. "Ever since I met her the other night, I can't get her out of my mind."

"So do I." Nino winked, "Every time I meet every single woman."

"No." Alejandro shook his head. "It's different. I've never felt like this before."

"I think I smell pure love, my friend," Nino said. "Who is she?"

"Oh, you wouldn't happen to know her."

"She does have a name, doesn't she?"

"Her name is Julia Belmonte."

Nino shook his head with a sigh. "If you are talking

about Julia Belmonte the top model, that girl is too spoiled for you."

"Ah." Alejandro gave a low laugh. "You need to get to know people before you catalogue them. I don't think Julia is the ice queen she seems to be."

Nino grinned. "You think?"

"You will see." Alejandro was quite sure about that. Maybe Julia had shown her strong personality that night, but he had seen her eyes, a soft, vulnerable glance when she'd thought he wasn't looking. Those emerald eyes showed a sensitive soul.

"That girl, I think she has left many broken hearts behind," Nino warned.

"That's because she hasn't met me before." Alejandro smiled. He knew he could control his own fate. Julia would be his triumph. She had class and beauty. He knew men found her irresistibly sexy, and women admired her sense of elegance and style.

It was quite obvious people loved her.

And he meant to be the one she loved back.

Chapter Six

On Saturday evening Alejandro dressed with more than his usual care in a classic black suit with an elegant tie, silver and black enameled cufflinks, and his favorite hand-made shoes. He always dressed to perfection, knowing it was important to look his best at all times. He paid attention to every small detail. It took him more than ten attempts to get his satisfactory tie knot.

He stepped out of the elevator and crossed the lobby to the bar, where Nino was waiting for him. Nino's exasperated voice carried clearly through the room, and Alejandro smiled at his friend's demand.

"Would you please bring me another coffee?"

The waitress looked pointedly at the cup in front of Nino. "I hope you can still sleep tonight after all that coffee."

"I hope it will keep me awake!" Nino said. "I am going to have a very long night—I need to be fresh." He spotted Alejandro. "Where have you been? I've been here waiting for you over an hour." It was obvious Nino was losing his patience.

Alejandro winked at the waitress. "I see you have good company. I could make you wait more."

Nino drained the last of his coffee cup. "Are you done with all your many phone calls? Ready to leave now?"

Outside the hotel, Alejandro couldn't resist teasing him. "That waitress was quite pretty, don't you think? Maybe we should stay here in the bar."

"Yes, but not as lovely as my Carla," Nino replied.

"Sometimes I don't understand you. If you love your fiancée so much, why do you never bring her with you?"

Nino laughed. "Because I am a free spirit. Carla is my angel. She likes the quiet life and I like her to be home waiting for me."

"Ah, and I guess that works for you?"

"So far, yes." Nino nodded emphatically as they got into the car and the driver pulled away from the hotel. "About forty five minutes to the party. It's in a beautiful villa on the coast of Lake Como. All the insanely rich people are there tonight."

"Good!" Alejandro was happy to hear that. Lavish parties were the kind of environment where he recharged his energy. He liked to be alert to the foibles of the wealthy people he had to spend time with, to determine their desires so that he could sell them whatever would fulfill. He liked to know how the world around him worked, and he knew how to control it to his advantage.

"The host is Marc Rotoglione. He owns some of the biggest estates in Italy," Nino announced.

"I am looking to buy some property over here. Maybe he could help me."

"If you want to make a good deal, Marc is your man. I'm going to introduce you tonight."

"Wonderful," Alejandro said. He never missed an occasion when it came to business. But tonight was different. He felt like a man on a mission.

Chapter Seven

The beautiful countryside of Lombardy blossomed around the car as Julia drove to Lake Como. This last week she'd been out almost every night, which was a lot for her, but the main collections were over, so she could afford some time for fun. Marc Rotoglione always threw mega-parties, this one for his nineteen-year-old fiancée. Julia suspected the young girl was using him, but Marc was in love with Elsa and spending millions on parties and gifts to make her happy. A week after the two had met, Elsa had moved into the villa, and Marc—twenty-four years Elsa's senior—was making all her wishes come true. Lately Elsa had been saying she wanted a big diamond, and of course she would have it. *What is it that happens to men when they are in love, why is it their judgment becomes impaired?*

Julia sighed. Men were so predictable. You just had to figure out the trick to make it happen, and really, it was all on-the-job training. Clearly Elsa had trained well.

The phone rang insistently, and Julia pressed a button on the dashboard. The voice of a woman reporter from one of the Italian lifestyle magazines filled the car. Julia had been promising her an interview for weeks, and now was as good a time as any. It would make the trip go faster, anyway.

"Miss Belmonte, lets skip the conventional get-to-know and come straight to the point. Why you are in fashion?" the woman asked, her voice was just and almost rhetorical.

"When I moved from Argentina, it had always been my dream. I had a lot of ambition as a young girl, and I was fortunate to be born with the level of beauty to be appreciated in the fashion world."

"And did your parents support your dream?"

"I've been lucky to have the support of many friends and family," Julia said, tenderly but firmly. She certainly wasn't going to have her private life splashed over the pages of a magazine, and she always avoided any questions about her family.

They talked about the fashion scene and Julia's opinion of some up-and-coming designers. Every so often the reporter tried to steer the conversation to something more personal, but Julia didn't tell her any more than what the media already had. She stayed polite and sweet, of course—she was always careful to present a sweet persona to the media.

"I'm at my destination—I'm afraid I must let you go," she said, relieved, turning into the grounds of the villa and parking. She took a golden compact from her bag, checked her lipstick, and lightly touched her hair before stepping out of the car and making her way to the front door. Her slim red dress, the hem just brushing her knee, gave her a seductive look—she knew it would kill.

With small steps, Julia arrived in the well-lit and elegantly designed garden of the villa, humming vibrantly with some country song. The flamboyant foliage swayed meticulously in the tranquil gust. The concrete path led to the center where it divided into two, leading deeper into the garden. A large swimming pool reflected the bright lights on the left corner. She saw Ruben sitting at the table near the pool and started to make her way through the crowd.

"I was waiting for your arrival." A voice materialized out of the thin air, "You are looking very sexy in that dress."

Julia turned as the voice continued. "You're going to be the shining light of my party tonight."

"Thanks, Marc." Julia smiled as she recognized his voice. "It's been a long time since I last saw you. How've you been?"

"He's been busy with me." Elsa appeared, then moved close to Marc and kissed his cheek.

"Oh! Happy to see you again, Elsa."

Elsa's voice was sarcastic. "Happy to see you too, Julia! Marc and I were waiting for you." She added softly, so only Julia could hear, "Of course I would have preferred it if you hadn't come."

"Well, here I am." Julia ignored the nasty words and smiled. Elsa had always been a bitch. "The party seems perfect."

"I organized the party myself," Elsa replied. That was another lie.

"Nice," Julia answered, edging away. The last thing she needed was to listen to mean-spirited Elsa and her stupid conversations. As she moved away, Julia heard Elsa giving Marc a hard time.

"Is there something between you and Julia that I should be worrying about?" Elsa asked.

"No!" Marc shook his head. "Julia is just a good friend."

"I don't trust her."

Julia rolled her eyes at Elsa's ridiculous jealousy, and then smiled as Marc's voice reached her over the noise of the party.

"God, Elsa, can you stop please? There's nothing between me and Julia. Can you stop doing the jealous fiancée and please take care of our guests? You are the only woman in my life…and I would like to make love with you right now."

Elsa flashed at the taunt. "We should just go upstairs."

"Maybe we should," Marc challenged.

Julia stepped away before she had to listen to any more, but Ruben was talking about it when she reached him. He greeted her with a gleeful smile.

"That was the most sensational scene. You should have seen Elsa's face behind you, after you left!"

"I feel sorry for Marc. Since he's been with Elsa, he's changed a great deal."

"Yes." Ruben could only admit the truth of that. "Let's enjoy the party now. It's been a very long week; we deserve some fun."

Julia agreed. "For that I need a glass of quality champagne." She made her way to the bar, and then passed through the jam-packed living room and onto the quiet terrace. She liked the idea of drinking her first glass of champagne undisturbed, leaving the gossip and chatting behind her. Here no one would disturb her; they were all busy drinking and dancing. Here she could be alone with her dreams and a good glass of champagne. *What better way to meditate.*

It was certainly a nice party, Alejandro noticed—Nino had not been exaggerating. He looked around; the party was everything his Italian friend had said it would be. The cream of Italian society was in attendance—celebrities and socialites, movie stars and politicians. The women were dressed in sexy dresses, and men in elegant suits filled the terrace and spilled out into the garden. Nino walked past him with an attractive blonde.

"No-one wants to bring his girlfriend to these parties," Nino said quietly to Alejandro, then disappeared into the garden with the blonde.

Alejandro smiled slightly. He couldn't understand this attitude. "I'll just go to freshen up with a glass of champagne," he said—he didn't want to get involved in Nino's affair. Tonight would be the night he would meet Julia again, and get to know her. He had made up his mind. This time he won't stand by like a zombie infected by a beauty-virus. He would speak, even if he ends up making a fool out of himself. He won't give up his arms without a fight.

Alejandro scanned the crowd—he saw Ruben at the edge of the pool, laughing loudly with two of his models, and he saw the crowd behind him bobbing their heads almost in sync with the rhythm of the music. Alejandro's eyes narrowed as he looked around for Julia, but she was nowhere to be seen. His mood plummeted.

Don't tell me I have come all this way for nothing. I should be working, not chasing foolish dreams.

"Hey Alejandro," Ruben called, waving him over. "How are you? I haven't seen you since the show. I thought you went back to New York?"

Alejandro shook Ruben's hand. "Good to see you again. I've decided to stay in Milan for a while. My business needs me here now."

"I can imagine you are a busy man," Ruben replied.

"And you are always in good company," Alejandro teased, indicating at the beautiful women at Ruben's table.

"That's my job." Ruben shrugged with a smile. "Julia is here too," he added, as if he knew Alejandro was searching for her.

Good. Alejandro's mood lifted. "It will be my pleasure to meet her again. I haven't seen her yet."

"She's around here somewhere. She went to get a glass of champagne. Check at the bar," Ruben said.

"I'll see you later, then!" Alejandro was excited at the idea of seeing Julia again. An elegantly dressed young waitress bearing a tray of glasses passed him. Alejandro grabbed a glass of champagne and scanned the bar, but Julia wasn't there. He went inside the villa, trying to figure out what it would be like to see her again.

How to handle the meeting? **Deep** in thought, he stepped through a wide door to the terrace.

She was there.

Joy surged through him. She stood looking over the garden, lost in her thoughts. Her head bent to one side, she was as beautiful as he remembered. The lights illuminated her perfect profile. He took a few steps closer, and then paused to look at her dangerously seductive body, impossible for him to forget. His heart almost skipped a beat at the thought of approaching her and breaking her reverie.

She stiffened as she became aware of his scrutiny, and then sipped from her glass. He walked closer.

"I love this kind of night, too. The shine of the stars never fails to thrill me." Alejandro spoke after clearing his throat.

She did not speak and he continued, "I spend a lot of time sitting outside, wherever I am, looking at the sky full of different stars. Often the time goes by like a flash, and before I realize, it's past midnight—but I could never have enough of this magic mystery of the sky."

His words were overly poetic even to him, but she smiled.

Finally Julia answered him. "I know that feeling," she said, without turning around.

Alejandro moved closer and placed his hand on the metal railing, his elbow brushing lightly against her arm. He wondered if she noticed.

Julia pulled back and turned, finally giving in to her curiosity. She gazed for a few seconds at the man with the deep, sexy voice. A thrill ran through her—he was a very good-looking man. Tall, his black hair shining in the low light, with gorgeous eyes of an incredible blue shade she had never seen before.

"We never exchanged a proper introduction," he said, looking deep into her eyes. "I'm Alejandro Quintana, and very delighted to meet you."

She knew very well that he was the man from the show the other night, the man she'd so profoundly pretended to ignore at the restaurant. She didn't want give him the impression that she remembered him. "I am Julia Belmonte. I don't think we have met before?"

"I wouldn't forget such a beautiful face," he replied. Staring at Julia, he seemed to sense that almost everything around her was unimportant to her. It was as though he could read her thoughts lingering in the cold aura around her.

His words broke the unbearable tension. "It seems to be a lovely party. Have you been here before?" he asked casually.

"Many times. Marc is one of my best friends. I always enjoy his parties. What about you?" she asked. "How do you know Marc?"

"I didn't have the pleasure of meeting him personally, but we have friends in common."

She gave a nod of acknowledgement. "So you've never been here before?"

"I came here years ago. Lake Como is one of my favorite places. But when I come to Italy these days, most of the time I am in Milan, where I have my office. Now that I met you I might come here more often." He smiled.

She smiled back. "Are you always in a hurry?"

"Only when I meet a special woman."

"Does that happen often?"

"Unfortunately, no," he murmured. "But maybe I have met her now." He gave her a long look, the kind of look that said - you are that special woman.

He moved closer to her. "I am sure many men tell you this, but I find you irresistible."

"Do you?" Julia looked at Alejandro—he was undoubtedly a very attractive and charming man. She moved back a pace and turned towards the balcony overlooking the illuminated garden.

"Maybe because I've never met a woman who had this impact on me before. I am sure you are excellent at breaking hearts, but I'll take the risk."

Julia smiled, bewildered at his rapid advancement "We just met. Let's take one step at a time." She tried to curb the tempo.

"I think I can manage that." He winked at her.

Julia had her share of desperate men trying their utmost to get into her list of significant people on their very first meet, but Alejandro appeared less desperate and more honest in his behavior. It was as if he was speaking his mind, without any filtration. Whatever originated at his mind came straight to his mouth. She hesitated for only a second looking straight into his eyes. "So, you're some successful businessman?"

"You know I am." He smiled.

Julia didn't have a clue about Alejandro's business empire, but flying words told her that he was one of the topmost business tycoon. She admired his self-assured attitude. "I guess you are used to being successful with women?"

Alejandro laughed. "As I said before, unfortunately, I don't meet special women very often."

"Oh, really!" she teased. "That must be very sad!"

"It is." The sexy voice thrilled her as he stared back

at her. "But not for long. Something tells me that my sad days are gone."

She decided to play. "Well, good for you."

For both of us, he thought. He looked at her quizzically, and then softened. "You got that right."

They smiled at each other, allowing the moment to dawn upon them. The music seeped from inside through the french door, which amplified every time the door sprung open. Nevertheless, the music was loud enough to compel everyone to speak louder than they usually do. But while they spoke they could only hear their own voices, as if the ambience had dissolved in the background. The beats, the chattering, the glass clinking, the wind hustling, seemed dull like a lullaby in mid sleep. Nothing around them was more important.

Alejandro Quintana made her feel good. Julia hadn't enjoyed herself like this for a long time. She felt fortunate to have his company, and rescued from the hordes of boring millionaires, whose conversation ended the same way as it started – their empire worth.

"How about another glass of champagne?" he asked.

"Yes, why not?"

"I will be back soon; don't run away."

"I would, but I hate to break a sweat." Julia smiled. "I wish I could fly off this terrace." She laughed.

Alejandro was fun to talk to. She wanted to enjoy speaking with him a little more. The party held no interest for her—she already knew most of the people, boring old rich people. Alejandro was so different from them. Rich? Yes. Boring? No.

After a moment Alejandro returned with two glasses of champagne. As she turned to take her glass, his hand touched hers again, and some kind of electricity she couldn't explain ran up her arm. She wondered if he felt it, too.

Julia held his gaze. "So how often do you come to Milan?"

"Every few months. I like to spend time here, but mostly it's for business."

"That's good," she said thoughtfully. "That's very good." She knew she was confusing him with her detachment, but she had learned to protect herself.

But her tone didn't seem to faze him. He held her eyes steadily. "If I invite you for dinner, I guess you're going to say you're very busy?"

"Exactly," she teased. Their eyes flickered away, then met again and her heartbeat sped up.

If only he wasn't so damn handsome. Perhaps she should have given him a chance at the restaurant, talked to him surrounded by people, instead of here, where it was so very intense to be alone. Confusion filled her thoughts. Luckily, Marc appeared on the terrace with his cigar, breaking the tension.

"Ah, here you are! I was wondering where you disappeared to."

"Too noisy inside," Julia said, glancing at Alejandro. He stood back politely and watched as Marc took her arm. He felt a sudden pinch at his heart as if a bug somewhere inside tried to alert him. He wished that the guy, whoever on the earth he was, would leave her arm alone.

"I know." Marc turned to Alejandro. "You should be inside, my friend. They are having a very good time. Two girls are dancing on the table and driving all my guests crazy."

"Wow!" Julia laughed. She thought that must be Natasha, another model—Natasha always liked to do that kind of stuff at a party after she had emptied a bottle of champagne.

"Good thing my old friend Nino is in there to keep those girls calm." Alejandro stepped forward and Julia sensed he didn't appreciate Marc's interruption.

"I'm sorry. Marc, let me introduce you to Alejandro Quintana. I don't think you two have met before?"

"I haven't had that pleasure," Marc replied, removing his hand from Julia's arm to shake

Alejandro's hand. "But I have heard a lot about you. You own that yacht company in New York?"

Alejandro felt relieved. The bug was gone, and his heart started pumping.

"Yes, you are right. The Signature Quintana is mine. And not just in New York—we are expanding all over the world. I have an office in Milan now, too."

"I might need your advice," Marc said. "I need to buy a good quality yacht for my fiancée, and she wants her name on it."

"No problem." Apparently Alejandro was always ready for business. He handed his business card to Marc. "I will be in Milan for a while; we can meet up and discuss all the details."

"I will call you tomorrow to fix an appointment."

"Looking forward to it," Alejandro said.

"I'll leave you now to enjoy my party; it was a pleasure to meet you."

Marc left the terrace, leaving behind him the foul smell of cigar smoke. Alejandro turned to Julia.

"I like your friend. He seems to know what he wants."

"He is a good guy, one of my closest friends."

"I am sure Marc knows he is lucky to have you as a friend."

A flattering rush of pleasure ran through Julia at the compliment. "We don't have really much time to meet up, but when we do, we enjoy each other's company."

"Sounds good," Alejandro said. Julia knew he was wondering if she'd ever had an affair with Marc.

"Shall I bring you another glass of champagne?" he asked.

"Boy! Someone's trying to get me drunk!" Julia laughed. She knew her boundaries. She stepped down before stepping into dangerous territory. She'd had two glasses already and she wasn't used to too much alcohol. She covered her mouth with her hand as a yawn overtook her. "I think it's time for me to go home."

Alejandro looked at her as if he could read her mind. Again, she was avoiding him. "I hope you are not running away from me. It took me forever to find you." His voice was sexy and full of promise.

"I am sure you will be able to find me again," she said with a smile.

"Believe me, I will," he replied.

"Call me to remind me of the date for that dinner." She took a card from her small bag and handed it to him.

"And it just a casual dinner. Please have no false impression."

"Thanks for the heads up. "Alejandro took the card, "I won't."

He held her hand and kissed it. A rigorous pulse ran through her spine. She defied her expression and took a step back.

"Thank you for the wonderful evening," he said gently. "I'll call you soon."

For a long moment they looked at each other, his deep blue eyes fixated hypnotically on hers. Before he could kiss her—she could see the intent in his eyes—she grabbed her bag and pulled away.

"Goodbye. I'll see you." She noticed that he moved toward her as she pulled away and hid a smile as she walked confidently back into the villa. Men were such babies when it came to women. And when it came to these moments, Julia never shied away from playing.

Chapter Eight

Julia called Samantha as soon as she woke up. "You won't believe what a strange coincidence happened last night."

"Tell me."

"Remember Alejandro? The American guy that Ruben invited to our table that night after the fashion show."

"The one whom you didn't cut any slack? Yeah." Samantha chuckled.

"Yeah well." Julia smiled. "He was at Marc's party. What a coincidence, isn't it?"

"You're kidding me!" Samantha yelled from the other side.

"You know I am not."

"This is fate, darling. You'll have to tell me all about it. I need to know everything, all the details."

"Mmmm," Julia murmured, remembering how good-looking he was. "We just had a few glasses of champagne and an interesting conversation."

"Interesting conversation?" She yelled again.

Julia could hear the curiosity in her friend's voice, and her mouth curved into a smile at the thought.

"I had a nice time. Alejandro is self-confident and assured. Very easy to talk to." She heard her phone clink. She picked it up and looked, her full lips curving into a smile at the glimpse. "He just sent me a text—we are having dinner together tomorrow evening."

Samantha laughed.

Julia grinned into the phone. "What are you laughing at?"

"Nothing," Samantha answered. "I'm just happy for you."

"Good that I can make you laugh. At least I distracted you from your paperwork." Julia imagined Samantha's office, piles of papers around her and Samantha barely pausing to breathe. That was the way Samantha worked, when she wasn't gossiping and dropping names.

Samantha shifted subjects. "So, let me tell you about the call I received the other day—from a very important business man."

She started talking about a man named Anthony. Julia had heard of him. She'd seen his photo in a magazine somewhere not long ago. He was handsome, but not as good-looking as Alejandro. Julia began to dream as Samantha talked about her famous client.

"And I just sent Anthony a text inviting him to my place. I promised him it would be memorable."

Julia laughed. "You are so naughty."

"Well, I would say I am happy to enjoy my life sometimes."

After breakfast the next day, Alejandro headed into the office. As soon as he finished a long but necessary phone conversation with one of his New York clients, he called his assistant. "Barbara, book a table for two for dinner at Il Mio."

He preferred Italian restaurants, where the oysters were always fresh, the truffles were served with champagne, and the wine was exquisite. The subdued lighting at Il Mio gave it a cozy but sophisticated nocturnal charm that invited intimacy. It would be the perfect place to take Julia for their first real date. *Or a casual dinner, as she dubbed it.*

Moving his silver pen over the papers on his desk, he wondered why Nino was late to the office. They needed to settle everything before the meeting. He pressed the button for Barbara's extension again.

"Barbara, have you heard from Nino?"

"He's just parking and he'll be here soon," Barbara announced. "And by the way, your table is booked for eight p.m."

"Thanks, Barbara. Send Nino in as soon as he arrives."

"I will."

Alejandro hung up and moved to the window. The sun caught his watch, reflecting a circle of light on the glass. He stared out, thinking of Julia and how much he looked forward to seeing her.

He turned as Nino opened the door and entered the room. Alejandro stepped forward to greet him. He couldn't wait to give Nino the news. "I am going to dinner with Julia Belmonte tonight."

"Julia Belmonte, the model?" Nino asked, his eyes widening.

"Yes," Alejandro replied, sitting on a comfortable leather chair. "I still can't believe she agreed."

"That's great!" Nino exclaimed.

"I can't wait to be with her tonight, just the two of us. Today is going to be a wonderful day," Alejandro bragged. His skin was flushed with excitement.

Nino grinned at him. "Love does strange things, my friend."

Alejandro returned the smile and started to speak, but the phone interrupted him.

"The investors are ready. They're waiting in the conference room," Barbara told him.

Alejandro thanked her and hung up the phone.

"Yes, it does, my friend," he said to Nino, then stood up and clapped his colleague on the shoulder. "But business first; the financiers are waiting."

Alejandro enjoyed doing business with Swiss investors. They were sharp and straight to the point. Jack Walker had prepared the contracts for them to sign, and everything was in order. Alejandro had one more appointment after lunch, and then he was going back to the hotel to get ready before picking up Julia at seven-thirty.

Yes, the day was going perfectly, exactly the way he planned. He wished Jack were here now. He would've bragged before him. Nothing was as pleasing as seeing Jack losing on his bet. He wanted him to tell that it surely could work out with Julia.

Julia was indeed a spectacular woman and it seemed that other men were intimidated by her. But of course she was particular about who she chose to go out with. Alejandro was persistent and always went for what he wanted. That was how he'd gained Julia's favor. His heart had done a somersault the moment he saw her at Marc's party. He knew she was the woman for him, and he had no doubt she felt it, too. He intended to spend as much time with her as he could before he returned to New York.

Chapter Nine

Julia called Samantha around six-thirty. "Darling, are you all right? You usually call. I haven't heard from you today."

"I'm okay," Samantha replied. "I'm still in the office. This case is driving me bonkers. Every day I discover something new—I just can't get to the end of it. I have no idea how it's going to go tomorrow in court."

"Don't be silly! You are the best lawyer in Milan. No one can beat you, and you know that. You'll give them a run for their money. Go home and have some rest. You need to be fresh for tomorrow."

"Maybe you're right," Samantha agreed. Julia heard the restrained sound of tapping which suggested that Samantha had taken off her glasses and was patting them gently on the stack of papers in front of her.

"Take my mind away from this case, Julia—what are

you up to tonight?"

"Dinner with Alejandro, remember?"

"Right, I almost forgot. What kind of business is he in?"

"He sells yachts. He has a huge company in New York. I think I told you already."

"Ah, yes, you did. Now I remember." Samantha was a typical lawyer. She liked to hear things over and over, just in case the information was wrong the first time, or the person talking let slip anything new.

"I don't have much time to talk. I need to get ready," Julia said. "I just called to see if you are okay. Alejandro is picking me up in an hour."

"He's going to pick you up from home? Great! Call me after dinner, okay?"

"I will, and you get out of that office." Julia sighed as she ended the call, thinking of Samantha spending so many nights with file folders and paperwork. Modeling might be hard work, but thank God, it was so much more fun. She took a long shower, dried off with a fluffy towel, and moisturized her whole body. She brushed her long, shiny hair, applied natural-looking makeup and painted red gloss over her lips. Opening her wardrobe, Julia stood and observed the rows of dresses in front of her, mostly gifts from the designers whose work she'd shown on the runway. She decided to wear her favorite navy dress, which fell softly just below the knee; it was sleeveless with a deep neckline. She put on her white pearl necklace and a silver bracelet, and slipped into stylish navy heels. Then she stepped back and looked into the full-length mirror at the front of the wardrobe. She felt good, and she knew she looked good. Her body was tall, lean and agile. The pearls around her neck finished the outfit nicely, giving her a classic look. Julia glanced at her watch just as the intercom buzzed.

Seven thirty. She smiled. Alejandro was right on time; she went to the door and pressed the button on the intercom panel.

"I am downstairs waiting for you." His voice resonated through the small speaker.

"I will be with you shortly," Julia said, thinking how life had a strange way of taking people in unexpected directions. Two weeks ago she would never have believed that she would go out with someone so soon after meeting them. Just a casual meeting, she reminded herself. She picked up her bag, and before she walked out the door she sprayed her neck with perfume, its seductive fragrance a sophisticated mix of sweet and smoky, with a hint of musk and flowers.

Alejandro caught his breath as Julia stepped from the elevator. She was beautiful. She smiled as he walked to greet her.

"It's nice to see you again," he murmured, as he gently kissed her cheeks. The seductive scent of her perfume was intoxicating. "You look very beautiful."

"Thank you. It's nice to see you too," she said, her cheeks turning a soft pink as he looked at her.

"I have booked a table for us at Il Mio. I hope you'll like it."

"Yes, it's a lovely place," she replied.

They stepped out into the fresh evening air. Alejandro opened the car door, and Julia slid elegantly into the front seat. Her long, toned legs filled his gaze, and he imagined her perfect body, free from the modest covering of her simple yet elegant navy dress.

God, she is a beautiful creature. I am a very fortunate man.

"I've been thinking about you today," he said, as he sat beside her and started the car.

"I hope they were good thoughts," she teased.

"Not all." He winked.

The motor was smooth and the two were quiet for a few moments as Alejandro steered the car into light traffic. The signal was red when they arrived at the intersection.

He turned to her, scanning her face as they waited. "Of course they were good thoughts."

Julia smiled.

"You are a very intriguing woman," he said. "A woman of mystery, that's what I like about you."

"Am I?" Julia's lips tipped up slightly in a seductive smile.

"You never take my compliments seriously! Or do you, and I just don't realize it?" It was obvious to him that she was used to receiving compliments.

"I do take them seriously," she said. "More than you know."

He reached over, put his hand on her knee and glanced at her. She pulled her legs away and he lifted his hands. He understood the indication. *It was too soon*.

He sensed that there was more than flirting between them. He wanted her, but he was unsure if she did the same. If she did, she was playing one hell of a game.

"What are you thinking?" she asked.

"I can't tell you. It's something special." He held her gaze.

"Very well!" She laughed, her eyes sparkling. It was going to be a good night.

Alejandro loved her sunny personality, but the memory of her seductive smile on the catwalk that night crossed his mind.

"You're a little cheeky!" A delightful giggle escaped her lips.

"And you like teasing me, don't you?" he replied. "I think we would be great together. We'll have fun tonight."

They reached the restaurant shortly after, and Alejandro pulled up to the entrance and gave his keys to the valet. Taking Julia by the hand, he led her inside. The restaurant was quiet and very elegant, and he smiled as heads turned in their direction, admiring Julia. The waitress led Julia and Alejandro to a secluded table, and gave them each a menu.

When the waitress left, Julia whispered to Alejandro, "This restaurant is perfect."

"I know, that's why I chose to come here. This place is perfect for our date." He said, then suddenly wondered if '*Date*' would be the apt word. He moved his hand over hers as it rested on the table. "What would you like to drink?"

"White wine."

"Good choice! Light and dry to suit the fish."

The waitress returned and Alejandro ordered the wine and starters of fresh oysters and crab.

"Fish is my favorite food," Julia said.

"That must be your secret for such a great figure."

"Eating healthy makes me feel good and think positive."

"I agree, and I find the same thing" Alejandro said, picking up his glass. He raised it for a toast. "To the beginning of many nights together."

Julia turned crimson at his pun and raised her own glass. "Maybe."

Alejandro glanced at her. He sensed her discomfort. He wouldn't want to freak her out on their very first date, but he could hardly help his urge. He couldn't afford to blow his only chance. He knew about her reputation. The fact that she was sitting before him was an achievement in itself. "I would really like to see you again—" his attempt to ease the moment was interrupted by a sudden ring on Julia's cellphone.

Julia's fished the phone from her side bag.

Alejandro shook his head, smiling. "I am taking a wild guess. That is your phone, and you are not about to answer."

"You're a good guesser. It's my friend Samantha. I'll call her back later." She hit the end call button and the melodious ringtone stopped.

Alejandro smiled at the fact that she didn't want to answer the call, a good sign that she was enjoying his company. Julia held his gaze and he could see the admiration in her face. But suddenly she looked vulnerable and dropped her eyes. Alejandro reached across the small table and placed his hand on her shoulder, wondering what thoughts were crossing her mind.

"Are you okay?"

"Yes," she answered, barely looking at him. She seemed distant, as if the current situation reminded her of some long forgotten past. A not to good past indeed.

"Did I say something I shouldn't have?"

"No. It's okay really." She said taking the last sip of her wine. "Your choice of wine is commendable."

"It is." He knew that she was trying to jump the subject of conversation, but he intended not to pry any further. "Thank you."

They finished the starters, and Alejandro leaned back in his chair to allow the waitress to place their main course and refill their glass of wine.

"Here they have the best fish in the city," Alejandro said. He took a fork and helped Julia remove a thick, moist filet from the bones of her fish.

"It looks delicious," she said, and glanced at him, still picking bones from her fish, to make it pleasant for her. *How romantic was that?* Julia reached for her glass of wine. "I will need you every time I eat fish from now on," she said, and winked.

I bet you would. Alejandro smiled sweetly. "Anytime."

Julia was confused. This man who owned so much, with so much money, seemed so benign and down to earth. *Even the most strong and powerful man can sometimes do things to impress a woman*, she thought.

In the restaurant, the stereo piped out classic Italian music. Julia was quiet as she finished her fish. Alejandro watched her take the last few bites and, when she set down her fork, took her hand.

"Would you like to go somewhere for an after dinner drink?" he asked, caressing her palm.

"I can't, I need to get home early tonight." She intended to pull her hand, but for once listened to her heart, and let him caress her palm.

"You must have a very busy day tomorrow," he said, noticing the blush that crept up her neck.

"Yes. I am indeed. But maybe we can have that drink another time."

"Sounds like a good idea to me." No need to rush things if he was going to see her again, and Alejandro was delighted to hear her say that they would meet again. His thoughts rushed ahead to the next date: he would bring her to the Opera in Milan. She had mentioned over the starters that she favored opera and classical music. She had good taste—she was young, smart, and beautiful—Julia was exactly the kind of woman he craved for.

Julia looked up and noticed his deep blue eyes fixated on her.

"What would you like for dessert?" he asked.

Julia hesitated for a second, indecisive, as the waitress showed the tray of desserts. Her hand hovered between fruit salad and a small piece of cake.

"Fruit salad," she said.

"No cakes. Everyone in fashion is on a diet." Alejandro smiled as the waitress set down their plates.

"You got that right." Julia smiled back.

After they finished the decoratively cut melon, kiwi, orange sections and strawberries, Alejandro paid the bill and left a generous tip. He turned to Julia. "We'll wait for the valet to bring the car and then I will take you home. I know it's becoming late for you."

"Thank you." Julia picked up her small evening bag and stood up.

Alejandro put his arm around her waist as they walked to the door, enjoying the envy on other men's faces as he ushered his beautiful date to the exit. She fit well in his arms, he thought.

"I had a lovely night," he said. "I have a feeling that we are going to spend lot of time together."

Julia laughed. "Okay, okay, I get the message."

Alejandro saw his chance and took it. "So…can I see you again tomorrow?"

There was a long pause before Julia finally said, "I can't meet you tomorrow, but I'm free over the weekend?"

"Sounds great!"

"I'll be at the Golf Country Club. Perhaps you can come by and we will have a round of golf together."

"I'll be there," he said. "I love golf, too."

Alejandro opened the car door for Julia, then shut it after her and walked around to his side. He started the car and turned on the radio. Some soft music played. Julia settled into her seat and looked through the window. It was a beautiful night without a cloud into the sky.

"I love this song." She hummed along to the radio.

"I can see you have a nice voice there." Alejandro shot Julia a smile and she giggled.

She was so relaxed and happy. It was wonderful.

"I just like singing, but my voice, it's not so good."

"Well, I think you sound great!"

She laughed and studied his profile thoughtfully. "I must admit you are very good when it comes to not telling the absolute truth."

"You better believe me. You have a great voice."

A moment from years ago flashed into Julia's mind—her teacher telling her she should choose to study opera instead of modeling. She had told Julia that her voice had great potential, and that she could become an incredible singer. *What would my life have been if I had chosen that path*? Julia wondered.

Alejandro pulled the car up in front of her house and turned off the engine. "It was a wonderful night," he said.

She felt comfortable in his company. "It was a lovely night for me, too."

An old romantic song played on the radio. Alejandro held her eyes for several seconds. "I love spending time with you," he said, reaching over slowly and taking her hand. Again Julia felt electricity passing between them.

"So do I." Blushing, she gently pulled her hand back, but he held her firm, then pulled her close to his body, his eyes still on hers.

"Do you have any idea how much I like being with you?" he asked.

Julia's breath caught in her throat. Yes, she knew,

she knew exactly how it felt! She felt the same, but somehow she hadn't even suspected his kiss. For a moment she resisted, her body rigid, not allowing him to get too close. But the warm pressure of his lips on hers persisted. He gently explored her mouth, his hands holding her shoulders lightly. Julia let go of her guard. She gasped for breath, but he kissed her again and slowly she let herself respond, warmth sweeping up her body. Her lips flowered beneath the insistent pressure of his mouth—she couldn't resist—and she lifted her arms to his neck to deepen the kiss. His heart beat strong against her breasts as he ran his hands through her long hair. He pressed his nose against her skin as if he couldn't get enough of her perfume, and then he pushed her hair back from her face and looked straight into her eyes.

"God, Julia, I never dreamed...I think I am falling for you. Maybe you'll say I'm crazy, but I think I fell for you the first time I saw you that night on the runway. In that moment I knew I'd found someone special."

"I didn't know I had this impact on you." Julia looked up to his gentle gaze.

"Now you know." He winked at her—he was incredibly sexy. His smile, with immaculately white teeth in perfect rows, sent a tremble down her legs, a feeling she'd never expected on a first date.

"You should smile more often," she said. "I need to

go now," her soft voice whispered regretfully, as she opened the door.

Alejandro stepped out and walked her to the building entrance. He kissed her cheeks, then he took a step back and let her go. His voice was soft. "I can't wait to see you again."

He held the door as she went inside, then turned back to his car. In the elevator up to her apartment, Julia smiled to herself. She had no idea how this was going to end, but she vowed she would enjoy Alejandro's company. Yes, she was very much looking forward to seeing him again.

Chapter Ten

From his desk, Alejandro called Jack Walker's cellphone. "I won't be coming back to New York for at least another few weeks." There was a time and place for everything, and that time and place was now and in Milan.

"But we have deadlines. You need to be in New York," Jack reminded him.

"Well that's why I'm paying you, to look after my company when I'm not there," Alejandro pointed out. "Keep me informed."

"I will." Jack sounded none-too-happy about it.

"Great! I need to run now. Julia's waiting for me, and I don't want to be late. We're playing golf."

"Who?" Jack asked.

"Julia Belmonte, the top model. I am sure you remember her?"

"I think I remember very well," Jack said, sarcasm

lacing his voice. "I hope you play golf better than she does."

"I'll try my best," Alejandro said.

"Watch out Alejandro—don't lose yourself," Jack said. "How much a woman can change a man!"

Alejandro wasn't sure why Jack was acting this way. *For God's sake, I pay him plenty of money; why can't he just do what he's paid for?* Maybe it was time to remind Jack that he was paid to work for The Signature Quintana, not to be Alejandro's personal advisor. Jack's skills were good, but there was no reason his behavior should change like this. Alejandro had worked hard for his success, but it had come at a price. Meeting Julia was like fresh air.

The coincidence was that Julia Belmonte had a similar view of her own success.

Julia had not slept well the night before; her mind buzzed, filled with the moments she'd spent with Alejandro, the remembered sensations flashing through her body. Normally she wouldn't waste time thinking about a date, but Alejandro was different. He had something special.

Ruben had called her. "Make sure you relax on your days off. You're shooting in Dubai next week. It's the Designer of the Year cover for Magazine."

"Don't worry, I won't disappoint you," Julia had assured him. She possessed supreme self-confidence, and knew how to handle herself in front of the camera. Through the years she had mastered the art of giving the best of herself when it was called for. She'd been born with that strength and drive, and she knew it was part of being a strong woman, not just a top model. Milan was the heart of fashion and Julia had made sure she was on top of it. She gazed at herself in the mirror above the sink in the bathroom. Although she hadn't slept well, her face was completely fine, as always.

The doorbell rang. She went into the hallway, trying to figure out who would come over without calling. She pressed the intercom button.

"Who's there?"

"It's me! Quick, I need the bathroom."

Julia opened the door and Samantha pushed past her to the bathroom. Julia didn't understand what was going on, but she was sure Samantha would explain whatever it was. Meanwhile, she went into the kitchen and made two coffees for when Samantha reappeared.

"Hey! You okay?" Julia put down the magazine she'd been flicking through while she was waiting.

"Yes, I'm okay." Samantha headed for the sofa and lay down. "I had brunch with a client at the bar next door...so many pastries and little cakes! I think I overdid it. My stomach never wants to see chocolate again. You know what the public toilets are like—I thought I'd pop in if you were home and kill two birds with one stone."

"You look tired," Julia said.

"I haven't had much of a break lately," Samantha replied. "And today I've got a friend from Rome coming to visit me and I'm not in the mood for guests!"

"And who might this friend be?" Julia teased.

"It's an old friend. We haven't seen each other for long time. We used to study together in pre-law."

"I'm guessing you have a story with this guy?"

"Do I ever." Samantha didn't look like she was expecting a happy reunion. "I was thinking maybe you could join us for dinner?"

"I can't come, I have other plans," Julia said, thinking the last thing she needed was spending an evening keeping company with Samantha and her ex.

"I would like you to come. Please? Let me know if you change your plans." Samantha was almost begging, and Julia smiled at her.

"I can't change my plans, but I am sure you'll be fine."

There was a long, awkward silence.

Samantha broke it. "I bumped into Corrine yesterday, she'd be happy to hear from you sometimes."

Julia dug around for an excuse. "I've been meaning to call her."

"What are you waiting for? She's our friend."

"I'll call her tomorrow. I'm going to the Golf Club today. I invited Alejandro for a round."

"I didn't know you were planning on getting so involved with him," Samantha said.

"Well, you're the one who insisted I give him a chance." Julia winked.

Samantha laughed. "And I was right. I was talking to Corrine about you today. I told her you're seeing someone, and she wasn't surprised that you've disappeared lately. Anyway, call her when you've got the time."

"I will."

"I am curious to meet this Alejandro," Samantha said.

"We can meet one of these days," Julia replied.

"That sounds good. Call me when you two can meet." Samantha checked her watch and stood up from the sofa. "I have to go now," she said, and headed to the door.

"I'll call you later."

"Okay. *Ciao*!"

"Ciao!"

Julia checked the time. It was just before noon; she had just enough time to get ready and leave. Setting the coffee cups in the sink, she glanced out the window. It was a beautiful sunny day, a great day for golf. *It's going to be fun to golf with Alejandro; he may not even know how to play golf,* she thought. Maybe it was just an excuse to see her again. *Oh god, if that's the case I am going to have lots of fun.*

Chapter Eleven

By the time Julia arrived at the Golf Club, Alejandro had settled into a group at the bar, chatting and making friends. She caught his eye and waved.

"Sorry I'm late."

Alejandro looked appreciatively at her as she crossed the room. Her ivory tunic swayed with the gentle flurry of air. Her feet jingled against the concrete path. "I was worried you'd changed your mind—I was about to call you to ask if you were still coming or not."

"I should warn you, I can't keep the time." Julia smiled and kissed his cheeks.

Alejandro kissed her back. "Are you ready to play golf now?"

"I've never been more ready," Julia said. "And you are ready to lose the match?"

"Well, I was thinking of giving you the opportunity to win, but now I've changed my mind." There was a challenging glint in his eye.

Julia put on her look—that famous cool look she used when she wanted to intimidate. Her green eyes raked over him. "Do you think I'd have allowed you to let me win?"

"Of course not," he said sympathetically. "But you might not have had a choice."

Julia's competitive spirit rose—she wasn't about to give him that pleasure. "Let's start the game then," she said with a wry smile. "Shall we?"

"You can be such a bossy person when you want to!" Alejandro admonished. "I wouldn't want to get on your bad side."

"Don't you worry about that I'll make sure you won't." She shot him a teasing glance.

Alejandro laughed. His perfect teeth peeked out behind his sexy smile lips, and his jaw-line stretched to give an even more impressive look. Julia felt a tremble down her back. The truth was that she loved teasing him—and Alejandro seemed to enjoy it, too.

Julia was wary of relationships. Her previous boyfriend of three years had been a pretty decent lover for the first two years. But then, because of his jealousy, his behavior had changed. He'd become edgy at the thought of her male companionship, her late night parties, and her 'friendly' rendezvous with colleagues.

For Julia, it was difficult to trust again, to believe that anyone else could be the part of her life and accept her lifestyle in its entirety. She wasn't sure yet if it was fortunate or unfortunate, but Alejandro was the man who made her feel good just being around him. Julia enjoyed his company so much that thinking of anything else was unimportant. As if her last relationship had never happened.

The club was still busy when they rounded the 18th hole and came inside, even though it was past six thirty in the evening. They gave their clubs to a caddy, and Julia took Alejandro by the hand and led him down to the bar.

Roberto Benetti was the last person Julia had expected to run into, and he seemed equally taken aback to see Julia. Roberto was accompanied by a girl who didn't look very classy. Julia looked at him with a frown. He appeared unkempt, his shirttail hanging untidily out of his trousers.

"Jesus, Roberto!" Julia exclaimed as she got close to him. "It's really you? I didn't know you played golf."

"Just...uh...visiting with a friend who is a member of the club," Roberto said vaguely spotting an appropriately dressed man standing beside her.

"I see," Julia replied, looking equally vague. "You look as if you haven't slept for a week," she said, and gave a sharp look to the girl, who was clutching Roberto's hand tightly.

"I had my birthday last night, and I'm still feeling a bit tired," he replied.

There was an awkward pause. Then Julia said, "Oh yes, I know the feeling…Happy Birthday!"

"Thanks," Roberto said, nodding at Julia and her companion who watched in silence, and then led his girl past them bidding his farewell.

Julia watched him go, thinking he looked embarrassed.

Alejandro jerked his chin at Roberto. "He looks still drunk after his party."

"Thank God, Samantha wasn't here to see him." Julia imagined Samantha having a hysterical crisis.

"Is he her boyfriend?" Alejandro asked.

"Her ex-boyfriend. But unfortunately, Samantha is still in love with him."

"I feel sorry for your friend."

"I know…" Julia shook her head sadly. "Anyway, enough about them." She took off her cap, and pushed back her long ponytail. "I am amazed! I didn't expect you to play golf so well!"

"I've had the good fortune to play some fabulous

courses in my life, and I learned a lot from that." He touched her arm. "You play very well too, you know!"

"Not as good as you!" Julia squeezed his arm back. "And that's the reason you won the match today."

He laughed. "Not yet," he said as he fixed his gaze on her face.

Julia felt suddenly intimidated by his penetrating look, like a little girl.

"I'll need to convince you to have dinner with me tonight," Alejandro murmured slowly.

Julia looked pointedly at her golfing clothes. "I'm not sure. I'm not exactly dressed for dinner."

"That's not a problem," Alejandro said. "I need to go by my hotel and have a shower and get changed, too. I'll come to you around nine."

"It's going to take me longer than you think," Julia said mockingly.

"No problem, I'll wait for you."

She smiled, then realized in that moment, he'd issued an invitation she couldn't refuse.

She was losing her control with him. *How annoying was that?*

They walked to the parking lot together, and kissed each other's cheeks lightly. After Alejandro drove off,

Julia sat on the hood of her car and looked out over the rolling greens. *Could she really be falling for him?* She hadn't thought it could happen so fast. *No, it can't be, we're just spending fantastic time together and that's all it is.*

Her cell rang. She glanced at the screen; it was Corrine.

"Hey Corrine, are you okay?" she answered, wondering why Corrine had insisted to Samantha that Julia should call her.

"Since you got engaged, you forgot about your friends? Why you didn't tell me anything?" Corrine said.

"What? Engaged? Why would you say that?" Julia asked.

"Because Samantha told me you're seeing someone."

"Yes, I'm seeing someone, but no, I'm not engaged! And surely you know that if I was getting engaged you'd be the first to know?"

"Glad to hear that. I must say, I thought you might be avoiding me after that discussion we had last time."

"Of course not." Julia had decided to forget that day. "I'm very busy, but I promise we'll have a nice long talk soon."

"I'm going to hold you to that. I need to know everything about this mysterious man who finally convinced you to go out with him." Corrine gave a long, drawn-out sigh. "You're so lucky."

No, you are the lucky one, Julia thought. You have your comfortable house in Lake Garda. Not to mention that because of your rich parents, you never worked one day in your life.

"Um, yes," Julia murmured. "I suppose I am lucky."

"You should come and visit me; the days are beautiful and sunny now. It would be nice to spend the day by the pool."

"We'll see," Julia said. She knew that she quite envied Corrine. How relaxing to do nothing but sit at the pool side all day long and beg for handouts from your family.

Chapter Twelve

Alejandro knew he was getting in way too deep with Julia, but still, she was much smarter than any girl he'd been with. She was passionate, independent and strong—he couldn't think of a better combination in a woman. There was an incandescent quality about Julia that he couldn't get enough of. The more time he spent with her, the more he liked her. He was already planning to invite her to the opera in Milan tomorrow; he had two tickets for the evening performance. His excitement built at the thought of spending more time with Julia. He enjoyed everything about her.

He waited downstairs at her building. When he saw her stepping out of the elevator, her slender hand pushing back the sensual curtain of her long hair, his thoughts began to whirl. He was tempted to get her in the car and drive her directly to his hotel, but no, that might upset her. Alejandro was known for his patience. He knew how to wait when he wanted something.

"Hello, *principessa*," he said.

Julia smiled.

Alejandro took her hand and walked her to the car, Julia following him with small, dainty steps. He held the door as she sat and tucked her legs in, then shut it gently after her and came around to the driver's side.

"You sure know how to treat a lady," Julia said, and squeezed his hand.

"I like to treat my lady well." Alejandro winked at her and put the car in motion.

"Did you grow up here in Milan?" Julia asked. "Quintana's not such an American name, I think!"

"I was born here, but after a few years my parents brought me to New York. I think it changed my life."

As they drove to the restaurant, he decided to tell her more.

"*My mamma* was a beautiful young woman. My father fell in love with her when he was very young. They were crazy about each other." Alejandro smiled proudly. "Can you believe that after fifty years together my father still gets jealous about my mother?"

Julia smiled a little wistfully. "That's sweet. I can't fathom to think about their love." How different her own story was—she had never seen that kind of immense love in her family.

"I have told *mamma* I have met a special woman. She

can't wait to see you." Alejandro already had big plans. He saw no reason why he shouldn't look to the future and put things in proper order.

"Those things take time," Julia said with a frown.

Alejandro nodded. "I guess they do, but the last thing I want in my life is to lose something by waiting too long." He knew Julia was the woman he wanted in his life. They were perfect for each other.

"What about your family?" he asked. "I'd like to get to know them." Julia hadn't yet talked about her family to him. He probed gently. "Where are your parents living? Do you have any brothers or sisters?"

"I've got a lovely mother, two sisters and two brothers."

"What about your father? You didn't mention him?"

"I've got a father, a real charmer. I haven't seen him in years."

"You don't speak to him?"

"No."

He was surprised to see the pain on her face. He knew at once that he'd stuck a critical chord.

"You don't have to tell me if you don't want to."

"Thank you." She was glad he understood her. There is nothing more fortunate to have someone with whom you can speak without actually speaking. "I don't really want to speak about that now."

Alejandro looked at Julia with deep respect. He knew it would be wrong to push her now. "I understand. Perhaps one day you will feel comfortable enough to talk about it with me." He pulled up and handed the keys to the valet, coming around the car to meet Julia and offered his arm. "Let's go into the restaurant."

"I've got a reservation for Quintana," Alejandro said to the black-jacketed maître d' standing at the door.

"I'll check for you, *Signiore*."

The restaurant was packed and Alejandro was glad Nino had arranged the reservation. Within a few minutes the maître d' was back, bowed to Alejandro and Julia, and a young waitress led them to a well-situated window table overlooking the turquoise blue pool which howled in the harsh wind.

"You know how to take a woman out in a grand style," Julia said. "And you surely know the best seats around those places."

Alejandro leaned across the table and took her hand, which was surprisingly cold. "I like being with you in glamorous places.

The jovial owner of the restaurant came to the table to greet them personally, presenting a complimentary bottle of champagne and treating Alejandro like a king, and Julia as if she was his queen. They began with caviar, and the dinner was impressive.

Alejandro felt better than he had in years, living a moment that a few weeks ago he had only dreamed of. He was with Julia Belmonte, and he knew without a doubt that most men would give their right arm to be in his chair. But he didn't want just a girlfriend. A fact that even spooked Alejandro at times, for once he was ready for commitment. Even though he'd seen enough married friends to convince him that staying single was the only way to go, with Julia he had reached an unfamiliar stage—he wanted more. The conversation was lively, and they talked about everything from politics to the latest fashions.

"Would you like a coffee?" Alejandro asked.

"Black." She squeezed his hand, glancing up at him. His watch read 23:45. Their young waitress approached their table and tapped her foot impatiently.

"One black coffee," Alejandro said, "and may I have the check, please?"

"Yes *Signiore*."

The waitress edged back to their table and presented the check. By the time Alejandro threw down his card and paid the bill, Julia had finished her coffee.

"We'll go?" he asked.

"Yes."

He pushed back her chair and tucked her arm into his. They were walking toward car when they heard someone singing an aria in the distance. Alejandro took her hand and twirled her into his arms. "May I have this dance?"

"We can't dance in the middle of the parking lot," Julia whispered.

"Of course we can. I don't mind." Alejandro acted as though they were in some kind of romantic movie. He put his hand on her back, and before she could object, Julia was dancing with him in a parking lot in the middle of the night.

"How romantic is this!" she said, looking up at him.

Alejandro bent his head over her fresh and clean-smelling hair and took a deep breath, inhaling her seductive perfume. He looked into her eyes. "I have tickets to the opera for tomorrow night. Would you like to come with me?"

"Wonderful!" Julia said. "I've missed going to hear music, now that you remind me."

Alejandro closed the door on her side and stepped into the car. "Is that a yes?"

"Yes." Julia could not help but say it. Even though

she still wasn't sure about Alejandro, she couldn't resist when it came to her favorite hobbies.

Alejandro reached for her hand and kissed it, holding it to his lips for a moment after. If only things will continue like this between us. Yes, that's exactly what I want, to be happy with Julia.

By the time he drove his distinctive car up to the front of her building, his dreams were taking him away.

"Hey," Julia said, squeezing his hand. "You are so quiet!"

"I am just thinking," he said. The truth was that he loved every minute with her, and his mind was filled with plans for his next step with her. "Let's go to Paris next week?" He couldn't help imagining what it would be like to make love with her.

"Wait! What? She exclaimed dazzled. "Well first of all, I am in Dubai for work next week. I leave on Sunday. And secondly… Well… Paris? Have we really come to that point?"

"Haven't we?" Alejandro asked concerned, "Where are we exactly?"

"I don't know." She bit her lips. "But it's just that we've met only on a few occasions, I do sincerely enjoy your company and you haven't been subtle about your fondness with me either, but still…"

"We should never wait for something if we already know it's for the best for us." Alejandro said, "Someone told me."

Alejandro had planned to return to New York ten days later.

"How long will you be in Dubai?" he inquired.

"I'll be there for the whole week."

"I'll still be here when you are back," he said. "And if you feel like it, we'll go forward with my plan. Only if you feel like it."

"I'll call you from Dubai," she offered.

A surge of joy rushed though him. "You will?"

"I promise," she smiled up at him. "You are certainly persistent...but I like it."

"I'll book the hotel in Paris for when you're back from Dubai?" he asked.

"I…I didn't say yes yet, but I promise to think about it." Her voice was hesitant, and disappointment crashed into his excitement but he covered it with a smile. *She said she'd think about it, at least.* Alejandro understood that she wanted to be in control.

"What time will we need to be at the opera tomorrow?" she asked.

"It starts at eight o'clock," Alejandro said. "I will pick you up at six-thirty so we can have a drink before."

"Great," Julia said, and turned to pick up her bag from the back seat.

Alejandro didn't want to let her go. Julia was becoming his addiction, wrecking abomination at his very soul. He moved toward her, and as she turned back he placed his hands on her shoulders. Before she could speak he lowered his lips to hers, insistent and strong. She kissed him back, her lips soft and her sensual mouth warm and demanding beneath his.

He knew she could feel that strong attraction between them, too. When she opened the door to leave, he pulled her back into the car and kissed her again. Her kisses were short and sharp as she laughed. The passion between them was strong, and he knew Julia would be a panther in the bedroom. Myriad thoughts flew through his head. *Yes, this was going to be a very passionate story.*

Chapter Thirteen

Dubai was very lovely this time of year, but very hot too. The skyline spread across the desert, with the spires of the Burj Khalifa visible for miles around. *This place is like a dream,* Julia thought. The hotel was extremely elegant and luxurious, and Julia made herself comfortable in her suite. After she'd unpacked and settled in, she chose a simple white dress and added low-heeled sandals for a walk along the beach. She loved feeling the warm sun in her bones—oh, yes, it was just what she needed. The wind played with her hair, and when she took off her shoes the sand was warm under her feet. Julia felt as free as a bird. She made her way down to the sea and walked along the edge of the water, the Arabian Gulf waves licking her toes. She bent down, picked up a small stone and threw it into the sea. Before she took another step, a tall man accosted her.

He spoke out of the corner of his mouth.

"You look like a princess."

Julia kept walking. Whether he was a creepy fan or a random stranger, it wasn't safe to talk to a man alone in the Middle East unless you knew him well.

"Maybe you need some friends over here, to show you around the place?"

"I have already friends here, thank you." Julia stopped, and turned to give him a withering look. The buttons on his white shirt were open and Julia could not help but notice his hairy chest.

Struck by her glare, the strange man stepped back and Julia hurried away. *Who the hell was that?* she thought, *and where had he come from?* The beach was empty and there was nobody else around.

The hotel was only five minutes away, and she passed Ruben in the foyer, fighting with his phone. She waved to him, collected her key from reception and went to her

room.

The next day Julia woke early to prepare for the shoot. After a luxurious shower in the huge lavishly marbled bathtub, she pulled her long hair into a ponytail and applied skin cream. Looking into the magnifying mirror, her face was fresh and rested despite the early hour, her youthful skin glowing. When she looked into the large mirror in the elegant white bathroom, she felt beautiful.

When she had begun her successful career, it hadn't taken long before she became the favorite of several top designers. She'd definitely paid her dues, and now she would reap the reward as the cover model for the Designer of the Year issue.

A few hours later, a girl with a small piercing on her ear applied Julia's make-up, as the hairdresser waved her hair with an iron. A skinny man hovered behind a camera set-up, and his assistant, the stylist and her assistants, and assorted gofers and hangers-on stood around watching Julia on the beautiful beach.

When she was dressed and Luca the photographer was happy with the light, they started shooting.

"You are amazing. You are the most fantastic woman in the world!" Luca knew what to say to encourage her, to help her connect with the camera, and beyond that with the thousands of women who would want to wear what she was wearing now. Julia held each pose for a moment, making intimate contact with the camera. The wind swayed her long dark hair and she made sure her deep green eyes were spellbinding and mesmerizing. This was the time Julia discovered the boldness within her, which only came out when she was in full control and in front of the camera, a place she loved to be.

After several rolls of film Luca called for a break. Julia collapsed into a chair and held up a spike heel. "My feet are killing me," she said, throwing her head back.

"Oh, don't worry, dear, I'll try to make you feel better." Her assistant rushed forward to massage her feet, bringing her a chilled glass of water, ready to attend to her every need.

Julia closed her eyes and tried to relax, but her thoughts drifted amiably to Alejandro. *You are falling for him and you can't do anything to stop this feeling.* The voice was so real! Her eyes flew open, trying to recapture reality. She had been lost in a dream. She was losing her control with Alejandro. How frustrating!

Ah…Alejandro. She smiled every time she thought of him. Was she really falling for him? It was a dilemma she couldn't work out. Usually she was the one calling the shots, but with him, there was comfort in yielding to his care, something she had never expected to feel.

When Luca called for an accessories change and the next set of frames, Julia's mind was still somewhere else.

Ruben gave her a knowing smile. "The last shots; we are almost there." He knew they already had the right picture for the Designer of the Year cover for Magazine, but it never hurt to take a few more shots.

Chapter Fourteen

Back in Milan, Alejandro was missing Julia already. He fantasized about her presence every day. She bought a permanent residence in his dream-world, mocking him at his depravity, laughing at his childishness. He felt like a kid who was promised a toy the next day and he couldn't help but feel sleepless the entire night. He'd tried to call her hotel, but couldn't reach her. That night he came back from his office and dined alone at the hotel restaurant, consoling himself, surrounded by his favorite cuisine.

He reached for his cell, and called Nino. "Get me a seat to London; I just set up a meeting with an important client. I want to be back in Milan Saturday night." Sunday, Julia would be back from Dubai.

He considered the possibility of going to Paris with her. He hoped that she wouldn't come up with some excuse. Eventually, late at night he lay in bed, eyes closed, unwilling to surrender to the peaceful darkness, fighting the fact that he had to return to New York soon, and facing the possibility that he would not see Julia for a while. He didn't want to leave her but he couldn't abandon his business. He had been away too long as it was.

His parents had called; wanting to know how much longer he'd be away. He had put them off, saying his business was taking him longer than he'd expected. He'd mentioned Julia again, and his mother was keen to meet her. More fascinatingly she was keen to meet the woman, who had imparted an alien personality in her son. She had never found her son so desperate about anything, other than his work.

"We are looking forward to seeing this woman who has distracted your attention from your business." His mother sounded pleased. "I have never heard you sound so happy."

"She's very smart, and beautiful; you'll love her." Alejandro was very excited by the idea of introducing Julia to his mother.

"Good," his mother said. "Make sure it lasts this time."

Alejandro smiled. "It will. Julia is a very special woman."

Early the next day Alejandro was on his flight to London. He was confident that the meeting with this potential client would be worthwhile. He settled back in the wide leather seat with extra leg space and closed his eyes. His thoughts about Julia were going to keep him very happy until he'd see her again.

Chapter Fifteen

For Julia it had been a very long week. She'd tried to call Alejandro before leaving for the airport, but his phone went straight to voicemail. After a quick shower she dressed in a pair of light jeans that clung to her beautiful curves and a simple white T-shirt. By the time she was ready, Ruben was knocking on her door.

"Are you ready?" his smooth voice hummed behind the door.

"Yes, I am ready." She unlocked the door and stepped into the hall.

"Did you get any sleep? Your eyes are swollen." He frowned.

"Not a bit. I woke up feeling like someone slapped my face."

"Your face is sweet in the morning, chubby like a little girl." He grinned.

"Don't make fun of me." Julia said, and reached for

her sunglasses.

"I'm only teasing." He smiled. "I don't know the reason, but these days you are more beautiful than ever."

"Could be the lovely weather," she replied.

"I think it's the result of being in love," Ruben said, laughing.

"Don't be ridiculous." Julia knew now she had been seen with Alejandro. The Milanese fashion world was so small, and she was such a figure within it, any change in her social life spread like lightning.

"Whatever the reason is, we've got amazing shots for the magazine cover," Ruben said as he followed her into the elevator.

"And that's what we were looking for," she replied, ignoring his allusion.

Alejandro had succeeded in making her feel unique and very special. Between dinners, golf and the opera, they'd discovered each other's likes and dislikes, and the last two dates had ended with passionate kisses. And now he wanted to spend a few romantic days with her in Paris.

They made their way to the ground-floor restaurant, where Ruben asked for crepes and Julia ordered black coffee and fruit.

"What are you thinking?" Ruben asked, picking up

his cup of coffee.

"Nothing," Julia said, banishing Alejandro from her thoughts. "This place is amazing!" she exclaimed. She looked around to take in every detail, wondering who designed the hotel. The furniture was minimalist modern, everything either black, white or stainless steel. She picked up a piece of exotic fruit, and finished her coffee.

Outside the hotel, a car was waiting to take them to the airport. Julia lay back on the seat and thought about Alejandro's proposal. She needn't decide about it, because she already had a decision long ago. *She was going to Paris.* She liked him, and yes, she trusted him. There was no reason to say no.

Julia watched the city stream by and lost herself in thought. She was a star in her own world and she usually didn't give a damn about anyone or anything. She enjoyed every minute of her lifestyle. But she knew this life wouldn't last forever.

Now she near the end of her twenty-fourth year, and maybe it was time to think about what she really wanted for her future. Until now she'd had fame and she'd had money. *But life cannot always be about those things,* she thought. With Alejandro she felt loved and protected. And Alejandro was the type of man she'd always pictured for herself. He was a real man, and he knew how to make her feel happy. Lying back, she pictured the two of them together, looking up at the Eiffel tower.

Chapter Sixteen

Alejandro was amused that his instincts were an honest indication. Julia did accept his invitation and in the most unusual way. Alejandro had pictured that he would have to persuade her stubbornly, make her realize that it was just a casual trip and he wouldn't let her feel uncomfortable anytime. Tell her that he won't put her in any difficult position until and unless both of them agree on advancing their relationship forward. But, on the other side of reality, before Alejandro could finish putting forward his proposal for reconsideration before Julia, she agreed spot on.

"I decided I am coming to Paris with you." she said mockingly witnessing Alejandro's bewildered expression.

Nothing could have pleased Alejandro more than Julia accepting his invitation to Paris. The flight was quick, and once they arrived at the airport, both men and women turned to admire Julia's elegance. She glided smoothly through the airport, noting well-designed lounge chairs and a beautiful vertical garden along one wall. Paris was always nice place to be in.

Outside the airport, Alejandro waved for a taxi and helped her in. "Hotel Du'Bleice, *s'il vous plaît*."

The taxi driver pulled away from the curb and into traffic, and they settled back for the ride.

Alejandro asked, "How was Dubai?"

"Oh, the usual—busy-busy," Julia replied.

"I can imagine," Alejandro said. "I tried to call you several times."

"I did try to call you back. I kept getting your voicemail."

"I flew to London and my phone was off, then I received your voicemail when we landed. It was a nice surprise for me when I listened to the message. Someone has been missing me." He chuckled

"So you like surprises too." Julia smiled.

"Who doesn't?" He drank in the vision of her—he had missed her smile.

The taxi pulled onto the Avenue des Champs-Elysees and drew up before the charming Hotel Du'Bleice. When they climbed from the taxi, he slid his arm around her shoulders as they walked toward the entrance.

The bellboy brought their luggage to the room. Alejandro tipped him generously and he left with a huge smile. Julia enjoyed the sight of the luxurious room, with elegant antique furnishings in white and gold, and a large marble bath. They freshened up, and went to the hotel restaurant for lunch.

After the meal, Alejandro turned to Julia. "Would you like to brave the paparazzi and do some shopping?"

"You bet." If there was anything Julia loved apart from her work, it was shopping.

They spent the day on the Champs-Elysees, that wide boulevard filled with the shops of all the greatest designers in the world. They bought clothes, shoes, and luggage from the most important designers. Of course the lurking paparazzi and photographers were all over them. Since Alejandro had emerged from the airport the flash of the cameras had been on them. The combination of a top model and a handsome, charming and successful yacht builder added a spice to their love story, one the press knew everyone would want to read about and dream of having for themselves.

But among the flash bulbs and the insistent voices calling their names, Alejandro knew one thing for sure: he needed to convince Julia to renounce all this one day, to stay with him and only him. He knew that only a very good plan would win her—it was something he had to think about. When he contemplated the future, he saw himself married, having kids, living happily in New York.

Later that evening Alejandro chose the place for dinner very carefully, a romantic restaurant where they could spend some intimate time.

"I'd like to introduce you to my *mamma*," he said.

Julia shook her head; Alejandro was moving too fast with his plans. She gave him a look, but his eyes were honest. "Is it not too early to introduce me to your mother?"

"I think is about time," Alejandro said, "and my mother can't wait to see you."

He has already spoken with his mother about me. There was no doubt in Julia's mind; Alejandro was taking this relationship very seriously.

Without waiting for permission, he held her face with his hands and kissed her, commandingly, with no room for hesitation or refusal.

"You could suffocate me," she said.

He still held her face firmly in his hands. The thought of having her in his arms gave him a thrill. "I like the way you behave when I kiss you and don't let you turn away."

After a delicious dinner they took a long walk down the boulevard. The paparazzi had faded away with the end of the afternoon and it was very romantic around them, with lights glowing from restaurant windows and soft music floating from the bars. Other couples were also walking in the warm night, stopping from time to time to hug each other.

Back at the hotel, Julia headed straight for the bathroom, adjusted her hair and brushed her teeth, then headed back into the room. Alejandro had taken off his jacket, undone his tie and placed them on the sofa. Now he stood at the window. As she came closer, he took her hands and pulled her close.

"Come have a look at this beautiful view," he said.

Julia walked closer to the window; the lights of the city spread out before them, brightening the room.

Alejandro noticed her soft movements and was filled with mixed emotions. He moved in for a kiss, but he wanted more; he wanted to make love to her. He had dreamed about this moment constantly. Julia wasn't just a one-night conquest. She was beautiful, talented, and most of all, special.

She gazed up at him, her emerald eyes dreamy and inviting.

He drew her hand close to his mouth and softly kissed it, then allowed his eyes to linger on her breasts.

She looked down and took her hand from his. His throat closed as desire rushed through him. He looked at her thoughtfully; she radiated a hidden sensuality that enthralled him. He reached for her hand again.

She stared at him in confusion—everything was happening so fast. "Maybe we shouldn't—"

"Yes we should," he said, piercing into her eyes. There was a long silence and then his fingers found hers; his hand twined against hers as she fell into his arms. He kissed her, gently canvassing her soft neck... He was filled with an enraged excitement. As the heat grew between them, he pulled her hard against him, cupping her face in his hands. He could feel her heartbeat against his chest, amplified, and her breath, riotous. His head bent and his lips took possession of hers, their tongues entangled. He stroked her hair, his hands lingering over the back of her neck. His hand reached down to her elegant dress. He unzipped it and the dress which covered her modesty till now, fell to the ground, surrendering to Alejandro's domination. Sexy, black lingerie filled his gaze. Before she could move, his hands were exploring her body.

"We should stop doing this," she said softly against her will, her body enjoying every moment of it. His fingers were desperately touching her body, their slow movements building her desire. He released her bra and her perfect breasts came into view, so natural and desirable. He kissed her breast and played with her hard nipples.

"I missed you," he moaned through a kiss, then lowered his arms and raised her body, bringing her onto the bed. "I missed you so much," he repeated savagely, his mouth even more fierce on hers now.

Julia missed him too, more than she could have imagined. She let him take the charge. She tried to resist occasionally, fighting against her desire, but Alejandro was in no mood to stop. Somehow he knew, *she wanted it too*.

"I've had fantasies about you this last week," he told her gruffly as his mouth explored her body. She opened the buttons on his shirt, exposing a perfectly muscled abdomen. Everything about him was incredibly sexual. She felt as if she had lost herself in his arms. She tensed, moaning her pleasure against his mouth. She felt his hands shaking under her body.

"I love you," he groaned, deep lines of emotion grooved on his face and between his eyebrows. "I knew I had actually fallen in love with you that night I first met you." It was a feeling he'd never had before. Julia kissed him. Taking his hand, she led his fingers to her mouth, and without words they began to make love. Alejandro took a moment to catch his breath when he saw how sensual and magnificent Julia was in action. Her skin was like smooth satin, her long, silky hair fanning out over the bed. She moved like a panther, arousing his desire sevenfold. Her fragrance was clean and fresh.

With a gasp of pleasure, Julia realized something. She realized how much she enjoyed his presence. She realized that his absence would irk her beyond anything. She realized that she was inviting him into her world. She realized that she was starting to fall in love. She was falling in love… with him.

She let go of the whirl of thoughts that filled her mind. Their encounter was an explosion of passion. They were living as if there was no tomorrow. She felt so free, so alive—she wanted this moment to last forever.

Alejandro saw the look of pure love cross her face and was transported to an even higher place of delight. Julia was his, and now the world was amazing.

Chapter Seventeen

After Paris Alejandro left for New York, and it was as though something went missing from Julia's heart. A void filled with blackness inhabited her heart. If there were any little doubts about her feelings for Alejandro, it was gone now. Now, she knew he was the one. She had fallen for him and she hadn't known it. Sometimes in life there were certain things she could never understand. Now she couldn't help wondering what he was doing, every moment of the day. She vividly remembered all the moments she'd spent with him in Paris. With Alejandro she had experienced something she couldn't forget. And now, being away from him, it was the perfect time to think about what this new feeling meant for her.

The ringing of the phone interrupted her thoughts. When Julia picked up and heard his voice, she couldn't believe it.

"Julia?" A familiar voice announced. A voice she

could never forget in seven lifetimes. A voice which was once her morning sun. You forget the person, but never to its entirety. There is always something which clings to the core of your very soul. In her case, it was his voice.

"George?"

What did he want from her now after all this time? Julia had completely forgotten about him and, after almost two years apart, had no intention of meeting him. After all this time he had never called her—he had practically disappeared—and now he materializes from nowhere, asking for a reunion.

"Is this some kind of joke you are playing on me?" she asked.

"I tried to call you many times after you left," he said.

That was a big lie, Julia thought. She'd had no calls from him, no messages. There had been some days when she had really missed him and he'd never called. Why he was calling her now?

"I need to see you," he said. "I have never forgotten you."

"George, you cheated on me, and you broke my heart," Julia pointed out. "What do you want from me now?"

"It was just a kiss between me and that girl, nothing more. I need to see you," he said. "And I will wait for however much time you need to forgive me."

"George, I am not going to meet you. I am happy with my life now. Please don't call me anymore."

"Please, Julia, don't hang up the phone. I really need to see you."

He was really stubborn, Julia thought. How could he be behaving as if nothing had happened, as if they could pick up where they had left off? Was it even possible he didn't understand how angry she was?

"Goodbye, George. Don't call again." She made her way into the kitchen and turned on the coffee machine. This wasn't at all the right moment. Why did he want to come back into her life now? *I'm happy with Alejandro.*

She thought about calling Samantha, but it was too early—she knew Samantha slept late on Saturdays. Julia decided to go to the gym for a hard workout. It focused her mind. At ten o'clock she called Samantha from the locker room.

"Hey, wake up, I need to see you. Come to my house for lunch."

"I am still in bed," Samantha said.

"I can hear that from your voice. But I need to see you today."

"I thought I'd come tomorrow instead, and spend the whole day with you."

"I need you today, Sam." Julia's voice was loud.

"Okay, okay, I'll be there for lunchtime."

Julia went straight home from the gym and got lunch ready for herself and Samantha. She couldn't wait to tell her fiery friend about George and his stupid idea of calling her. *What would give George any thought that I was still waiting for him? I will never forgive him for what he did to me.*

Julia heard the doorbell ring and checked the time. *Must be Samantha—she certainly took her time.* She opened the door, and Samantha rushed inside.

"I hate busy traffic," she said, throwing her bag on the small table in the hall.

"Happy to see you too," Julia said.

Samantha shook her head. "Sorry sweetie, I got stressed after the journey."

"That's okay."

After few moments Samantha calmed down. "What are we having for lunch, then?"

"Seafood," Julia said.

"You are amazing, Julia, you know that?"

"Yes, I know, but anyway, let me tell you the news. Guess who called me this morning?"

"Who?"

"I said 'Guess'."

"Okay, the President of the United States?" Samantha said with a raised eyebrow to mock her.

"George decided to come back into my life. I was shocked when I heard his voice."

"Your ex-boyfriend?" Samantha narrowed her eyes. "George called?"

"Yes, I wanted to tell him he's an asshole, but I didn't."

Samantha picked up a forkful of spaghetti but paused before it reached her mouth. "Do you still love him?"

"Of course not! That person doesn't exist for me. You know me, I am not the girl who changes men at every step, but I couldn't bear to stay with anyone after he cheated on me."

"That's true. I am slightly different," Samantha said with a smile.

"Slightly!" Julia teased. They both laughed.

"What about Alejandro? Did he call you from New York?"

"Yes, he calls me almost every day. It's been a month since he left – I've started to miss him and that scares me a bit. I don't need another distraction."

"You're right," Samantha said. "But you don't need to take everything so seriously. Nobody but you takes this life so seriously!"

"I think I am falling for him, and I don't think that's a good idea," Julia replied.

"Stop being so much about control and enjoy your life." Samantha placed the fork on her plate and gave Julia her full attention. "And what's wrong with falling in love?"

"I'm not sure. Everything happened so fast. Maybe I should take it more slowly. But I can't stop thinking about him. Alejandro is so romantic, and…he's sensational in bed," she added, smiling.

"And that's very important." Samantha smiled back. She saw how Julia's eyes gleamed when she was speaking about Alejandro. "I have the feeling Alejandro could be the right man for you."

"I am not thinking of getting married yet," Julia said.

"Never say never. Don't be surprised if in the end you find out that Alejandro is Mr. Right."

Julia laughed at her. "Isn't it a bit early for those kind of thoughts?"

"Believe me, honey, when it happens, you won't ask yourself if it is too early."

Julia threw her pragmatic friend a look. "Yeah, yeah, I get it," she said, taking another sip of wine. She liked Alejandro alright, but on a second thought she wasn't so sure whether she really loved him to the extent to picture a future with him. In the heat of moment, she did consider him as her Mr. Right, but now because of the distance between them she started having doubts. He lived in New York and she lived in Milan; how often could they see each other anyway?

Chapter Eighteen

Alejandro was sitting in his office at The Signature Quintana in New York when Daniel Jordan, one of his oldest clients, called to ask if he could send an industrialist friend "to see some boats."

Alejandro happily agreed; he knew Daniel worked with the biggest millionaires in New York. But strategy was everything—when the industrialist arrived, Alejandro kept him waiting in the outer office for half an hour. Finally, he escorted the industrialist to his private office to show him the portfolio of yachts on the flat screen monitor on the wall. As they flashed through the pictures, Alejandro could tell his tactics had worked—Pique their eagerness by the delay and send a message that he wasn't too desperate to make the sale. Knowing Alejandro didn't "have" to make a deal, the industrialist asked the price for the most luxurious model.

Usually Alejandro left room for bargaining in his

first price—it always made buyers feel a little more secure when they believed they were getting a deal. But when Alejandro named the first price, the industrialist said he'd take it.

As a businessman, Alejandro was unique. His ability to close the deal in a short time was the product of his years of experience. He adored his yachts, and was more than capable of making others feel the same way, conjuring up a seductive world of glamour and luxury around himself and The Signature Quintana. He had an extraordinary gift for making friends, and he'd put as much energy into developing that talent as he had his financial acumen. After the meeting, Alejandro called Jack and told him that at the end of the week they'd have to fly to Miami to supervise the delivery of the yacht he had just sold. Then they'd throw a party at Alejandro's villa in Miami Beach, where Daniel and a few important friends would attend.

"Come into my office and I'll give you all the details," Alejandro said. Then he picked up the phone again and rang Julia, but it went straight to voicemail. He didn't want to leave her a message; he wanted to speak with her. He sat in his office and thought.

Was Julia taking their relationship as seriously as he was? They'd been so close and now she seemed so distant. The last time they'd spoken, he'd sensed that there was something that disturbed her. He hadn't wanted to pry, but now he felt compelled to hear her voice and see if everything was okay.

Jack came into the office and Alejandro brought his focus back to work, greeting Jack with his usual cheer.

"I just closed the deal with the investor that Daniel Jordan sent us," he said.

"You've never missed one yet," Jack said, looking over to Alejandro.

"We have to celebrate this with a party in Miami." Alejandro winked.

"Of course," Jack agreed.

"As you see, everything's going well here," Alejandro said. "And that makes me think that soon I can fly back to Italy."

Jack nodded in understanding. "Tell me, how's it going with your girlfriend? Is she your girlfriend now?"

"Julia." Alejandro smiled. "She is the most perfect woman I have ever met. Apparently my wishes to meet the perfect woman have come true. That woman takes me to the next level."

"You really love her, don't you?" Jack asked. "I've never seen you as happy as you are right now."

"I just can't stop thinking about her. Those few weeks in Italy, I spent the most amazing time of my life with her. I can't live without her—she brings me to life and desire like nothing I have ever experienced."

"The risk of following your instinct was worth it," Jack said.

"Sometimes you need to follow your heart, even if this foolish love lasts only for a moment," Alejandro said.

"Well said," Jack replied.

"I've never made love to a woman the way I did with Julia." Alejandro said. "Since I left Milan, she's been constantly on my mind. I feel as I've left a piece of me there and wherever I go, something inside me is missing. I miss her so much! I need to go back and bring her here with me."

Julia was becoming his addiction. But he couldn't worry about that now. What mattered was that Julia was making him the happiest man in the world.

Chapter Nineteen

Julia looked into the mirror and refreshed her lipstick before the show started. In the hectic backstage area, models were running through the dressing rooms as if their tails were on fire, to be given the last touches before they went onstage. They talked hastily and rushed from one person to other to make sure that they look perfect.

"I don't understand why all of those girls go crazy right before the show starts," Ruben said.

"I guess they just want to be perfect for the cameras and the public," Julia replied.

"I guess so," Ruben said. "You have always the right answer."

"I know." Julia smiled.

"You are a smart girl and you know that," Ruben replied. "You're the top European model, maybe the best in the world, and last year you topped the earnings list—for the fifth year in row—and you always fly first class."

"I wouldn't call myself the smartest girl in the world, but I was smart enough to sign with Ruben & Fashion. It's really thanks to you."

Ruben chuckled. "Sweetie, you're a strong woman, who knows how to take chances when they come. You're one of my best models, and that's easy for me to say."

Julia was one of those girls who knew how to take full advantage of any situation. She always knew what she wanted and she never gave up until she got it. Whenever an opportunity presented itself in front of a box of chocolates, she shoved both her hands in it and made sure she got every last one of those that her hands could grab at. When she looked at the teenage wannabes around her, who hadn't yet discovered the cutthroat side of the modeling business, she was proud of herself for making it this far, for being able to stand out as special and different from her colleagues.

"All set," the dresser said, as she gave a final twitch to Julia's long dress. The dresser turned to the next girl. "Good to go, Natasha?"

"I'm not ready," Natasha said, her hands searching desperately in her bag. "Can I borrow an aspirin from you?" she asked the model next to her, a new girl trying to keep her balance in her mega-high-heels.

Julia looked at the new girl and rolled her eyes. Natasha was a good model but she had no class when it came to backstage etiquette.

The new girl stayed quiet for a moment, until Natasha broke the silence. "Well, are you going to give me that aspirin?"

Unsure about dressing-room manners, the girl looked desperately at Julia. Julia shook her head slightly.

The girl took a breath and spoke. "I don't have any aspirin with me; it's something I don't usually take. Maybe you should keep some with you," she added with a flash of boldness, "if you're going to come in hungover."

Natasha was too shocked to respond—usually she intimidated the new models, running roughshod over them and borrowing all manner of personal items while the girls were too shy and nervous to refuse. But this new model had done the unthinkable and Natasha had nothing to say.

Julia was amused. It was fun to see Natasha's face when someone said no to her. Julia smiled at the new girl and gave her a wink. From the dress rack, Ruben started to laugh.

"It's not funny," Natasha said. "I need it."

"Maybe you should have brought it," Julia said

softly, giving Ruben a wicked glance. She was sick of seeing Natasha treating the new models badly when the girls were young and scared.

Natasha saw Julia's look. "So you agree with this baby?"

Julia shrugged. "Kind of." She turned back to her own mirror for a final check. Everything looked great.

Natasha shook her head infuriated; the wind WAS out of her sails.

Julia remembered the first time she'd met the Russian girl, with her strong voice and tall, slim body. Natasha had a beautiful feminine look that was sometimes ruined by her strident voice. They'd bumped into each other in the VIP lounge at a Milan club—it was difficult not to notice Natasha, who was already drunk and loudly socializing at one table after another. When she made it back to the table next to Julia's, Natasha began yelling at a man seated there.

"What the fuck is this dude doing at my table? Don't you see that I am trying to have fun here? Do I even know you?" Natasha then took a long sip from her glass of champagne, and as the man rose to his feet, she clutched his arm to avoid falling down.

"You don't remember me?" the guy asked.

Natasha shook her head vigorously and looked at

him closely. "I don't know you. How can you come to sit at my table without asking my permission?"

The guy gave her a skeptical look. It was quite obvious he was there by invitation, and equally clear that his host, that would be Natasha, was too drunk to remember him. The guy turned crimson with embarrassment.

At her own table beside the scene, Julia was amused.

"Maybe I should introduce myself," the guy gently said to Natasha, looking for some way to cool her down.

"Excuse me!" Natasha said, and then frowned deeply in thought. Julia could tell that her mind was trying to remember if she'd had some affair with him in the past. Natasha gave the man another look. "Don't tell me we were lovers, because I will disappoint you. I don't remember you at all."

He began to laugh. "No, we didn't have an affair together. I mean, not yet," he added.

Julia had registered Natasha's height and beauty and wondered that if perhaps the Russian girl was also a model, but she knew one thing for certain—Natasha was too drunk to know what she was doing. Julia watched for another moment, but her interest faded and she turned her attention back to her own party. In the end she didn't much care who this girl was and what she was doing with her life. *She's a big girl—she should know how to take care of herself.*

Chapter Twenty

At seven-thirty, Alejandro climbed into the seat of his silver grey Z24GT. His phone rang.

"Your private jet is ready and waiting for you," Jack said.

"Great! I'll be there shortly," Alejandro replied. "In the meantime, go get a cup of coffee. Get as much cream as you like," he added mischievously.

Jack Walker had gotten early to the airport in New York, and he'd already had his morning coffee. He checked his watch, and then looked across the terminal, his attention caught by a group of young guys crowding each other and making a lot of noise. As they approached, he stepped aside to let them pass. One of the guys regarded him with suspicion. Knowing he had lots of time to kill and being unable to think of anything better to do, Jack decided to walk to the bar. He might as well order another coffee.

"Black?" the bartender asked, as she set his cup down, already turning away. Jack touched her wrist and winked. "With cream, sweetie."

The girl blushed and left. She came back with a few creamers, and Jack smiled as she set them down. But she gave him only a quick professional smile, shooting him a look that gave no ground, and moved on to the next customer.

Jack nodded to himself none-too-happily. He hated to admit it, but he wasn't getting any younger, and his impact on the ladies wasn't what it used to be. It was diminishing with each passing day. Well, no-one could step back in time. And he'd certainly had his day. He chuckled as he remembered dating three strippers at the same time—Candi, Dakota, and...what was the brunette's name? Ah, for the days when women fell at his feet. *Old memories*. He toasted himself with the coffee—"Where there's life, there's hope"—dropped a five on the table and headed for the gate.

Alejandro had reached the airport and he and Jack settled into their seats on the private plane. Jack had to satisfy his curiosity. "Any idea who Daniel Jordan is bringing tonight? Any special guests from Miami Beach?"

"Two of his close friends want to talk about business," Alejandro said, trying to remember their names. "And Daniel informed me that they are bringing a certain sexy movie star with them." He smiled, knowing his thoughts would be on Julia.

"Sounds good," Jack said. "We are going to have fun then."

"Work first, before the party," Alejandro replied.

The first order of business when they hit Miami was to go directly to the port. Daniel Jordan's friend, the industrial billionaire who'd bought the mega-yacht a few days ago in Alejandro's New York office, was coming to collect the vessel from the Port of Miami. When the older man arrived and stepped out of his car dockside, he was dumbstruck by not only the immense size of the luxury yacht, but the charm and beauty of the design, both outside and below decks. It was like nothing he had seen before. The inexplicable level of finishing and intricate design with minute details added to the perfection. The interior was no less than a palace chamber, adorned with chandeliers, velvet sofas and carpeted flooring which added to the suave aura.

"Jordan told me you sell the most singular yachts in New York, and now I can tell him he was right," the old billionaire said.

"Every one of my yachts is unique," Alejandro replied.

"I've got a number of friends interested in yachts; I might bring some of them to see you."

"Of course," Alejandro said. "And by the way, don't forget about the party at my villa tonight." Alejandro had no problem blurring the line between personal and business. Most of his clients became his friends, and remained friends.

The old billionaire liked the idea. "I'm delighted. And I consider that a very good start for our business relationship," he said. The men shook hands. Jack chuckled, admiring Alejandro's business acumen and smooth social manners.

What better way to make new friends? For Alejandro, throwing a party at his Miami Beach villa was always a good moment to combine business and pleasure. The party flowed with champagne and cocktails, with Alejandro moving from room to room making sure everyone had a good time, playing an ideal host who tended to their guests every request.

As good a host as he was, Alejandro was still born for business. Although it was a long night of chatting, laughing, and entertaining, the next day he was ready to get back to work. He and Jack enjoyed the morning sitting on the terrace of an exquisite restaurant in Miami Beach, having an early lunch before embarking on the jet back to New York.

Below them, walking on the beach and playfully holding hands were two lovers. With a pang of discomfort, Jack thought of Cindy. *How could she have treated him so disrespectfully?* As if his thoughts had been spoken aloud, Alejandro looked across the table, raised his glass of champagne.

"La vita e' *bella!*—a toast for our success," he said.

Jack smiled ruefully and raised his glass. That was Alejandro's attitude toward life. He always looked to the positive side of everything.

Alejandro was passionate about life, and his business, and that passion had brought him homes around the world, luxurious cars and a pre-eminent position in the yacht-building industry.

Back in his New York penthouse, Alejandro called Julia. "Hey."

"Hey," she responded. "Where were you last night? I tried to call you."

"Went to Miami for business and then I slept there in my villa," he replied, deciding he didn't need to mention the party. "That old industrialist I told you about, he took his time when we got to the port, and I ended up staying in Miami Beach overnight. But never mind about me. How are you?"

"I'm okay," she said softly.

"Missing me already?"

"Yes, I do."

"I like to hear that. I miss you too."

"When will you be back in Italy?"

"I'll fly to Milan next Thursday. Then Friday we can fly to Monte Carlo for a weekend. Please tell me you are saying yes."

Julia reflected for a few seconds on her calendar. Dinner with Samantha on Saturday night. A few hours of horseback riding on Sunday…seems like nothing very exciting. "I'm saying yes," she said.

"Perfect! I'll call you tomorrow." He jumped in eagerly.

Alejandro missed her so much. He knew that when he went back to Milan he would ask her to move with him to New York and marry him. He had high hopes that she—perhaps eventually—would accept. Why not? He had all the right credentials, and he was an extremely driven man. Nothing could stop him. And he couldn't wait to introduce Julia to his family. He knew they would love her. There was an incandescent quality about Julia; she captivated the attention of both men and women. After shaving and showering, he called his mother and announced that tomorrow he'd come home for lunch.

"Make sure you do that, this time," his mother said.

"I will," Alejandro promised.

"Your father wants to come to your office one of these days."

"I know, he called me yesterday. He said he wanted to speak with me about a new project."

"Your papá is a smart man, but he has to understand that he's not young any more, to do this kind of business."

"I know, *mamma*."

"You need to speak with him because he is not listening to me."

"Leave it with me, *mamma*. You take care."

"Lucky I got you," she said, before hanging up. Signora Quintana glanced around the house. It always gave her a feeling of achievement to note what she and her husband had accomplished. Their beautiful house was spacious yet cozy; the rooms featured antique red banquettes imported from Italy. The silver candlesticks held long white tapers, and were placed on Brazilian wood tables. She sat on a velvet sofa and let her mind drift back to the old memories.

Chapter Twenty-One

Monte Carlo was an absolutely amazing place and obviously Alejandro had booked one of the BEST hotels there. Hotel L'Olardene was an exquisite palace located in the city center, one of the greatest hotels in the world. The luxurious services it offered ranged from gastronomy to its wonderful rooms and an incredible spa. *Tonight he would ask Julia to marry him and go to live in New York together.* Emotion ran through his body at the thought.

At the entrance to the hotel, Julia looked up at the noble architecture and remembered the last time she had come to Monte Carlo. She, Samantha, and Corinne had ended up in a casino all night, and Corrine had lost a great deal of money at roulette. *That was one of the most outrageous nights of my life,* Julia thought, shuddering at the memories. Corrine's parent should be hugely thankful to Samantha for being able to convince Corrine to stop playing. They never knew how close they came to bankruptcy. Samantha undoubtedly saved Corrine's wealthy parents a small fortune. Still, even if Corrine was practically a gambling addict, they had spent some exciting moments here.

After walking into the luxurious room, Julia glanced out the window. "I must say, this is one of the places I most enjoy visiting."

"I love this place too," Alejandro said, turning to her. As she stared out at the Monte Carlo view that never failed to thrill her, he came behind her and gently put his arms around her waist, resting his head on her shoulder. She remained absorbed in the gorgeous sea view and the blue sky above, vaguely alert of Alejandro's affectionate presence. The sun moved slowly closer to the horizon as evening approached, purging an enchanting shade of orange and red.

"It's such an attractive place," she said.

"Guess why I chose this place?" Alejandro asked, moving her hair to her other shoulder and kissing her neck.

"Because you wanted to surprise me?" She glanced over her shoulder and sweetly winked her right eye at him.

"Am I too predictable?" He winked back, knowing that the surprises hadn't even started yet. The biggest one would be putting an engagement ring on her finger—he wondered what Julia would think about it.

Alejandro was wise enough to realize that asking her to give up her modeling career and move to New York with him might be premature. One shot at a time. Julia had a brilliant career, as much at the top of her field as he was of his, and she might not want to make a radical change in her life right now, whether she loved him or not. But the truth was that Alejandro had never liked long-distance relationships. He needed her in New York with him. It would take all his courage to be straightforward with her tonight, when he proposed. Determined not to worry, he glanced at his watch; it was past seven.

"Hey," he said, squeezing her shoulder. "Would you like to have a bath with me before we go for dinner?"

"I...I think you should have yours and then you can scrub my back for me after," she said, teasing him.

"Mmmm...please," he insisted.

"Mmmm...I don't know," she said thoughtfully, touching her lips with her finger.

"You are a very stubborn woman."

"Just because I don't want to take a bath with you?"

"No, you will have a bath with me!" he said. With his strong arms already around her waist, he lifted her as easily as a child and tossed her onto the huge bed. She tried fending him off with a pillow, but was no match for his commanding hands. He undressed her with fast movements, throwing each article of clothing over his shoulder until they flew around the room.

Julia started to laugh. "What a brutal man you are!"

"And you like this, don't you?" Alejandro said with a challenging look. "I've got you."

"Really? You think you've got me?"

"I do, don't I?" he said, pausing for breath. Her beauty left him breathless, her nakedness, and her chocolate-tanned skin. She had the most perfect body he had ever seen.

Julia held his gaze for a moment, and then the passion between them could no longer wait. He began to kiss her, and she moaned with pleasure. Never had she felt love this intensely; never in her life had she experienced this level of passion.

Julia wished that their magnificent love-making could last forever. Nothing made her happier than being with Alejandro. She smiled to herself, thinking of how she loved him. This was the relationship she'd never had before, what she had waited to feel in her heart. Alejandro kissed her navel, and then traced his lips downward. Julia rolled her eyes as the overwhelming emotions came flooding in. She closed her eyes and lost herself in the indescribable emotions between them.

Later that night Alejandro took Julia for dinner at an exquisite restaurant in Monte Carlo, with a sophisticated atmosphere, and delicious cuisine.

"What a perfect place to be," Alejandro said, reaching for her hand across the table. The night was going exactly as he'd wished. His thought was interrupted by the waiter approaching their table.

"Does Monsieur desire another bottle of wine?"

Alejandro looked across to ask Julia if she'd like the same wine or to try another, but before he could say a word Julia's cell rang quietly in her purse.

Julia glanced at Alejandro with a regretful smile. "Sorry—a model must always be reachable." She opened her bag and picked up the phone. *Why was Ruben calling her now?* She excused herself and stepped away from the table. Alejandro said something to the waiter but his voice was inaudible.

"Yes, Ruben, what's up?"

"Are you ready for tomorrow?" he asked. "You didn't forget we're filming for that television appearance, did you? It's great publicity."

"What?" Julia shook her head, bemused. She had completely forgotten about the talk show booking. "I...I can't be there, I'm in Argentina right now. I came to see my mamá; she is not feeling so well." Julia hated lying, but sometimes it was needed.

"You're joking!" Ruben said loudly. Julia felt embarrassed, realizing how loud Ruben's voice was, hoping Alejandro wasn't hearing him scream over the phone.

"Unfortunately I'm not," she said. "Sorry I can't be there tomorrow. I know this puts you in an awkward position, but I need to stay with my mamá for a few more days."

"Okay, okay, I've heard enough," Ruben said. He sighed, and Julia knew he was thinking about whether they could reschedule. She was confident he could—Ruben knew everyone. Ruben sighed again. "At least you could have called to let me know. I hope you will take excellent care of your mother," he added, and clicked off the phone.

What a risky conversation, she thought. Ruben wasn't stupid, and Julia was pretty sure he didn't believe her excuse. She was a terrible liar. But she couldn't make herself care too much—Ruben would sort out her absence somehow, and she wanted more time with Alejandro. She hadn't seen him for a while, and every moment filled her with bliss.

She decided to just switch off the phone. Back at the table, she dropped the mobile in her handbag and smiled at Alejandro. "Sorry."

"No problem. Hope everything's okay?"

"Yes, nothing that important." Julia decided it wasn't essential for him to know what the call was about.

"Good!" he said. "Let's dedicate this night just to us."

"You're right, let's enjoy our time together." Julia stared at him for a moment, lost in his eyes, remembering the day she'd met Alejandro, and that feeling when he held her hand for the first time on the terrace outside Marc's party.

As if he'd read her mind, Alejandro took a sip of champagne, then leaned toward her, placing his warm hand over her delicate one. He knew Julia loved sitting outside the restaurant best, and he'd booked a table on the terrace so they could people-watch as the beautifully-dressed men and women streamed in and out of the casino. He had to admit, the little boy inside him was enjoying spotting the luxurious cars driving up.

Julia gave the casino a long look, the sparkling lights giving her immense satisfaction.

Alejandro saw her gaze and chuckled. "I'm taking a wild guess—that casino you've been looking at since we sat down is more special than I am?"

"Hey," she said, with a casual shrug, "I was just looking around." Memories of the night with Samantha and Corrine, in that very casino, still whirled in her head.

"You've been staring at it since we sat down. That casino looks more important than me tonight."

"Come on!" Julia groaned. "Don't say that, you're making me feel bad."

"Am I?" he said, giving her a long look that sent shivers up and down her body.

She moved forward and kissed him.

Alejandro kissed her back, and slipped his hand gently over her face before gazing into her eyes. *Maybe now was the right moment to ask her?*

Julia broke the moment. "Hey," she said softly. "Want to come horseback riding next week?"

He nodded. It was a measure of his love that he didn't even mind her interrupting him, though that was his pet peeve. "Yes, we can do that. But now I have something important to ask you." His face became serious. He pulled back his chair, came in front of Julia and got down on one knee.

"What's going on?" Julia asked, obviously realizing 'what was going on'. The one-knee stance was popular worldwide. "Why are you kneeling?" She asked anyhow, looking down at him. He was so charming and romantic, wearing his elegant suit and on bended knee before her.

Alejandro kept her gaze. "I've been thinking

constantly about how much you mean to me."

Julia was speechless, but that didn't faze him.

He continued to hold her eyes with his. "We've been seeing each other for a few months now. Perhaps you'll think it's too early for me to ask you this."

"Ask me what?"

And here it comes.

Alejandro took a small box from his pocket. "The first time I met you I had already fallen in love with you. From the start I knew you were the perfect woman for me. Don't ask me why—I can't explain it. But I know we were born to meet, born to be together. And I can't imagine the rest of my life without you by my side."

He took Julia's hand, and she felt his hand tremble. His blue eyes were incredibly sincere. She opened her mouth to speak, but Alejandro gently put a finger over her mouth. "Please don't interrupt me." His words were firm, but his voice was soft and appealing. Julia saw that there was something special about him tonight.

Alejandro raised her hand with his. "Julia, love of my life, will you marry me?"

The idea of a proposal had never crossed Julia's

mind. *Was this really happening?* It was so soon—such a short space of time. "Did you just… ask me…?"

"Yes. I did. And I will ask you again and again, a hundred times over, until you say yes." Alejandro found himself impatient for her response.

Julia knew he wasn't a traditional guy, but this proposal was memorable. His voice was the most serious and the most loving she'd ever heard.

"I enjoy being with you," Julia said, looking sagely at Alejandro, still on his knee. "It is fun, and believe me, I feel wonderful every time I'm with you." She tossed back her long, jet-black hair.

Alejandro narrowed his eyes. *She's going to refuse me*! He felt a blush rise in his cheeks. He found himself holding his breath as Julia took a moment to reflect, and then her eyes were looking into his, her mouth curved into the most romantic and sweet expression as she said, "Yes, Alejandro. I will marry you."

She said yes! "Yes!" Alejandro exclaimed with happiness. He gently slid the engagement ring on her finger. "I want you to wear this ring for the rest of your life."

"It's a beautiful ring," she said. "And it fits perfectly—my fingers are so skinny, I am always losing rings!" The rare pink, round-cut diamond sparkled with unrivaled brilliance. "Beautiful," she breathed again, as the stone caught the candlelight.

"A beautiful ring for a beautiful woman," Alejandro replied. He rose from his kneeling position, gently bringing Julia to her feet, and swept her into his arms to kiss her, holding her tight. All the eyes around them bore down at them. A round of applause erupted through the hall.

Their waiter looked up from a nearby table. "Congratulations!" he called out.

For Julia, the night was magical. Every detail of this incomparable place was perfect for the occasion. Alejandro had planned so well.

Alejandro could not believe how incredible the time was together. They laughed and talked and fed each other bites of food, exactly as people in love so often do. He felt lucky to have earned this romantic and special night, to have earned Julia's consent to marry him. Julia felt like a teenage girl. Her stomach tickled with butterflies. Alejandro was happy—Julia brought to his life that rare combination of passion and love that made magical every moment. "I love our life together," he whispered in her ear.

She nuzzled against him, cheek to cheek, and replied, "I love the way your voice sounds whispering in my ear."

"I am happy you love it, because this is going to be the first voice you'll hear when you wake in the morning," he said.

Julia had never expected to fall so much in love, but it had happened. She felt transported by a crazy passion. She was ready to throw caution to the winds, to be foolish in love for her whole lifetime, the passion between her and Alejandro beyond all boundaries.

Back in Hotel L'Olardene's Diamond Suite, Julia felt happy and dizzy at the enormous changes now taking place in her life at high speed. *What's going to be next?* She thought. *Would Alejandro come to live in Italy with me?* She'd never really thought about their living arrangements before.

"You okay babe?" Alejandro asked, seeing her sunk in distant thought as she stood near the bed, staring at her reflection in the mirror.

"I'm okay," she said in her soft, sweet voice.

Her voice stirred desire within him—suddenly Alejandro wanted nothing more than to touch her, feel her skin against his. It didn't matter that they had made love before dinner. Desire was a spoilt child. He reached for her, and began stroking her hair, feeling the long tresses slipping between his fingers. His warm breath enclosed her spirit in a tiny shell. He inhaled her fragrance, and kissed her neck. She felt a tickle run down her spine. He turned her towards him. Their gaze met. Their bodies longed for each other. Their lips met, twisting and tasting every bit of flavor. Julia moaned against his mouth, her entire body nearly melting, possessed by an almost intolerable heat.

Alejandro's hands traced to her back, unbuttoning her gown. The gown disappeared below in an instant. Letting the fabric slide to her waist, he cupped her breast in his palms and began playing with her already-hard nipples. *Oh yes, he adored her perfect, natural breasts.* He ran his tongue over their softness, savoring the sensual flavor. An unlimited urgency of desire overwhelmed him. Smoothing her hair back, he slipped the shoulders of her dress down further, gently pinning her arms, making her subject to his need. She was irresistibly sexy.

Sliding her dress off completely, he pressed his skin into hers, feeling their bodies throbbing in rhythm; his hands explored every inch of her. He kissed her passionately, her breath calling his desire, his hand moving agonizingly slowly on her body as he covered her flat stomach with hot kisses. He could feel his urgency reflected in her, her body begging him.

He lifted Julia up and she wrapped her legs around him. He stepped forward and pushed her hard into the wall. She gasped and called his name—"Alejandro"—her eyes full of deep passion. She ran her fingers over his head with a delicate touch as his tongue savored her. His strong arms pulled her higher and she whispered his name again, feeling pleasure run through every inch of her body. Alejandro touched her mouth with his fingers, and she pressed her lips around them, yearning with pleasure. He felt Julia's nails move over his back, and he kissed her with an insurmountable level of yearning.

"I love you," he murmured between kisses.

"I love you too." Julia realized, with a sharp feeling in her stomach, it was the first time she'd loved someone the way she loved Alejandro.

It was in that moment of extreme passion, of kissing and touching, that Julia gave herself to him unconditionally and without reservation.

Alejandro looked into her face, her eyes closed, her beautiful lips releasing erotic sounds of pleasure, and knew she was the most sensual woman he had ever seen. Her hair fell over her closed eyes, and her face reflected the depths of pleasure he gave her. *This girl was born to be loved,* he thought. And then passion exploded between them, and the world around them disappeared. In that moment of euphoric orgasm they could only feel themselves, fully infused with sexual pleasure.

They lay on the bed, spent, Alejandro stroking Julia's hair, Julia circling her nails on his chest and smiling a slow, dangerous smile.

"I love the way you smile after we make love," he said, kissing her face all over.

"That because you're an incredible lover," Julia said, her green eyes sparkling as she kissed him back.

"How would you like to celebrate our engagement? Should we have a party?" he asked, keeping her head on his shoulder, still playing with her hair.

"Oh," she said softly, passing her hand over his chest. "I really want something intimate, just with our close friends."

"In that case we need to keep our secret locked down until we leave for New York." He kissed her head, thinking that with all the paparazzi Julia attracted, it was going to be a bit difficult keeping it quiet.

"Leave for New York?" Julia looked up with surprised eyes. "No, you stay here," she corrected.

"But sweetheart, I can't be in Italy all the time. I want you to come with me to New York instead."

"I need to think about that," Julia said.

She needed to think about that. Alejandro knew that most other girls would be packed before the offer was finished if someone offered a 5th Avenue penthouse overlooking Central Park. But Julia Belmonte was not most of those girls. She was A top model at the prime of her career, a strong and independent woman, not easy to impress. Alejandro refused to let her answer faze him. *She will come with me to New York; she will have to.*

Chapter Twenty-Two

Back in Milan, Julia grabbed for her cell while still asleep. "What?" she mumbled into the phone.

"*I'm outside the door,*" Ruben's voice whispered.

"Ruben?"

"Yes, it's me. Can you open the door?"

Julia had returned from Monte Carlo only two days ago. She'd sent a message to Ruben, but he hadn't gotten back to her yet. She threw on a silk dressing gown and went to the door. Opening it, she stared for a moment—what was Ruben doing on her doorstep?—then led him into the apartment.

"You okay?" she asked.

"I want you to see this before the press starts calling you and asking a hundred questions," Ruben said, and tossed a magazine onto the table.

Julia had no idea what he was talking about. "What's

happened?"

"I want you to tell me. I went to buy the newspaper this morning, and then this magazine cover catches my eye."

Julia immediately reached for the magazine, the latest issue of a French gossip rag. On the cover was a picture of her—obviously taken with a long lens—kissing Alejandro in one of the restaurants they had dined at in Monte Carlo.

The headline blared: "Secret Lovers Sneak Away—Top model Julia Belmonte falls for American billionaire."

Julia threw the magazine back on the table. "I don't have a clue where they took this picture. And I couldn't care less about gossip." She smiled. "The positive thing is that Alejandro and I both look damn sexy in that shot."

Ruben sighed. From the gleam in her eye, he'd bet Julia was losing interest in modeling, that her time with his agency was drawing to a close. *They all do this when they fall in love.*

He grabbed the magazine and read aloud. "After signing with Milan-based agency Ruben and Fashion, Julia Belmonte's career grew exponentially. She's shown for top designers around the world, been the face of two major cosmetics campaigns, and boasts the biggest social media following in the industry. But now it seems the world of haut couture may lose her to a hottie! Alejandro Quintana, the legendary yacht-designer—"

"Blah, blah, blah!" Julia interrupted. "I am fed up with this gossip. My life has been so much happier since I met Alejandro. Maybe if I decide to move to New York with him it will be even better."

"What do you mean 'Move to New York with him'?" Ruben blurted. "You can't just walk out on me. You just can't!"

"Okay, first of all, I don't like the way you're criticizing me, and secondly, Yes I can."

Ruben moved to the window and stared out. "I am sad to hear that. I don't want to lose my best model."

"I know," Julia said, lowering her temper. "I appreciate everything you've done for me. And I haven't decided yet what to do. My career—I am so confused."

Ruben watched her closely. "You love him?

"Yes, I do."

"Then that is the answer. If you love Alejandro and he makes you happy, you should follow your heart."

"You think I should go to New York?" Julia asked.

"Damn right you should," Ruben said, reaching down to pick up his car keys.

"Okay. Maybe I'll do it," Julia said. In that moment, she decided that she definitely would. *When will I feel like this about any man ever again?*

"We'll call you later. And say hello to Alejandro," Ruben said, hurrying toward the door.

Julia stopped him before he left. "Ruben?"

He turned and smiled at her happiness.

"Thank you," she said. "I needed to hear I was making the right decision."

She was half-impressed, half-thrilled at how Ruben had taken the news. But now happiness poured into her heart. The idea of moving to New York felt amazing. Being a top model had been a major kick, both on the catwalk and on the top-selling magazine covers. But after so many years, it was a job rather than an adventure. The thrill was gone. She lay back on her bed for some more sleep and to think over her plan, but the insistent buzz of her doorbell awoke her again.

Maybe Ruben forgot something?

She rolled out of bed and headed for the door, some sixth sense telling her to stop before she opened it, to see who it was. She looked through the peephole and stopped. Dead still. George—her ex—was outside the door.

God! What he was doing outside of her apartment? And how had he found out where she lived?

The doorbell continued to ring as she stood silently in the hallway trying to figure out her next move.

It occurred to her there was only one answer, and that was to do absolutely nothing and hope George would go away and not come back. The last time he had called she'd told him not to call her again, to forget about her. He had continued to pursue her, phoning several times a day—thank goodness for caller ID—and eventually she'd blocked him.

Apparently his last girlfriend hadn't been enough for him, and now he was on Julia's doorstep. And what was she supposed to do about that?

Exactly nothing.

George was just an unpleasant memory, and she had so many better things to think about. She stepped back softly and made her way back to bed.

Chapter Twenty-Three

Julia could not help but be pleased with herself. She had not answered her door to the early caller, had not given in to him calling her name in the hall. Her only fear was that George might be capable of springing the lock of her door. What an insane situation. Fortunately, after twenty minutes the ringing doorbell had stopped and George had gone. Now it was late afternoon and Julia felt much safer.

She called Samantha, who Julia knew would be driving through town on her way home.

"I meant to call you," Samantha said. She was curious to find out when there would actually be a party. Was Julia still giving herself an escape route by not "officially" announcing the engagement? Giving up the career she loved so quickly, almost without thinking about it, seemed such a random thing for Julia to do.

"Is Alejandro in town?" Samantha asked, pulling up to a red light.

"Yes, but he had an important business dinner tonight," Julia replied, her phone tucked between shoulder and ear as she folded designer label jeans and put them into a large suitcase. "Why?"

"Cause I was thinking of picking up your favorite pizza and coming over."

"Sounds good," Julia said. It had been a while since she and Samantha had a girls' night in. "What time will you be here?"

"About half an hour," Samantha replied.

"That's great! See you!"

After stopping by Il Fornello for a thin crust with basil and tomato, Samantha headed straight for Julia's house.

"So," Samantha said, throwing herself into a chair at the kitchen table. "I'm dying to know—how was your romantic weekend in Monte Carlo?"

"Very interesting," Julia said, as her doorbell chimed.

"Are you expecting someone?" Samantha asked.

Julia stood up. "I'm not expecting anyone." She rushed to the door, but quietly—heaven forbid it was George again.

"The pizza is getting cold and I'm starving," Samantha yelled after her.

When Julia came back into the kitchen, Alejandro was right behind her.

Samantha was surprised. Hadn't Julia assured her that Alejandro had some important dinner tonight?

"It's Alejandro," Julia said briskly.

"Uh, hi," Samantha said, smoothing her hair with one hand and adjusting her skirt with the other, embarrassed that she wasn't looking her best this evening. *Damn Julia, she always looks amazing.*

"Hello Samantha," Alejandro said, proffering a firm handshake and a friendly smile. "It's such a pleasure to meet you again."

"Samantha just brought a pizza," Julia said, smiling delightfully at her friend. "Would you like some?"

"I already had dinner with my client earlier." Alejandro said, bending to kiss Julia on the cheek. "Are you packed? We need to leave Milan early tomorrow to miss the traffic."

"Almost finished."

"Well, I hope you'll have finished everything before bedtime," Alejandro chided, and the two exchanged an intimate look.

Oh my God! Samantha thought. *They're acting as if they're going to get it on, right there on the kitchen table.* She couldn't help feeling that somehow she'd been left behind. It wasn't that she didn't like Alejandro; he was warm and friendly, quite lovely in fact. So what was it?

Am I jealous? Do I feel as if Julia is abandoning me?

They'd been friends since Julia came to Milan. They'd shared everything—all their thoughts about men in their lives, about dreams and problems.

Samantha sensed that their friendship was slipping away. Alejandro was so important in Julia's life, and there might not be any room left for her. The thought saddened her, truthful as it seemed. She wished that she too had someone to giggle at and feed pizza to. Someone who would exchange the same intimate look as Julia and Alejandro were doing right now. She even wished her ex-boyfriend, Roberto, was here with her.

But no, Roberto had another woman in his life now. And that was a problem that Samantha couldn't get over. Life was a bitch.

"So! Who wants a slice of warm delicious Pizza!" Samantha shrieked purposely to break them from the fantasy world.

Chapter Twenty-Four

Breakfast in Lake Como was like something from a dream world. Julia and Alejandro sat out on the bar terrace overlooking the lake. July had just made an entrance and the sunrise was marvelous, sparkling on the water between the mountains. Here everything was noble and gracious; everywhere she looked there were uneven hills, covered with clumps of trees, randomly grown and flourishing, where mankind had not yet planted their life-stealing hands. The air was filled with scent from the ancient orchards of gardenia and magnolia.

"This place is so beautiful—and very relaxing," Julia said.

"Glad you like it," Alejandro said, pleased with her astonishment. "Marc Rotoglione sold me a lovely villa over here."

"Why haven't you ever told me you owned a villa here?" Julia shook her head.

Alejandro had known Julia would love the villa.

"I didn't tell you because I wanted to surprise you. And I told Marc to keep the secret, too."

"I thought Marc was my friend," Julia snapped.

"Well, now he's my friend too." Alejandro winked at her. "I sold him a modern yacht at a very convenient price, and then he gave me a good price for this villa."

For a moment Alejandro was all business. Julia smiled at his intensity.

"You are full of surprises," she said.

"I like to surprise you and make you happy. "

Looking at the gorgeous landscape, Julia felt she was living in a dream. She loved every minute with Alejandro. She felt a happiness she'd never felt before.

When they'd finished breakfast and lingered over their coffee, looking into each other's eyes, they took Alejandro's car on a drive along the coast and up to the villa. When Alejandro turned into the drive and the gates slowly opened, a vision appeared before Julia's eyes. A beautiful villa, set like a jewel in the hills around the lake, with views to die for. Words were not enough to describe this amazing estate and its surroundings.

Julia couldn't imagine the price this unbelievably beautiful place must have fetched. She was impressed. *How rich could this Alejandro Quintana be?* The view left her speechless. And Marc, her best friend, had never told her about Alejandro's plans. *How annoying was that?*

Alejandro smiled with satisfaction at how his new place had delighted Julia. He liked to do things in his own way. He always had, but now, since he had met Julia Belmonte, he'd turned his single-minded focus to impressing her.

He led her through the gardens, where they walked down gravel paths lined with precisely manicured hedges interspersed with flower beds in a riot of colors. Surrounded by exotic plants, beautiful fountains bubbled softly.

"This is truly an amazing place," Julia said.

"I'm delighted you like it." Alejandro glanced at the slim woman beside him, imagining being here with her at sunrise, or watching the sunset holding her in his arms.

As they walked along the marble wall of the villa, Julia saw niches in the walls, each hosting a striking sculpture. They crossed a wide terrace, where Alejandro opened a pair of glass doors and ushered her inside. In the spacious, high-ceilinged salon, an old painting attracted Julia's attention. She stepped closer to see it more clearly. It was a figure of a girl reclining on a chaise, one hand holding her hair back to the side.

"Do you like it?" Alejandro asked.

"Yes. It's very beautiful," Julia replied. She studied Alejandro's face. "You look surprised."

"It's my favorite painting too," Alejandro said. "I see we have a lot in common," he added.

"Well I was bit worried we didn't," Julia teased.

He smiled back. He liked her sense of humor.

He'd been serious for far too long, and Julia was the right woman to make him laugh.

Julia turned back to admire the painting. For fun, she did quick mathematical calculations in her head, trying to figure out how much it was worth.

It was an incredibly beautiful work of art.

Alejandro took her by the hand. "Let's go, darling. There are more things inside the villa to show you."

God! she thought. Everything around her—sculpture, antiques, *objects d'art*—was precious.

She turned to Alejandro. "I should be congratulating you on having chosen this wonderful villa."

"This is our villa," Alejandro replied.

Julia looked to see if he was serious, and saw nothing but deep sincerity in his eyes. Once again she realized that Alejandro was doing everything within his power to make her happy. He had surely made up his mind to tie their fates together. She smiled from within at the thought. Her heart suddenly felt relieved. She took him by his arms.

"I like the way you think about us and our future," she said softly, glaring intently at his eyes.

Alejandro eyes drank in the magnificent being by his side. There was nothing more satisfying than spending time with her. "You are my lady, and I will do everything to protect you and make you happy."

Sounds like a fairy tale, Julia thought.

Chapter Twenty-Five

Paris was the last fashion show, the last catwalk for Julia, and it was unexpectedly memorable. Her face glowed with happiness. Her smile lit up the room and made even her rivals feel happy for her. Her colleagues congratulated her—the news of her engagement had taken sail.

"I must say, when I heard the news I thought it was a joke," Natasha said. "Everyone here knows how much you love modeling, how it was your first true love, and you put your heart and soul into building your career."

"You've got that right," Julia said. "But now I found someone who made me happier." She could have shouted with joy.

"I'm glad for you," Natasha said, tightening her lips.

Julia could not help but notice the jealousy on Natasha's face. "Okay, enough about my life now."

She said a last few goodbyes, waved, and with her

luggage headed for the street to get a taxi to the airport.

On the way she called Samantha. "Where are you? I've been calling and calling!"

"Guess," Samantha mumbled into the phone.

Julia suspected she already knew the answer. Samantha's highs and lows were radical, triumphing at each new conquest, then despairing for a few days after, bemoaning the "totally random sex."

"Guess."

"Don't wanna guess," Julia said, putting her big sunglasses on as the taxi pulled up to Departures. Grabbing the oversize luggage and making her way into the terminal, she felt a little irritated by Samantha's behavior. Was there anything she could do to change her friend's character? Nothing came to mind. She and Samantha were living in two different worlds, and as much as Julia tried to influence Samantha into better choices, she'd finally realized it was never going to happen. After all, everyone is entitled to their own choice of lifestyle.

By two in the afternoon Julia touched down in Milan. Amid a forest of camera flashes, Alejandro bundled her into the car. When he deemed they'd driven far enough to escape the paparazzi, he pulled over to the side of the road and gave her a passionate kiss, breathing in the familiar smell of her skin. She always smelled so good. It reminded him how much he had missed her while she was away.

"It's been too long since I last hugged you." He said, studying her body. She was dressed for traveling in a pair of jeans and a pink top. As always, her height was only enhanced by her stylish high heels. The sophisticated design of her glamorous sunglasses gave her class and style. Alejandro felt proud.

Julia noticed his eyes scanning her, and smiled. "I've only been away one week."

"Which felt like a thousand years." He replied. He pulled back onto the road and felt her lips slip over his neck. His hand kept her head placed on his shoulder as he accelerated. With Julia's life so exciting and enigmatic—he never knew what to expect. He thought of her from head to toe and decided there was nothing he would change on her. She was perfect just the way she was.

"I spoke with Jack in New York yesterday," he said, pulling up as the traffic snarled. "He'll come to our engagement party, too."

"Sounds good," Julia said. She rummaged in her bag for the guest list she'd scribbled on the flight from Paris. "Did you speak with the florist?"

"Already done, my love," Alejandro replied.

"I want small arrangements on every table, with fresh tulips coordinating with the color palette. I think it will tie things together."

Alejandro noticed her anxiety and patted her thigh. "Everything will be perfect," he assured her.

"I just want everything impeccable for our day," she softly said.

Hearing her sweet voice, Alejandro felt his desire for her growing. He lifted his hand and stroked her hair. "I missed you."

"I missed you too," Julia whispered into his ear.

Alejandro whispered back with deep sensuality, "Can't wait to get home and make love with you."

Julia felt a tingle deep in her abdomen. Yes, that was exactly she wanted to do, too.

Forty minutes later they had rushed through the door, unable to resist a moment longer, flinging their clothes on any piece of furniture they passed, making foolish love.

"You're irresistible," Alejandro said, and pulled her toward the bedroom. The way Julia kissed him drove him nuts. He scooped her into his arms and she wrapped her legs around his waist, her mouth reaching for his chest, his neck, his ears.

"I missed you," she whispered again, flushed and

breathless.

"And I am foolishly in love with you," he replied, lightly dropping her onto the bed. He engulfed her body with his and felt her tremble beneath him. Slowly he ran his hand down her body.

She felt as if a series of electric shocks followed his touch. It was too good to resist and she melted beneath him. His powerful arms wrapped around her as he commanded her with his need. She felt he was giving her everything, and yet she couldn't get enough of him. Their connection was incredible—their passion, their love, their respect knew no boundaries, and now their bodies surpassed all limits together.

"I'm giving you my schedule," Julia informed Samantha on the phone. "I'll be going back to Lake Como today, and staying there until after the engagement party. Then I'll be taking off for New York with Alejandro."

"I still can't believe you're leaving," Samantha said.

"I know," Julia replied. "But you can come to New York to visit me."

"Of course I will."

Samantha felt she was losing her best friend. And to New York! The distance was so great. Yes, they could phone, but it wasn't the same as having her friend right here. She didn't want to burden Julia with her feelings—it wasn't fair to lay that on her right before the engagement party. After all, she told herself, it wasn't as if Julia had planned to abandon her, or even to leave Milan—but it was all happening so fast. She couldn't blame Julia. If Samantha found a man who made her as happy as Alejandro made Julia, she'd drop everything in a minute, too.

Chapter Twenty-Six

As she reached her office Friday morning, Samantha was ready for a break which broke her usual routine. Today she'd go to the office, issue some work to her assistant, and then take the rest of the day off. There was plenty to do in the office—there was always plenty to do—but today what she needed most was to shop for a new dress and a nice pair of heels for Julia's engagement party. She needed to look her best for any prying eyes looking for a date. Her phone rang in her bag. Anthony, she thought. She'd called him last night and he hadn't picked up. Maybe now he was calling with some excuse. He'd fallen asleep, he hadn't heard the phone, *whatever*. Despite herself, she rummaged in her bag to glance at the caller-ID.

Not Anthony. Corrine.

"Samantha!" Corrine's voice was even louder over the phone. "You know Alejandro and Julia are throwing an engagement party?"

"I certainly do know," Samantha replied. "Did you

get an invitation?"

"Yes, I just got it in the mail. So formal!" Corrine said. "I was surprised Julia didn't call me to tell me about it."

"Well, she sent you the invitation, right? She can't call everyone, she's busy these days."

"The party is this weekend! I was so surprised," Corrine pointed out. "Julia's never seemed like the kind of girl who wants to settle down, especially so quickly after meeting this guy. And the fact she is dropping her sky soaring career for him is giving me sleepless nights."

"I know," Samantha said. "But love always makes people change. It can do wonders. Anyway, keep the news secret. Julia and Alejandro want something small just to announce and celebrate their engagement, so not everyone's invited."

"That's so Julia," Corrine said. "She always wants to keep things intimate, just among the nearest and dearest friends."

"That's the best way to celebrate an engagement," Samantha agreed. "I think she was smart to limit the guest list to just her close friends. You know how private she is—she doesn't want to have a bunch of gossips at her engagement party. By the way, do you know how to get there?"

"I can read, silly. The address is on the invitation."

"If you want, we can go together?"

"That would be great!" Corrine replied, sounding almost expectant of this proposal.

"Okay then. Come to my house tomorrow and we'll leave together from there."

"Great, see you tomorrow then."

"Bye!"

"Bye!" Corrine clicked off the phone thinking how lucky Julia was. *She and Alejandro have been together only a few months and they already got engaged!* Corrine couldn't believe everything had happened so fast. They'd flown to Monte Carlo, Alejandro had seduced Julia with a fancy ring on her finger and it was done. Why was Julia so lucky? Everything seemed to drift to her side all the time. Mostly, Corrine was surprised Julia had given up her brilliant career—she'd never expected that from Julia. *This Alejandro Quintana must have a strong influence on her. Why can't I find a real man, too?*

Corrine let the phone slip down on the bed, closed her eyes and allowed her mind to dream. *Why not me?*

Then almost suddenly, as if it was her mind retaliating against her, she realized. That one thing she did, utterly unforgivable, and she hops Julia will never find out.

Saturday morning dawned clear and bright. Samantha grabbed a cup of coffee and started getting ready for the occasion. Yesterday she'd bought a pink dress that showed off her streaky hazel eyes, heels and a small bag to match. Just as she was done admiring herself in the mirror, her phone buzzed. *Unknown caller.* When she picked up, a familiar not so friendly voice spoke from the other side.

"Julia is getting engaged." Said the hoarse voice, "And you kept it from me."

"George?" Samantha said picking up her senses, "You don't need to know anything about that. Julia is happy for the first time in her life. You stay away from her."

"I still love her!" he yelled. Samantha felt her heart jump through her skin.

"Stay away George." She said, "If you really love her. Just… Stay away." She hung up the phone without listening to his protest dearly hoping that he didn't know where the party was being held. Julia would not be happy seen him in there.

Minutes later, Corrine knocked at the door of her apartment. Samantha flushed her mind of the recent activity that took place. George would never find out where Julia's engagement party is. And he appear too drunk to think clearly anyway. He needs to go home and get some sleep. God knows where he had spent the night before. Or maybe he had drunk vodka instead of coffee for breakfast. Ah, I can't be bother to think of George now. Today is going to be a great day! Samantha couldn't help feeling excited—this was an important day, her and Corrine were going to celebrate her best friend's engagement.

"Your dress looks good," Samantha said as she opened the door. Corrine was wearing an electric blue dress with elegant nude heels. "You're ready to go?" she said. "Do you want to come in and take another look before we leave?"

"No, I'm okay." Corinne replied. "We can go."

"Great!" Samantha said, and reached for her keys and her bag. Once they were in the car, Corrine again launched into the story of the time Nick, her ex, had walked out of her life.

Samantha didn't really need to hear it again. "Oh, you should have listened to me that time you came into my office to bitch about him."

Corrine sighed. "You were right." She stared out the window at the villas appearing on the Lake Como coast, beautiful vistas of the hills stretching out behind them. Samantha stole a look at her. She wondered if Corrine was thinking about the same thing as she was. Samantha was the only one who knew about Corrine's wretched secret. But she never judged her for it. A l*eopard can never change its spots.*

"What a beautiful sunny day, perfect weather for Julia's party," Samantha said, as she pulled the car into the long drive in front of a huge villa. She parked behind a long row of luxurious cars.

Corrine had to admit, the day was beautiful and she wanted to be present in it. She felt a real thrill kicking Nick out of her mind. *You never know who you'll meet at a party, right?*

The two beautifully dressed women made their way into the garden. Among the hedges and fountains, Samantha saw Alejandro moving from group to group, welcoming his guests. Given the opportunity to assess him from a distance, she looked at him critically. He was certainly a handsome man, his elegant, silver-grey summer suit cut perfectly to his body. His hair was cut shorter than the style, but it suited him, and the bright blue eyes sparkling in his tan face gave him a very sexy look. As if he could feel Samantha's gaze, Alejandro looked up and smiled at her. Samantha waved, and he crossed the garden to greet her.

Behind Samantha, Corrine checked out the billionaire she'd heard so much about. She indulged her own thoughts for a moment, wondering what such a sexy and charming man would be like in the bedroom.

Fortunately, Samantha interrupted her thoughts. "Hi

Alejandro! Congratulations."

"Thank you," he said, and kissed her on both cheeks.

"I haven't seen Julia?" Samantha asked.

"She's coming down in a minute."

"Great! I'm sure she looks gorgeous, as always," Samantha said.

Alejandro proudly smiled. "She does!"

Samantha remembered Corrine behind her. "Ah, I almost forgot, this is Corrine, a friend of Julia's and mine."

Great, Corrine thought. Exactly the kind of man I'd like to be with. Now that I find one, he turns out to be my friend's fiancé. Totally bad luck.

"Nice to meet you," Alejandro said politely, and they kissed each other's cheeks.

"It's my pleasure," Corrine replied.

Alejandro's eye was caught by another guest entering the garden. Jack Walker was taking a stroll, lapping the vicinity, as if looking for someone in particular.

"Ladies, I wish you to have a great time and enjoy the party," Alejandro said. He stepped back and turned away.

Alejandro was barely out of earshot before Corrine

burst out, "Oh my god! He is so hot. I can't get enough of tall guys—and he's built! Have you noticed those arms, and that perfect ass?"

Samantha gave her a straight look. A l*eopard can never change its spots.* "Make sure your ridiculous fantasies do not arrive at Julia's ears. I don't want to imagine what she'd do hearing you speaking about her man like that."

"I was just saying how good-looking he is," Corrine complained. "There's nothing wrong with looking!"

"Well make sure your fantasies end here and stop looking, because if Julia notices you looking at her man with those eyes, she's going to kill you."

"Calm down, I was just admiring him, that's all."

"I hope so," Samantha snapped.

"You are so uptight," Corrine said. "I'm going to find the ladies' room. See you later."

Samantha watched Corrine walk away and shook her head. Corrine was always so man-crazy.

As Alejandro was walking towards his parents tending to his guests en route, he saw a commotion at the main gate. A small crowd had gathered which consisted of people who had gone that there to have a quick smoke. The rest of the party was unaware due to the music. As Alejandro advanced towards the gate, the voice of the man was starting to register in his ears.

"Let me in!" The man shouted. He looked drunk and judging by his appearance he hadn't even taken a bath in over a year. His hair was disheveled and his eyes were bloodshot. He smelled foul from a distance and could barely stand on his feet. The bouncers pulled him away while he kept yelling, "Let me in!"

When the bouncers returned Alejandro approached one of them, "Who was he?"

"Ah, nobody, I think it was some crazy fan of Miss. Julia." He said while cleaning himself of the dirt, "It happens when their idols get married. They go nuts. Happens all the time. No big deal, everything's under control. Enjoy the party Sir."

Alejandro nodded and walked away from the spot. He decided it was of no use to let Julia know about the incident. She didn't need to stress about some crazy fan. Julia was his in every aspect of her life. His mind filled with conviction. In no time at all, he'd totally forgotten about the guy at the gate.

He walked to his parents and sat before them. They had their undivided attention towards him.

Samantha followed the path beneath her feet—this was a beautiful garden and she wanted to admire it. She stopped at a bed of gorgeous orchids around a small fountain, and heard voices. One of them was Alejandro, and the other…? She risked a peek around the fountain and saw Alejandro speaking with an older lady, and a man in a classic suit. The man stood a little to the side, his chin resting dully at his palms, listening thoughtfully and nodding on cue from time to time.

"You have to tell her now; she needs to know that you will never allow her to model again," the woman said.

"If I tell her now she might not be happy with that," Alejandro said. "What if she doesn't want to stay with me then? I don't want to lose her."

"Well, son," she said, "do what you think best. But you must remember, never lie to your woman because one day she will discover it and she will never forgive you."

"Listen to your mother, son, she is right," said the thoughtful man.

Samantha was shocked at the words she was hearing. She wasn't hiding herself, exactly, and she couldn't help overhearing, she told herself. It wasn't like she was eavesdropping—people with private conversations shouldn't have them outside! Intent on hearing what came next, Samantha was startled and gave a jump when a man spoke.

"Nice fountain!"

"Yes it is," Samantha replied, catching her breath

and trying to look relaxed, as if she hadn't just had a man practically jump on her out of nowhere. Before she knew it, the two of them were walking down the path, admiring the abundance of spectacular flora the garden hosted.

The man eyed her appreciatively. "Let me guess," he said. "I bet you're a friend of the bride."

Samantha nodded. "Yes. I'm Julia's best friend, actually," she added. "I suppose you're a friend of the groom?"

"Indeed. I am Alejandro's…well, good friend." He smiled. "Jack Walker. Nice to meet you."

Samantha glanced at him. "Seriously? I've heard about you from Julia." Julia had told her about Alejandro's friend Jack Walker. In a way it was Jack's doing that they were all here—because of him, Alejandro had gone to the fashion show where he'd first seen Julia.

As they walked, Samantha stole glances at Jack. He looked about fifty-four, tall, dark blond hair with a nice smile; a little robust, but his body was proportionate. And his American accent made him sound even more interesting. Samantha gave Jack a flirtatious smile. "One thing Julia forgot to say about you…"

"What that might be?"

"She forgot to tell me that you are quite an

interesting man."

Jack looked amused. "I think this evening is starting better than I hoped."

Samantha opened her fashionably small bag and took out a business card. She scribbled her mobile number on the back and gave it to him. "If you need any help while you're in Italy, just give me a call."

"Thanks, I'll do that." Jack took the card and put it in his pocket.

"If you'll excuse me, I've left my friend alone—I should go find her. Heaven only knows what she's been doing without me. She likes to have a very good time."

Jack smiled. "See you later."

Under a marquee with cocktail tables, Samantha found Corrine at the bar, surrounded by men. Samantha shook her head and went over to extract her friend.

"Excuse me gentlemen." She drew Corrine away from the bar. "I leave you alone for five minutes!"

Corrine looked over her shoulder and mouthed *call me*. To Samantha she asked, "Where have you been? I was looking for you."

"I walked around admiring the garden. It was…delightful."

Everything went quiet around them. Heads turned

toward the stairs at the villa's entrance, jaws dropped in astonishment. Julia paused for a moment at the top of the stairs, smiling in welcome. Her slender, elegant figure was clad in a stunningly cut, aqua-green dress, long and strapless with a high side slit. She'd done her long dark hair in soft waves, pulled to one side, her diamond earrings flashing against the ebony of her hair. As she descended the stairs, every eye admired her class and elegance. For a magical moment, Julia had captivated their attention with her charm.

Julia made her way into the garden, greeting her guests. She loved seeing people from every corner of her life gathered together for the first time. She had flown her mother in from Argentina, and saw *mamá* talking with Alejandro, hopefully getting to know him better. Meanwhile, her older sister Lucila had moved over to Samantha's group and was casually chatting with Corinne. Julia felt a moment of alarm as she considered the stories they could exchange. When it came to gossip, Corinne was very good at putting rumors around. But the little group was surrounded by noise and laughter, so Julia could only guess what they might be saying. She brushed away the worry and welcomed more guests with her warm smile. At least everyone was enjoying the party.

As Julia moved toward her sister and Corinne, Samantha intercepted her.

"Samantha! I am so happy you are here."

"How could I miss such an important event?" Samantha paused, wondering if it was really a good idea to tell Julia about the conversation she had overhead in the garden. But she couldn't ignore what Alejandro had said either. *How could he agree with his mother that he should stop Julia from any kind of modeling in the future*? Maybe it would end their love story—but Julia was her best friend, and she needed to know this before leaving for New York. "I need to tell you something very important."

Julia frowned slightly at the urgency in Samantha's tone. "What is it? Is everything okay with you?"

"Nothing happened to me, I'm fine," Samantha said. "It's just—I was just wondering—once you move to New York, will you still work at all? I mean, will you do any modeling?

Julia relaxed. "I'm not sure if I'll go back to modeling, but it wouldn't be for a while. I want to enjoy my time with Alejandro, maybe even expand our family soon!" She smiled.

Samantha widened her eyes in surprise. "Are you pregnant?"

"No, of course not! I was just making plans." Julia winked.

So Alejandro stopping Julia from modeling isn't a problem…for the moment. Samantha decided there was no reason to repeat the conversation between Alejandro and his mother. Or maybe she should just tell Julia? Either way, it sounded like it made no difference now.

"What it was that you wanted to tell me?" Julia asked.

"Ah…I was just—" but as soon she began to speak, Alejandro materialized behind Julia and put his hand around her waist.

"I imagine you are having a nice conversation, ladies, but I need to steal Julia for a moment. I'm sorry to interrupt." He took Julia by the hand and led her away.

Samantha's thoughts buzzed furiously—had Alejandro noticed her listening behind the fountain? The other guests began to clap, and she followed suit mechanically with them. Alejandro was mounting the stairs to a microphone that had been placed there, Julia by his side.

He took the microphone and the crowd fell silent. "Today is a special day for me, and I thank all of you for coming to celebrate this important day of my life with me."

"When I first met Julia—" he cleared his throat "—it was the most magical moment of my life. I knew immediately she was the woman of my dreams." He raised his glass and saluted Jack Walker. "And for this, I can't give thanks enough to my friend Jack Walker, who basically forced me to go to the fashion show that night."

A murmur of laughter ran through the crowd, and Jack smiled sardonically, raising his glass in return.

Alejandro continued, "If it wasn't for Jack, I wouldn't be here, with Julia, to celebrate this day. We've had an unusual courtship—usually when two people meet, they get to know each other first before knowing if there's a connection. But when I first saw Julia, from that very first moment I knew: I wanted her to be with me for the rest of my life."

A cheerful round of applause followed. Julia felt she was about to burst into tears.

"I've never met another woman as perfect as her, and deep inside, I felt she was my soul mate. That night, after the show, I caught myself wondering how to get close to her, wondering if she would ever feel for me what I felt for her. I knew I had found my princess and I couldn't let her go. I stayed in Italy, to find out who this girl was who had stolen my heart."

Julia turned crimson, and stared at her heels. She bit her lips until Alejandro pulled her closer and looked at the crowd as if learning the expression of his audience who just witnessed his masterpiece.

"I remember Jack flying back to New York alone—

grazie mille, Jack—and hearing him say he couldn't believe I'd go so far for a woman. Trust me, Jack…" Alejandro winked at his friend ."I'd do it all over again."

"But now, I am standing here announcing my engagement to the most wonderful being in my life. I feel so lucky, I can't believe it—and I'll admit, I am still worried that she might slip through my fingers. So, friends, family, guests, before she changes her mind, please join me in raising your glasses to the future Mrs. Quintana." He lifted his glass to Julia, and as everyone drank, she threw her arms around his neck. They exchanged kisses, and phones and cameras popped out everywhere for photos. The garden illuminated with flashes.

When the guests calmed down a bit, Alejandro reached for the microphone again. "I'd like to invite Julia's best friend, Samantha Lombardo, to come up and say a few words."

The guests clapped as Samantha went up the stairs to take the microphone.

She looked at the crowd with expectant eyes as if she was going to give a speech on something that would curb the problem of global warming. She cleared her throat and began, "When Julia first asked me to give a speech at her engagement party, at first I thought I'd have no idea what to say. But then I realized, yes, I do have a few things to say about this couple." Samantha looked at Julia and Alejandro with mock sternness, and Julia giggled at her friend's pretend-serious expression.

Samantha continued, "When Julia first told me she was in love with Alejandro and was going to move to New York to be with him, my first thought was, are you drunk? You're going to leave *Milan?* You're going to leave *Italy*? I mean, look at this place!" Samantha gestured to the beautiful hills surrounding them, and the view of the lake. The guests chuckled appreciatively.

"But what my feeling really was, was that I was afraid to lose my best friend. I admit it, I did hope she'd change her mind—sorry, Alejandro."

Alejandro laughed at Samantha's honesty and humor. He knew it could be hard for two women to stay friends when one of them got married.

Samantha spoke again. "A long time ago, Julia and I had first moved to Milan, and both of us were struggling. Julia was still a new face in the fashion world, and I had just joined my firm here. We didn't have any other friends, we hadn't moved into our apartments yet, we didn't know anyone—we only had each other. One night we started crying together—the wine may have had something to do with that—" she paused as the crowd burst into laughter, "—and we promised ourselves we would never abandon each other. So when Julia met Alejandro, I was worried at first. Their love seemed too perfect to be true. But, the more time I spend with them, the more I see how much they love each other. How perfectly they fit together. And if I have to give up some of my best friend, I'm happy to share her with a man who's crazy about her."

Again, she turned sternly to Alejandro. "I've decided I like you—for now." At this Samantha couldn't keep her face straight and giggled before composing herself again. "And you make my best friend happier than I have ever seen her." She looked at Julia. She was already looking at her with her eyes filled with immense admiration. For an instance Julia witnessed the same Samantha who she'd met the very first time.

"Ladies and gentlemen, friends and family, I know you are as happy as I am to see Julia and Alejandro joining their lives together. That they will be there for each other whether it's a beautiful sunny day, or a fierce storm. That they belong together—" Samantha's voice caught and her eyes welled up, "—and will make each other happy for the rest of their lives. And now I need to finish this speech before these tears ruin my makeup, because it cost me three hundred bucks to get this pretty face."

The garden echoed with jovial laughter. Julia stepped forward to hug Samantha, both laughing and crying at the same time. "I love you," she said into Samantha's ear.

The guests lifted their glasses to the happy couple,

and Alejandro kissed Julia again, holding her tight in his arms.

"As always, your dream has come true," Alejandro whispered. "All your close friends are here today."

Julia smiled with satisfaction, and looked around the guests, now chatting in groups and drinking champagne. White-jacketed waiters circulated with trays of hors d'oeuvres. She spotted two women in deep conversation. "Our mothers look like they get on well."

"I have noticed that," Alejandro said. "And just so you know, your mother liked me. We had a nice conversation earlier."

"Glad to hear that! Mamá has a very modern mentality. I'm sure you enjoyed talking with her."

"I did indeed, especially when she told me that story of the time you almost burned down the kitchen."

"Oh no, she didn't tell you *that* story!"

"Oh yes, she very much did! But don't you worry; I will never ask you to cook your specialty for me. You have many more qualities other than cooking." He winked and squeezed her arm.

"In that case, you will have to cook for me." Julia smiled with satisfaction.

"Not a problem," Alejandro said. "I am excellent at hiring people to cook."

"Good point!" Julia said.

Alejandro put his arms around her waist and pulled her closer. "Have I ever told you how important you are to me and how much I love you?"

Julia looked up at him. "Yes, you mention that every day."

"I like to remind you every day, just in case you forget." He looked into her deep green eyes which had the capability of pulling him into an un-dismissible numbness. He felt there was nothing in the world more valuable than Julia.

She looked at him, filled with the desire to kiss him again. But a shadow passed over Alejandro's face, and she stepped back. "Is something bothering you?"

Alejandro saw her clear gaze and knew he couldn't sidestep the issue any longer. "There's something I want to tell you before we go to New York."

"What is it?"

"I would like you to—take a break, at least for a short time, from modeling. So we can have more time for us, and to travel together."

"We can do that for a while," Julia replied, "but I can't promise you I'll stay away from the fashion world forever."

Julia didn't mind staying away from the catwalk for a few months, perhaps even a year. It was time for a break. *But was Alejandro taking control of her life?* No, she told herself. This was just a short span of time. She'd always ended up as the dominant force in every relationship she'd had.

Chapter Twenty-Seven

Just a few days after the engagement party, Julia and Alejandro settled into the private jet, their destination New York.

Julia glanced through the small window. The sun was just rising in a clear blue sky, and the day promised to be cordial.

She turned away from the window and leafed through the magazines Alejandro had bought at the airport. As had happened so often before, she saw herself on a cover—it was Magazine's Designer of the Year issue, the shoot she'd done in Dubai. A sticker on the cover announced this was a second printing, that this was now the top-selling magazine in the world this month. She stared at her perfect image on the cover—a self that seemed a million miles away—then flicked through the pages to find her brief interview and the pages of editorial she'd shot.

Julia let out a sigh of dismay. Suddenly she'd

realized—she would no longer be the top supermodel. People would soon forget about her, as they forgot about Linda, about Cindy and Christy, and before those girls, the first to be called "supermodels," the public had forgotten Dovima and Twiggy and Suzy. It was Linda who had said, "I never get out of bed for less than $10,000 a day," and Julia had vowed that would be true for herself, too. And it had been. Well, now she'd be getting up for love and love alone. She was the fiancée of a billionaire and soon to be his wife. There would no doubt be parties to host and galas and charity balls to attend; surely that would take up a great deal of time, not to mention if there were children.

And she was happy with Alejandro; he was perfect man for her—a true lover, who cared for her needs. After all, if one day she got bored with the life of a wealthy socialite, she could always return to modeling in New York. She had made that clear to him. She knew what she wanted when she wanted it, and certainly no man had ever stopped her from doing what she enjoyed.

Alejandro's mother's words drifted back into her mind. "My son is a lucky man," she'd said, clearly happy to meet Julia. She and Alejandro had met his parents at the airport when they came for the engagement party. The last time Alejandro's parents had visited their native Italy had been thirty years ago, and his parents were happy that Alejandro had chosen to celebrate his engagement party in here, especially in the beautiful Lake Como.

"Since he met you, Alejandro does nothing but speak about you," his dad, Eduardo, had confirmed with a wide smile and sparkling eyes.

Julia flipped through the rest of the magazines without focusing on the images, lost in her own thoughts, and then fell asleep without her knowledge. Alejandro had his arm around her, and now it was stuck. He laughed softly, and watched her sleep, her face relaxed and sweet. He cuddled her gently without disturbing her slumber, and when Julia woke up the plane was touching down in New York.

As the plane taxied to their gate, Julia went into the jet's small lavatory to refresh her look after the long flight. When she came back twenty minutes later, her face was still sleepy.

"You will need a few days to get used to the time change," Alejandro said.

"I know, that's always the hard part for me when I travel."

Alejandro noticed she could barely keep her eyes open. "I promise you, as soon as we get home you will feel much better."

The chauffeur met them at the curb and put the bags in the trunk, then drove through Manhattan to Alejandro's house.

They stepped out of the private elevator and Alejandro opened the door. Julia barely noticed the house as she made a beeline for a long, hot shower. In the kitchen, Alejandro brushed aside the chef and prepared a warm cup of milk with cinnamon for his bride-to-be.

Thirty minutes later Julia felt refreshed, if still not totally awake. Wrapping herself in a thick terrycloth robe, she stepped out of the bathroom and stopped for a moment, mesmerized by the luxury around her.

With his love of surprising her, Alejandro had told Julia very little about his penthouse on Park Avenue. Julia walked softly through the rooms, peeking in the doors of four bedrooms, three additional baths, a game room, and a hallway leading to the servants' quarters. The kitchen gleamed with stainless steel appliances. When she stepped into the living room, she caught her breath at the beauty of the high ceiling, made entirely of glass panels. She'd be able to see the stars, maybe, if the city lights weren't too bright. Alejandro's home—their home—was beautiful beyond words.

After ten minutes of following her small, damp footsteps, Alejandro found Julia out on the terrace in a bathrobe, with her hair still wet.

"How do you feel? Did the shower help?" he asked.

"I feel much better now."

"Great. Here is your milk with cinnamon as you like; in the meantime, I'll have a shower too. I've given the staff the day off so we can be alone in our home together."

Julia put her hand on his chest and played with his tie. "Mmmm…" she said, "try not to be too long, I don't like waiting." Her seductive expression toying with his heart.

"I'll be back before you know it." Alejandro gave her a wink.

Julia turned back to admire the view. Over the roofs of the buildings on the next two streets, she could see the tops of the trees in Central Park, and beyond them, the ornate roofline of the Museum of Natural History. *If I can't accept being with Alejandro, one hundred percent, I will miss some of the best moments of my life.* She had the feeling everything was going to be okay.

Chapter Twenty-Eight

"I'm so satisfied with my life now!" Julia sang over the phone. "I'm so happy with Alejandro!"

"That's great!" Samantha tried to sound enthusiastic, but this phone call only reminded her how much she missed Julia's voice. They'd barely spoken since the moment her best friend had left for New York. "It's nice that you called—I know you must be so busy with planning for the wedding. And with Alejandro." She spoke with not so subtle indication.

"I am never too busy for you, Samantha. You're my best friend, and don't ever forget it." Julia paused. She could hear the wistfulness in Samantha's voice. Impulsively, she asked, "Why don't you come to New York to visit me?"

"What?"

"Come to New York!" Julia insisted.

Samantha considered the proposal. She had her

schedule lined up for a visit to New York for some business affairs. "Actually, that might be a good idea! October's not too busy for me. A trip to New York would be great. I just need to organize my time here, and then I'll let you know."

"Glad to hear that. I'm sure you are going to love it," Julia said.

"How is Alejandro, is he still crazy about you?" Samantha asked curiously.

"Oh, he is the most perfect man I ever met," Julia replied. "I am so happy living here with him. And New York is a wonderful place to live—so vibrant and exciting! Alejandro's penthouse is fabulous—I never dreamed I'd live in such an incredibly beautiful place. Imagine me waking up every morning overlooking the city that never sleeps!"

"Sounds wonderful," Samantha said, smiling at her friend's exuberance. "That's the life that suits you, and I'm sure you know how to make the most of it."

"Jesus!" Julia exclaimed, "You just reminded me I need to run, Alejandro is waiting for me in his office downtown."

"Okay, I'll text you when I know the dates I can come," Samantha said.

"Great! Make sure you don't change your mind," Julia replied. She hung up and phoned the driver to meet her in front of the building in half an hour. She did her makeup and dressed quickly, throwing on a pair of sexy heels, and in thirty minutes she was in the car and on her way to Alejandro's office.

By the time she reached Alejandro's office, she'd checked her makeup again to make sure everything was perfect. She passed a lipstick over her full mouth until her lips glistened. When the car pulled up in front of The Signature Quintana building, she stepped out, smoothed the skirt and jacket of her sharply-tailored sky-blue suit that perfectly fit her gorgeous curves, unbuttoned one button of her white shirt to reveal just a hint of the curve of her breasts, and then, finally ready, set off for a meeting with Alejandro and his investors. She'd made a bet with Alejandro that she could easily get the latest spoiled, indecisive billionaire to sign the contracts and close the deal today.

Jack Walker had spent a week with the buyers. Four brothers who had made up their minds to buy six boats, practically a fleet, for "family vacations," and because of that they wanted a huge discount. One that they would not be getting. Alejandro had already made a fair price, and if necessary, they would walk away. But Jack and Alejandro hoped that, with Julia as their secret weapon, the deal would go through.

The glass doors closed behind Julia, as she entered the eerily cold and silent conference hall. Every man at the table looked up as if they had never seen a woman, whispering among them. Julia smiled—they were hooked, and she would reel them in.

Alejandro noticed the looks—he knew Julia was the kind of woman who could make your head spin at the snap of her finger. The woman who always asked for more and no man would be able to say no.

Jack Walker got up and indicated a chair for Julia at the long table, between him and Alejandro.

"Hi Jack, it's good to see you!" She kissed him on both cheeks, nodded in greeting to the other four men she'd never met, and sat next to her fiancé.

A copy of the contract was laid out on the table, ready to be signed.

"You look very attractive," Alejandro whispered. "Your hair looks different today!"

"Oh! Thank you," she said, and smiled. The stranger's heads followed her like drones.

Alejandro admired her move over as it revealed her classic profile, with a few strands framing her face. Julia's beauty struck him anew, and he gazed at her as she scanned the contract placed in front of her.

"Gentlemen," Alejandro said to the table, "allow me to introduce The Signature Quintana's new Director of Sales and Marketing. I'm sure she'll make an impact on our meeting."

She did already, the thought erupted in the stranger's heads.

"Congratulations on your new director," one of the men said, with an appreciative look at Julia.

With that, Alejandro knew what the meeting held. Julia would get the result she wanted—the result The Signature Quintana wanted. And not just from a pretty face—she had a sharp business mind and knew how to say the right words to close a deal. Since he'd started inviting Julia to be present at contract negotiation meetings, they'd never come out bested in any transaction.

Once the deal was closed and the meeting at an end, one of the buyers quietly congratulated Alejandro. "Your marketing director is an amazing woman."

Alejandro could not help but agree with him.

"I've never signed a contract for such a huge investment faster than I've done today," the buyer added. "This woman had the power to convince all of us. That's an incredible talent!"

"I said the same thing when I first met her," Alejandro replied.

"Keep her close to you as much as you can; she is a real treasure."

"I will," Alejandro said. As they shook hands, he

noticed Julia and the youngest of the four brothers talking and laughing in the corner of the room.

After the post-meeting pleasantries wrapped up, Alejandro and Julia took the car back uptown, where Alejandro's parents were waiting for them.

Alejandro asked her casually on the drive, "So that youngest brother seemed very interested in you."

Julia felt a blush grow up on her checks. So, Alejandro was starting to get jealous. She wasn't going to tolerate that by any means. "Well, after I convinced him and his three brothers to sign several million dollars' worth of contracts, I thought it might be interesting to find out if anyone else in the family wanted to buy some yachts," Julia replied sarcastically.

Alejandro hesitated for only a second. "I hope you won't fall for someone else…because I couldn't survive that." He gazed at her as if seeing her for the first time.

For a moment Julia was speechless. Then she shook her head. "Don't be ridiculous."

"You think I am?"

"I can't fall in love with every man who talks to me, when I'm already in love with you." Julia found her voice rising. *Why was Alejandro doing this?*

Alejandro noticed her getting upset. "Okay, let's keep calm, maybe I'm overreacting."

"Are you jealous?" Julia couldn't help wondering how Alejandro would react if he really did see her with another man. He was being totally unreasonable—since she'd met him, there had certainly been many occasions to look at another man, even flirt, but it had never crossed her mind. *Why was he coming up with this today to ruin everything?* And her day had started so well!

Alejandro looked away. "I never want you to forget how much I love you and care for you."

"How could I ever forget?" She sighed, and played with one of the strands artfully escaping her chignon, winding it around her finger. The car slowed as they hit traffic.

Alejandro turned back to face her, and spoke seriously. "Since the day you came into my life, everything's been perfect." He kissed her cheek. "I just can't get enough of you."

Julia nodded silently.

Alejandro took her hand and brought it to his chest. "I apologize for my behavior. I promise, that will never happen again."

The car moved, and Julia's mood shifted into confusion. What a strange day this had turned out to be. She wasn't sure about anything anymore—she'd never seen Alejandro this way before. Jealousy was exactly what she couldn't accept in a man. A bad memory of

George, her ex, crossed her mind and she frowned. *I hope Alejandro never makes this kind of scene again. I'm not going to waste my life having a man be sick with jealousy by my side.*

Chapter Twenty-Nine

Alejandro's parents lived in an enormous pre-war constructed building in Manhattan, with a large front garden in Italian style.

"My mother loves the garden," Alejandro said as they pulled up. "No matter what season, she must always outshine the neighbors."

As they stepped from the car, Alejandro's mother Angela came to greet them. She wore a pale yellow suit. Julia admired her style—Angela was in her sixties, but a beautiful woman nevertheless. Her golden brown hair was cut short in an elegant style and her almond eyes sparkled with enthusiasm.

"Hello darling," she said, greeting Julia with a hug. "I am so happy you two made the time to come and visit me. I know how busy you are."

"We'll always make time to visit you, no matter how busy we are," Julia replied. She glanced around the garden. "This place is lovely."

"Eduardo hired an Italian gardener to do all this," Angela said. "We brought him over from Milan especially for the job."

"My father has a passion for nature," Alejandro said.

"More like an obsession." Angela said with a jovial laughter.

"Speaking of papà, where is he?"

"Ah, he is in the basement somewhere. You know him, always worried about choosing the perfect wine for a special occasion."

"Oh, right," Alejandro said, grinning.

"Let's go inside," Angela suggested.

Just as they were about to enter the house, the door opened and Eduardo emerged from inside. A peculiar confusion clouded Julia. Was this Alejandro's father? But he looked so different from the personality she encountered at the engagement party. He no longer seemed to be sixty-five years old, but much younger. His skin was tanned deep olive and his salt-and-pepper hair shined. Eduardo wore a white shirt and cream trousers, which contrasted his tanned skin. His brown suede shoes perfectly matched his belt.

For a moment, they stared at each other.

Finally, Eduardo broke the silence. "Welcome to my house!" He came forward with open arms.

"Hello Eduardo!" Julia was cool and collected as they exchanged a hug. "How are you?"

"I am very good. Angela and I just came back from our Italian holiday—I feel like a new man!"

"You certainly look like a new man!" Julia agreed. "It's amazing what a change a relaxing holiday can make in a person."

"Plenty of relaxation at Lake Como," Eduardo said.

"And you've got quite a tan," Julia said.

"I had almost forgotten how beautiful my country is," Eduardo replied. "It brought me back to life." He shook hands with Alejandro. "Let's go in for a glass of good wine and some good food. I am starving, and your *mamma* has cooked a very nice meal."

"She still cooks her Italian specialties for you?" Alejandro asked.

"Yes. And she came back from Lake Como with a new recipe." Eduardo winked.

After dinner Julia got up to help Angela, leaving Alejandro and his father to continue their business conversation.

"How did you spend your time in Italy?" Julia asked, as she and Angela went into the kitchen to cut the cake and prepare coffee. Angela was a very good cook indeed, Julia noticed. The cake was beautifully iced, and the inside looked light and beautifully textured.

"Oh, Alejandro was such a good son to have us stay. We really enjoyed ourselves," Angela replied.

"You spent the whole month in Lake Como after the engagement party?"

"With a few trips to Milan to see old friends. Eduardo thoroughly enjoyed himself."

"I am happy you had such a lovely time," Julia said

"Thank you, darling. We had that sort of holiday where you lay by the sea with your cocktail to relax and feel good. The weather was so beautiful; I so enjoyed that time of the day when the sun was setting, feeling the breeze of the sea brushing gently against my face." Angela's eyes filled with nostalgia.

"I am glad you two had a wonderful time," Alejandro said as he emerged from the living room with a smile on his face.

"I was just telling Julia how much we enjoyed Italy," Angela said. "And you have brought a bit of that beauty home with you, son. Your bride-to-be is gorgeous." She smiled at Julia.

Alejandro nodded, and looked at Julia, measuring her fantastic long legs, and her perfect body. *And best of all, she is mine,* he thought.

Julia glanced up and gave him a seductive smile.

For a moment, Alejandro remembered the events of the morning again—why had he upset her like that? He was lucky Julia was a real lady, that she was funny and spontaneous and able to transform everyday moments into something special. But still, disturbing flashes of jealousy sometimes overcame his reason. Sometimes he felt trapped by her beauty.

Chapter Thirty

The day of Samantha's visit to New York had arrived sooner than they both expected. They both had been so caught up in their daily endeavors that time flew like a hawk. Julia met her at the airport, and took her through a bit of the city before they went to a restaurant for lunch. There was so much to talk about, even before they got home.

As usual, Samantha's love life was a mess.

"I hardly dare to hope he will come back to me," Samantha said sadly. Since she and Roberto Benetti had broken up, she'd started an affair with a married man. Now he, too, had abandoned her.

"He told me so many lies, telling me it was all over with his wife. But the whole time, he was still living with her. I loved him so much. I tried to be happy with the little shreds of life he could share with me."

"Since Roberto Benetti left you, you've completely lost your head," Julia snapped. "It's been one bad relationship after another, first the divorced man with the child, and now an affair with a married man!"

"You're right, it was a bad decision. But now I'm alone, and starting a new story with a new man is so hard! I don't want to be alone forever, but I don't think I can ever love another man. I feel like my heart is an open wound. Maybe I can heal a bit here in New York."

"Maybe it will leave a scar and you will stop making such stupid choices!"

Samantha's eyes filled with tears and Julia softened her tone. "You are my best friend. You deserve better than that. I hate to see you choose one bad man after another—I would rather see you spend the rest of your life alone."

"I hope not," Samantha replied.

Julia sipped her wine and took a long look at Samantha. Was her friend always going to play games in love, or would she ever be able to face the truth and have a real relationship? Samantha's face seemed serious. Then her eyes crinkled and Julia realized Samantha was full of irony. Julia gave her a very serious look, and said, "There is nothing sadder than not having sex for the rest of your life."

Samantha couldn't help but laugh.

They both broke into a laughter until they could hardly drink their wine. Samantha's face cleared, and they were able to talk about the things they'd like to do in the next few days around town.

"Did he ever try to contact you after that day?" Samantha's expression suddenly charged with intent. Julia need not ask her as to whom Samantha was referring to. It was undoubtedly George.

"No." She said. "Why do you ask?"

"Just curious."

"I've had my share of bad luck. But I can guarantee Alejandro would never turn out to be like him." She said, and then suddenly her mind drifted elsewhere, wondering about something she had always tried to uncover. "I never found out who the girl was who George found more beautiful than me."

"Yeah, about that," Samantha bore her eyes at Julia, "I've been meaning to talk to you about that."

"What do you mean?" Julia felt clouded with confusion.

"I know, Julia." Her voice suddenly shaking,

"I've known all along."

Julia stood still like a mannequin, barely changing her expression or her stance.

"I thought it would break you apart, so I decided to keep it from you. I wanted to tell you that day when you told me that you were in love with Alejandro and you'll move to New York with him. In that moment I knew George was out of your life forever and it wouldn't hurt you. But I didn't have the courage to tell you. Then you were busy with your engagement party and I didn't get the opportunity to tell you then or since.

She lowered her gaze, and then raised it again, looking at Julia's eyes demanding answers "It was Corrine."

"What? Who! Corrine! No, that can't be....it's not possible...this is a joke...I can't imagine...I...the knowledge barely managed to lodge itself in Julia's conscience. She felt enraged, and the same time she felt cheated, not by one, but two. Two people at whom she had utmost trust.

"I am sorry." Samantha looked sorry, "When I saw how happy you were with Alejandro, I was on cloud nine. I knew you deserved every inch of it. That's when I decided I would tell you the truth." She paused, and then added in almost a whisper, "Are you mad at me?"

Julia felt betrayed, but Samantha was right. Alejandro was the best thing that ever happened to her. Even if she was fooled by two closest people of her life, she was glad that she had someone with whose virtue she could let it pass into her past. Alejandro. Samantha was right. She definitely deserved him.

Julia cupped Samantha's face in her palms and

smiled, "I am not. You're the only one who stood by my on every blind turn. How could I ever be mad at you?"

Samantha hugged her tight, breaking into tears. Julia consoled her. She couldn't change the past for what it has been, but she could surely shape her future for what it was going to be.

Samantha opened her mouth to say something, then she stopped.

"What? There is anything else I should know about?" Julia asked.

"Ah, no...no... that is all I know." For a second Samantha thought to tell her about George and his stupid idea of coming to her engagement party. Thank God the bodyguards had stopped him at the gates before he could come inside to ruin the whole party. *No, Julia doesn't need to know about that. George belongs in the past, leave him in there.*

 "Maybe we should go home; Alejandro is waiting for us," Julia said, picking up her sunglasses from the table.

Samantha saw the excitement in her eyes. "You love him so much, do you?"

"Yes, I do." Julia turned to look at Samantha as they waited for the valet to bring her car. "Alejandro has his defects as every one of us has, but I never loved someone as much as I love him." She walked around the white Z24GT sports car and got in.

"I can see that," Samantha replied, as she jumped into the sleek little car.

"He makes me happy in all my senses," Julia said. Her mouth instantly curved into a smile, remembering the first time she and Alejandro made love.

As soon they got home, the doorman took Samantha's luggage to the elevator. When they arrived upstairs, Alejandro was waiting in front of the elevator.

"I was wondering where you two ended up," Alejandro said.

"We stopped at my new favorite Italian restaurant for lunch," Julia said. "We were talking so much I didn't realize the time had gone so fast! I was thinking—"

Samantha interrupted. "New York is so exciting! I want to take this opportunity to see as much I can while I'm here."

"Why not!" Alejandro replied. "Julia's practically a native now—she knows the best places in New York. I am sure you two will enjoy sightseeing." He smiled and added, "Just don't get her too tired; especially now she's taking care of two." Alejandro put a hand possessively on Julia's tummy.

A baby! Samantha narrowed her eyes. "Why you didn't tell me anything about that?"

"I was about to tell you, but you started with your story and then I forgot." Even to Julia's own ears, it sounded like an excuse, but she had wanted to keep her pregnancy a secret for at least the first three months…just in case. But now Alejandro had come right out with it. She couldn't be mad, though—he looked so happy.

"That's such great news!" Samantha said. "I am so happy for you. Now, Alejandro, you know I wouldn't allow her to get tired at all."

"What are you talking about?" asked Julia. "I'm not sick or anything, I'm just pregnant."

"I insisted she must renounce her obsession with her image, and stop all her exercising with too many sports; she must stop putting herself in danger," Alejandro said. "But she is a very stubborn woman."

"You're looking good, Julia, and your body hasn't changed at all," Samantha said. "I never would have guessed."

"I'm only seven weeks, of course my body hasn't changed! But I do need to be careful what I eat and—" here Julia gave Alejandro a stern look "—continue to do some activity."

"Sweetheart, you do lots of activity, you spend

almost every day in the gym," Alejandro pointed out.

Julia sighed. "Let's get you into your room, Samantha." She led her friend to the guest suite, thinking hard. Alejandro was exquisite, but maybe lately he'd become too protective. *I am not a small girl*, Julia thought. *And I feel perfectly well*.

Chapter Thirty-One

The next day Samantha woke up and threw on her yoga pants. Julia had arranged a private yoga lesson with her Portuguese instructor.

"He's beautiful to look at," Julia told Samantha. Maybe looking at a gorgeous man would distract her.

Samantha had scoffed "You think that's all I think about?" But she did take extra care of her hair that morning, and applied a full layer of foundation. At the last minute, she changed into a sleek fitted shirt instead of her exercise tank which exposed her curves, thinking to herself, *you never know.*

She left the guest suite and walked through the living room, gazing at the luxurious house. Julia was sitting outside on the terrace, with a big glass of dark green liquid. *I'm sure it's some uber-healthy combination of fruit and vegetables. Probably full of kale, ick.*

"Hey Samantha!" Julia fluttered her hand as she saw her. "Did you sleep well, darling?"

"Yes, very well, I was a bit tired after the flight. At least with jet lag I'm up early."

Julia glanced at her and smiled. Of course she dressed up for a new venture.

"So, where is this hot instructor?" Samantha asked.

"He just texted, he's on his way. The cook left breakfast ready in the kitchen for us after, but would you like some juice before?"

"Yes I would like some juice," Samantha said, "As long as it's not that strange combination that you have! It looks awful. What is it, a kelp cocktail?"

Julia laughed. "This 'awful cocktail' gives me loads of energy. I feel extra-healthy; don't you want some too?"

"Just a simple orange juice if you don't mind."

"There's fresh orange juice in the fridge," Julia said, taking a sip from her glass. "Let me get some for you."

"No, you sit here; I'll go get it," Samantha said. She stepped back and disappeared inside the apartment, reappearing a minute later with an equally large glass of plain orange juice. She sat in a deck chair and took in the view. "This place has such an amazing panorama!" Samantha looked back into the house, where a view of the gorgeous, sunny living room was framed by the French doors from the terrace. "Sometimes I wonder how it feels to live in all this luxury."

"I guess you just get used to it," Julia replied.

"I guess it's just amazing," Samantha said.

Julia looked out over the rooftops to the park, noticing the bright trees purged with autumn colors. She could only see the tops from the penthouse terrace—it was like a fiery lake between them and the Upper West Side.

"So you're going to have a baby," Samantha said, as she noticed Julia lost in thought.

"Yes," Julia replied tracing her stomach gently. *There is a being inside me. A whole human being.* "Alejandro wants to get married by the end of the year."

"Well there's only three months left—you are sure you want to get married so soon?" Samantha gave Julia a quick look. Julia didn't look all that excited about the idea.

"Of course, I'm sure." Julia imagined Alejandro playing with the baby around the house—maybe even two babies, if they had another one soon. Since Julia had told him she was pregnant, Alejandro had been jumping out of his skin. He had a clear idea of how their family would be. It had all happened so fast—a simple date, a whirlwind engagement, and now they were planning a wedding. But then, one of her biggest dreams was to have a good husband and a perfect family.

The Yoga instructor arrived and Julia introduced him to Samantha. He was handsome, Samantha noticed, although slightly short. At least he wouldn't be too distracting. She grabbed a yoga mat, eager to start the lesson. It had been a while—she felt her muscles stretch and realized how much she'd missed exercise.

A glorious house, a beautiful day, and a baby on the way—it is really a perfect life, Julia thought.

A few hours later Julia and Samantha, elegantly dressed, had headed out in the car for a beautiful day in New York City. Samantha found herself forgetting her heartbreak and enjoying every minute of the day. After lunch they went shopping, and as the evening drew near they went to meet Alejandro. One of his friends was throwing a party, and he was waiting for Julia and Samantha there.

They saw Alejandro at the bar with Jack and another man. Julia watched him, noticing how even after a lifetime in America, he still talked like an Italian, gesturing with his hands as he spoke.

Jack glanced over Alejandro's shoulder as he saw Julia and Samantha arrive, taking a stroll and checking out the vicinity as they gradually approached them. He nodded toward them, and Alejandro turned to smile at Julia from across the room. His classical profile looked like the bust of a noble Roman emperor come to life.

Julia thought how attractive and important he looked in just his basic movements, and she smiled back with her unique charm.

That's my girl, thought Alejandro. He loved the way she flirted with him in public. Everyone in the room might be drawn to her, but between them there was something special, and that give him immense satisfaction.

"This woman makes you very happy," Jack said.

"Absolutely true," Alejandro said. "She's the reason why I wake up each morning."

"You're so crazy about her!" Jack said.

"I am more than crazy. Julia turned my world upside down. She's changed my life completely—I feel like I'm flying without wind."

"That must be a nice feeling." Jack smiled as Julia and Samantha arrived.

Julia was stunning in a fluttery white dress. Alejandro loved his fiancée's impeccable dress sense. Her hair, her makeup and her accessories were perfectly coordinated and she looked incredible.

"Hi sweetie!" she said.

Alejandro kissed her on both cheeks. "Did you two have a good day?"

"Yes, we did. Samantha loves New York."

"Good," Alejandro said.

Jack stepped forward to greet Samantha. "Long time no see, beautiful lady."

"How are you doing? I haven't seen you since the engagement party."

"I'm good," Jack replied. "I haven't been back in Milan; I've been keeping busy here," he added.

"It looks like it," Samantha replied. She looked around and witnessed how life sprung from every corner. *There was always something going on around here in New York. You could never get bored in this city.*

Chapter Thirty-Two

The week flew by until Samantha's holiday was finished. In the elevator down to the car, Samantha made a sad face. "I'm going to miss this life here."

"You need to come back soon, then," Julia replied.

Alejandro glanced at his watch. "We're going to be late for the airport."

At the curb, Samantha gave Julia another hug before she got into the car. Julia felt a bit tired, and went back upstairs, where she plumped herself down into the comfortable bed and read a thick book, waiting for Alejandro to come back.

Later, when she heard the elevator doors shut softly and the front door open, she pretended to sleep. Alejandro's footsteps came closer, and his hand moved over her breasts. Julia sighed with pleasure. He started kissing her slowly.

"Are you sleeping?" he murmured.

"Yes…" she murmured back.

"Oh, really?" Alejandro stroked his hands down the side of her body, and then in one smooth gesture slid her ivory silk nightgown over her head. He bent his head to kiss her breasts, savoring the perfume of her soft skin.

Julia felt her desire growing as Alejandro played with her body, and she let out a soft moan. Now that he knew she wanted him, he held her arms over her head, ravishing her body with his kisses, forceful in exactly the way she liked. He reached with one hand to turn off her reading light, and the darkness enveloped their passion.

When she awoke, still in Alejandro's arms, it was late morning and Alejandro's hand was slowly rubbing her stomach. He obviously loved the idea of becoming a father.

"How long have you been awake and stroking my tummy?" Julia asked.

"Mmmm…I don't even remember."

"Mmmm…you don't remember, do you?" She cuddled his head. "I need a huge breakfast. I'm starving."

"I'll get a good breakfast ready for you," Alejandro replied.

"Don't forget the fresh juice!" Julia said, as she rolled out of bed and wrapped herself in a big towel.

"I think by now I know exactly what you like."

"You mean you're actually going to impress me with your specialty?" she teased. "I didn't know you were such a chef."

He laughed weakly. "Not really, but I will do my best."

After showering, Julia went through the kitchen and out to the terrace, where Alejandro had arranged the breakfast table. A vase of flowers stood in the center. Fresh juice was ready in a pitcher, and cereal and light yogurt were in a bowl in the exact quantity that Julia wanted. He had arranged exotic fruit in a modernist steel basket. Smiling at her arrival, Alejandro poured out the coffee.

"It seems like everything is perfect," Julia said as she sat down. She leaned over to murmur in his ear. "Last night was…incredible."

Alejandro smiled. "You almost killed me."

"Yes, I kind of realized that," Julia smiled back and bit into a strawberry.

"You know, I was thinking how to make room for the baby." Alejandro picked up a pencil and began to sketch the apartment floor plan on a napkin. "We could have a nursery here, and another one here, for our second baby."

Julia looked at his drawing and nodded. "Perhaps it would be better to start with one here." She took the pencil from his fingers to make her own drawing.

Alejandro knew she was making the point that she wanted to be in charge. He smiled. "If it's a girl, you will make the room as you like. But if it's a boy, then I will make his room the way I like." Said the negotiator in him. He set his coffee mug down firmly.

"Fine," she said, knowing that Alejandro would always ask her for advice.

"Deal," he agreed.

Chapter Thirty-Three

"I'm going with Julia to my villa in Miami Beach for a while. We want to spend some relaxation time over there," Alejandro said.

"Hmm…you mean, you want more action?" Jack winked. "Taking a woman on vacation always makes everything better, am I right?"

Alejandro smiled—he couldn't help but think of last night with Julia. For him, it wasn't important where they were in the world. New York, Milan, Miami—wherever Julia was, he would be happy to be there.

"It's not about that," Alejandro replied. "New York is so fast-paced it's making Julia tired, and now that she's expecting she needs to relax more. Besides, November's a great time to spend in Miami, and it is close enough, so I can always fly to New York when the business needs me. I'll even be in the same time zone."

"That should be all right," Jack agreed. "Besides,

we're selling a ton of boats down there. Couldn't hurt to be the man on the ground."

"And by the way," Alejandro said, "You must come to our party at the villa next weekend."

"What party?" Jack asked. The last Miami party had been quite a scene—billionaire investors, actresses in sexy dresses, all dancing on the bar. He wouldn't mind another party like that. He could use some more long legs in short dresses.

Alejandro interrupted Jack's thoughts. "Julia is turning twenty-five. I want to celebrate her birthday at the villa. And I know she'd love to see you there."

"Wouldn't miss it for the world," Jack replied. He thought how Alejandro had changed; he was practically a different person since Julia had come into his life, and he smiled at the memory of Alejandro's face when he first saw Julia on the catwalk.

Now Alejandro hardly came to a single event or party without Julia. Jack had to admit it, he was even a little jealous of their relationship and their unprecedented love. It seemed like Alejandro had always achieved everything he craved for in life, and for this Jack envied him sometimes.

Julia drove into the basement garage and took the elevator to the penthouse. Alejandro wasn't home yet.

She decided to surprise him by cooking dinner. *I am going to show him that I am not so bad in the kitchen. I am going to redeem myself.* She tossed her car keys onto the counter and opened the fridge to see what she could make. *I can do grilled salmon and salad; it's fast and good.* She put up a list of all the ingredients she needed, and in order to make a hassle free dish, she wrote a To-Do list. At the end of the To-Do list in capitals she wrote: No burning houses.

She washed her hands and began to wash the salad when her phone rang in her bag. *Maybe Alejandro finished his meeting earlier than I expected.* She wiped her hands on a tea towel and picked up the phone.

Samantha's voice came through her cell. "Hi sweetie!"

"Samantha! Did you get home safe? How was the flight back?"

"Looooooong," Samantha answered. "Now I'm just trying to shake off jet lag and get back into my routine."

"I know," Julia agreed. "That's the worst thing after a trip. It's a shame you couldn't stay longer."

"I wish," Samantha replied. "But my job called me back here. *C'est la vie.*"

"Next time take a longer holiday," Julia said, as she went into the living room and threw herself down across the large sofa.

"Definitely," Samantha said. She was pleased that Julia was already inviting her back to New York. It made her feel like their friendship would stay strong despite the distance.

"It will be great if you could be here when I have my baby."

"I can arrange that," Samantha replied. "I still can't believe you're having a baby in six months!"

"I know," Julia replied, "I am so excited!"

"Well, I just wanted to let you know I'm safe and sound. I'm going to try to sleep now. Bye sweetie!"

"Bye Samantha!" Julia hugged a pillow across her chest and looked through the glass ceiling. It was dusk, and the first star peeked from behind the clouds like a small child from behind her mother. Her dream of a baby someday had somehow turned into reality now, and she loved it. She was looking forward to staying in Miami Beach with Alejandro until the baby was born— she loved the sun and chilling out on the beach. Alejandro had even promised to spend more time at home, only flying to New York for the most important meetings. Those for which he couldn't be substituted by Jack.

"Jack has the experience and skills to close the deals even without me," Alejandro had assured her. "I don't want to be far away from you, you might need me."

Julia laughed. "You can't stop working just because I am pregnant!"

"No, but I can avoid being away from you as much as possible," Alejandro replied.

Knowing how protective he was with her, she wondered how Alejandro would act with their children. *He would be a great father.* Then a sudden selfish thought occurred to her and it made her awry. *Would he love their child even more than her?* She glanced at the ornate gold clock on the mantelpiece; it was nearly eight. *Better go and get that dinner ready.*

And then after she still needed to finish packing. Tomorrow they would fly to Florida.

―――

"Well," Alejandro said, leaning across the table, "I will never again say that you don't know how to cook."

"Are you sure? It was such a simple meal," Julia teased him.

"Simple but good," Alejandro teased back.

"Simple but good," Julia repeated. "I like that."

"Now you have to learn to make my mother's recipes."

"Oh, yes?" Julia's eyes flashed, but Alejandro liked provoking her—she was even more beautiful when she started to get angry. And somehow or other they always ended up in bed after those conversations. Obviously, they both enjoyed stirring things

up…in more ways than one.

The next morning they boarded Alejandro's private plane, ready to take them to Miami. Julia wore a dangerously low-cut white top, and as she leaned forward for a water bottle in the plane, Alejandro couldn't keep his eyes from straying to her generous breasts. Julia noticed his gaze and held her pose a moment longer, then winked a deep green eye and smiled seductively, knowing how much Alejandro liked her body.

And Julia certainly knew how to drive him nuts.

Chapter Thirty-Four

Miami was a beautiful place, with spectacular palm trees and the clearest and warmest water in the U.S. Alejandro's villa was in South Beach, along a stretch of beautiful white sand, with a magnificent view to the horizon. The perfectly-restored Art Deco villa sat in lush tropical gardens, and an infinity pool looked over a stretch of secluded beach. Julia fell in love with the villa as soon she saw it.

She was enjoying the peaceful atmosphere, especially after the busy streets of New York. She looked through the bedroom window to see Alejandro coming up to the terrace with a big smile on his face.

"Come on, get your bathing suit! We're going out on the yacht today," he called up from the garden.

"Okay, I hope I can still fit into my bikini!" Julia replied, laughing.

"Of course you will, you're only three months and a

bikini is two pieces anyway."

They both laughed, enjoying the moment. Julia called down, "You'll have to wait, I can't find my sunglasses."

"I saw them on the table by the pool," Alejandro replied. "We'll get them on the way out."

"Okay, where are your board shorts? The long red ones."

"No, I've got my blue trunks in the yacht because I need to get my legs out, they're so white."

Julia laughed. "That'll teach you for wearing long trousers instead of shorts by the pool yesterday. And no shirt! No wonder your back got burnt."

"I've got sunscreen today."

"Do you want me to rub some on your back now?"

"You can do it on the yacht in your sexy bikini."

They headed to the car and Alejandro put the picnic basket in the trunk. As they drove to the marina, he glanced at Julia's body. "You look so beautiful, especially with that tan on your long legs."

"I wish I had this tan all year round," she replied.

"Your wishes are my dreams too, *amore*. So, how are the two of you feeling today?"

"We're good! I hardly had any morning sickness today."

"Glad to hear it. But you must make sure you're eating enough for both of you."

"I do! You didn't hear me when I woke up at four this morning. I went downstairs and had three pieces of fruit bread toast."

"Oh did you? You should have woken me up, I would have made it for you."

"You looked so peaceful sleeping, I didn't want to wake you."

"You can wake me any time, babe. And by the way, I'm a bit concerned. I think maybe you're doing too much exercise."

"It's not like I'm jogging anymore. And the doctor said I can do light exercise."

"Okay. But take it easy, precious."

"I will."

They arrived at the marina, where Alejandro pulled into the parking lot and they walked down to the jetty.

"Today I want to stay in Biscayne Bay and show you the view from Key Biscayne," Alejandro said as he took Julia's hand and helped her step into the yacht. He took the picnic basket and jumped onto the deck. "Do you want to put a life jacket on, sweetheart?"

"No thanks, I'm a good swimmer," Julia replied.

"Hold tight, there will be a little bump when I start the engine."

"I'm ready."

The yacht sailed up the coastline in the blazing sun. Julia undressed, revealing a gold bikini. Alejandro whistled before ripping off his own shirt and reached for the sunscreen.

"Wait, I'm going to help you put it on," Julia said, and walked toward him. "Everything is so beautiful here." She looked to the islands they were passing between, with their lush green shorelines. "This is exactly where I want to be."

"I knew you'd like it," Alejandro said.

"You know me so well," Julia replied, smoothing sunscreen over his body.

The bay was truly an amazing place, with the sun shining on little ripples in the water. It was peaceful, with the only sounds the soft splashing of the waves against the boat and the gentle breeze. Julia was mesmerized by the crystal-clear water, where she could see fish swimming in their schools. As they came into the open water at the mouth of the bay, the immensity of the ocean met the horizon so far away they seemed to be whole as one. It seemed to her she was looking into endless space.

Julia yawned and stretched. "I'm going to lie down on the rear deck." Julia made her way along the side of the boat, then climbed up to the back deck and laid out her towel.

"Okay, I'll drop anchor and be with you shortly," Alejandro said. He stopped the motor.

It became blissfully quiet as soon as the noise of the motor cut out. Julia lay on her towel and listened to the whisper of the cool blue water caressing the yacht, like a smooth melody. The wind blew through her hair, and the tangy smell of saltwater filled her lungs. She felt good.

"I feel a bit thirsty," she called. "Would you bring me a bottle of water from the fridge, on your way back?"

"I will," Alejandro said as he began lowering the anchor. As soon he felt it touch bottom, he checked the instrument panel to confirm everything was okay, then went down into the galley. From the fridge he took a bottle of water and another of vintage champagne. He brought two glasses with him and went back above deck. He agreed with Julia—this was a perfect day, and a nice, mellow way to celebrate three months of her pregnancy. On the rear deck, Julia was basking in the beautiful sunshine, her body tanned and glowing golden brown, the wind playing with her long dark hair.

"Your water is here, sexy lady," Alejandro said,

smiling as he appreciated her beauty.

"Thank you. What we are celebrating?" she asked as she noticed the bottle of champagne and the two glasses Alejandro held.

"We need to celebrate this gorgeous day with a glass of champagne," he said, opening the bottle and pouring two modest glasses. He passed her a glass less than half full. "This is for our future and for every minute we will spend together," he said as they clinked glasses. "And by the way, you're not allowed to drink more than half a glass." Alejandro winked.

Julia could not resist teasing him. "Mmmm… This is very good champagne. I think I will have more than half a glass."

Alejandro looked at her, knowing how Julia liked joking. "I can see I'm going to have to be the responsible one," he teased back.

"Well next time you should only bring me what I asked for."

"I'll keep that in mind."

"Good! And don't you forget it, because soon you're going to have even more responsibilities. You think you can keep up?" Julia laughed.

"Funny girl," Alejandro replied, as he pulled her to his chest. His hand moved to the back of her head, and his strong fingers laced into her hair as he kissed her with frantic desire. His hand slipped inside her bikini top, and Julia felt her body melting as he rolled her nipple between his fingers. Sex was always exciting between them, and although Julia was pregnant, she still made love to him with all the intimacy they shared leaving no stones unturned to give him the best time. An uncontrollable passion resided between them giving birth to a sensual lust for each other. With Alejandro she lost any self-consciousness; she was aware of only him, and how she loved him unconditionally.

"I want you so much," he said between kisses.

"I want you even more," she whispered. She slipped her hand between Alejandro's legs, and he groaned at her unexpected touch, at how special she made him feel. Julia kissed him hard, sensually, and made love to him as if it were the last time. The sun played over their shining bodies and the murmur of the water played a romantic symphony. Afterwards, they lay in each other's arms and felt the wind freshen.

Alejandro placed his hand over her rounded stomach. "Our baby is growing!" he said with satisfaction.

"Mmm…yes," Julia said. She adjusted her suit and stood up, leaning into the strong breeze. "Let's go for a swim?"

"Maybe that's not such a good idea. It's pretty

windy, and the water isn't calm anymore," Alejandro replied.

"That's okay, I'm a good swimmer," she winked.

"Are you sure?" Alejandro said.

"What do you mean by that? Of course I'm sure." Julia shot him a look. Was he trying to control her again?

"Okay, but you have to promise me you'll stay near the yacht," he said.

"I can't promise you that," Julia said, and dove off the side of the boat, her tan body cutting through the water like a hot knife against butter. The water was refreshing and not too cold, and Julia felt good. She splashed in place for a few minutes, slicking back her hair, and then began to swim.

Alejandro noticed the distance she was getting from the yacht and how the wind was pushing her even farther. He shouted from the deck, "Can you come back near the yacht? The wind's getting stronger!"

"It's not too strong!" Julia shouted back confidently. She was enjoying her swim and loved the feel of cool water on her skin and its salty taste. Alejandro rolled his eyes, then dove off the deck and swam after Julia to bring her back to the boat. Julia did her best to control her amusement, knowing how Alejandro was prone to exaggerating any dangers to her, especially now that she was pregnant. He splashed through the now-increasing waves to reach Julia, and took her by arms. "What's happening with you? You're behaving like a little kid."

She shot him a look. "Am I?"

"Let's go back to the yacht right now," he said sharply.

Julia shook her head. "Okay, okay," she said and started swimming back to the yacht. She climbed the ladder and swung onto the deck, where she picked up her towel and dried her body. She noticed Alejandro staring at her and said, "I am fine."

"Dammit, you don't know how dangerous it is when the wind picks up like that!" he said.

"Well as you see, nothing happened!" Julia replied and dropped the towel.

Alejandro turned to the railing and stared into the distant blue water, running his hands over his hair.

Seeing his genuine worry, Julia softened and went close to him. "I am sorry," she said, curling her arms around his body and kissing his muscled shoulder.

Alejandro's eyes glittered as he turned to look at her. "I don't want you to do that ever again."

"Okay, it won't happen again," she said softly. "I didn't mean to scare you." He saw honesty in her eyes.

"Okay." Alejandro touched her head and kissed her

hair.

Julia felt protected and safe with him. She relaxed into his arms for a moment.

"Maybe we should go home now?" he asked.

"Okay. I'm going to get out of this wet suit and put my shorts on. I'll be back up in a minute." Julia turned toward the stairway to the lower deck, and as she did a wave slapped the yacht hard. Thrown off balance, she slipped and fell head-first into a bench.

"JULIA!" Alejandro roared and rushed over and saw Julia holding her stomach, where a red scratch was already beginning to appear. "You okay?" he asked frantically and gently probed the wound. "This damned wind."

"There was some water on the deck, and I slipped in it."

"Do you feel pain? I mean, do you feel like anything's wrong inside?"

"Not so far, no, it's just the scratch burning a bit."

"Should we go to the hospital to see if everything's okay?" Alejandro suggested.

"I'm fine," Julia said. "Let's go home."

Alejandro helped her up. "Maybe it would be good for you to go lie down below deck?"

"I am fine," Julia replied. "I don't need to lie down."

"Are you sure?"

"Yes, I'm okay."

"Okay, then sit here on the bench, but be aware of the movement of the boat and the wind."

"I will," Julia replied.

Alejandro weighed anchor and started the motor. While he piloted the yacht back to the marina, Julia sat on the bench, wrapped in a towel. She was quiet, feeling that she'd upset Alejandro enough for today. From time to time, he turned to see how she was feeling. Julia could see panic in his face. She looked away, blushing guiltily at the accusation in his deep blue eyes. He had been right when he warned her about the strong wind, and she didn't think it was funny to tease him anymore. Her thoughts wandered, and the movement of the water lulled her to sleep.

Alejandro watched her curl up on the bench. She looked impossibly sweet and helpless. He realized he probably shouldn't have yelled at her earlier.

After docking, he woke Julia with a gentle touch on her arm. "Hey sweetie, how do you feel?"

"I'm okay," Julia said softly as she opened her eyes.

"Good," Alejandro said. "I got very scared when I saw you on the floor."

"I noticed that," Julia replied, "but now I'm fine, and I'm starving."

"Good sign!" Alejandro smiled. "I'm happy you feel better now. Let's go to eat at that chic Italian restaurant you like."

"Great," Julia said. "I can't get enough of that place. Actually, I can't get enough of all the places here," she added.

She enjoyed Miami Beach's thick blend of life—the symphony, theaters, and chic restaurants. She loved the day-to-day immersion in the trends and design of the beautiful people, how even the streets were a paradise of prestige and glamour. Miami Beach was a dream life made real.

After the exquisite meal at her new favorite Italian restaurant, Julia truly felt better. By the time they were back home, Julia's good humor had returned. She glanced sidelong at Alejandro, knowing that he was as excited as she about her birthday party.

"Tomorrow night this villa will be full of people celebrating your birthday," he said.

"Right." Julia smiled. "It's funny that I don't even know most of their names!"

"Tomorrow night they will all be introduced to you," Alejandro replied. "I can't wait to present you to all of my friends."

"I'm looking forward to it," Julia replied.

Alejandro had invited lots of friends who Julia had never met before, and she was curious to get to know them. He'd told her it would be a mix of VIPs flying in from New York and some who were based in Miami, which had a wealthy social scene all its own. He'd organized the whole party himself, wanting Julia to relax and enjoy it as the guest of honor.

"Do you think there will be space enough in the garden for all the guests?" she asked.

"The garden and the poolside will have to be enough. If they want more fun they can spread out on the private beach," Alejandro said.

"Not such a bad idea." As he parked the car in the front driveway, she looked at him for several seconds—Alejandro had changed her life. With him, she felt happy and loved.

Chapter Thirty-Five

"Good morning!" Alejandro said. He came across the room, clad only in his black boxers and a white towel draped around his neck. Julia glanced at his body. His firm chest and six-pack abs seemed sculpted to perfection. Muscles rippled across every part of his exquisitely shaped body. She admired his strength and beauty—he was a man of any girl's dreams. Alejandro's eyes shone like the blue of the sea against his tanned skin, and his lips were very attractive and captivating. His right hand was behind his back as if he was hiding something.

"Good morning!" Julia said softly.

"How do you feel today? Is your tummy okay?" he asked, as he sat on the bed close to her.

"I am okay."

"I am so happy to hear that," Alejandro said. He kissed her on the cheek and from behind his back produced an elegant, blue velvet box. "Happy Birthday amore!"

"Thank you," Julia said, holding the box.

"You don't want to open it?"

"Of course I want to." She opened the elegant box and an enchanting diamond necklace stared back at her. "It's beautiful," she said as her fingers touched the stones. She moved forward and kissed him, enjoying the fragrance of the aftershave he always wore. It felt good to start the day in his arms.

"I love you," she said, kissing his cheek delicately.

"I love you too," he said, gazing into her emerald eyes. "I've never been so happy as I am when I am with you."

Julia kept his gaze. "You make me happy, too," she said, thinking that she couldn't be happier. Alejandro loved and protected her in a way no one else had ever done before. "Anyway, now that we are both happy, I'd better get up and get ready—it's a long day for me today." She slid out of bed and headed for the shower, Alejandro following.

"Yes, I know it's a long day, but I can help you with that," Alejandro said, meeting her eyes in the mirror above the sink.

"I appreciate it, but no you can't," Julia said. "I need

to go into Coconut Grove to do some shopping, and then go to the salon."

"I'll come with you," Alejandro said. "You need a strong man to carry all your bags, right?"

Julia giggled at the thought of Alejandro loaded down with shopping. "Are you sure? Maybe you want to stay home and settle any last-minute things for the party tonight?"

"I don't need to stay home. The caterers are already here and they'll take care of everything," Alejandro replied.

"It's better if I go alone," Julia insisted. "Can you pass me a towel please?"

Alejandro handed her a large white towel and Julia stepped out of the shower. She dried off, then moisturized and sprayed her body with perfume. She brushed her long hair and then got dressed.

Her fiancé followed her and watched her movement filled with delicacy, enjoying the view from a distance. Her tummy was growing but she still had an extremely attractive figure, and her face glowed.

Julia noticed him checking her out and smiled. "If you come with me, you're going to get bored waiting around while I shop, and even more bored at the beauty salon."

"Why would I be bored? I always come shopping with you. I like to see you trying on the dresses, so I can tell you which ones I like."

"I know, but I don't want you to see my hairstyle today until it's done," Julia said. "It's a surprise," she said, and gently pinched him.

"I have no choice, then," Alejandro mock-pouted.

"I am afraid not," Julia said, smiling. "And by the way, I hope you don't mind that I'm taking your car?"

Alejandro smiled back. It didn't matter which car she chose to go in. Julia had a way of making her decisions work out with her incredible charm. She was smart and unique, and that's what he liked about her.

"Shame," he said with a resigned gesture. "I was hoping to come with you."

"Not today, honey," she whispered into his ear. Her breath on his skin gave him a pang of desire.

"Let's go downstairs and have breakfast together before I leave," she said.

"At least I have the honor of breakfast in your company," Alejandro teased.

"Always," Julia said as she winked at him.

Thirty minutes later after the exquisite breakfast Alejandro prepared for them. Julia took off in Alejandro's black Lex170GTX Super Sport. It was an incredible feeling to drive the fastest car in the world, especially on the streets of Miami Beach. Smoothly cruising past the prominent architecture and extraordinary views was a fantastic sensation.

Julia gave the car to the valet in Coconut Grove, then she went to a couple of chic shops. After trying and discarding several different styles, she bought a gorgeous emerald-green silk dress. The color made her tan skin look sensual, and brought out her emerald eyes. In another shop she picked out some sexy black lingerie to surprise Alejandro with after the party. She had something in mind for him tonight, and she was beyond excited at the idea. She knew he'd be very happy about her surprise, especially when he saw the black silk and lace that he loved on her. Julia felt immensely happy about her life with Alejandro—she couldn't have wished for better. Her stomach rumbled, and she glanced at her watch. It was already 4PM—where had the time gone?—and she stopped at a small French restaurant to have something to eat.

After shopping she went to the day spa to make herself relax with a good massage, then have her hair and nails done. She was enjoying having a day on her own—except when Alejandro called her every thirty minutes to check if everything was still okay. He'd called several times before she'd chosen the green dress, sounding anxious. He told her again to be careful driving such a fast car. "I know you're a good driver, but when you drive in Miami Beach you need to be aware."

"I will," Julia said. Suddenly she wondered how Alejandro would react if she came back with a dent in his expensive car. The truth was, she loved driving the cool, sporty car. The sophistication of a beautiful woman in a fast car always captivated the attention of the people on the street, but what she loved most was the sensation of freedom when she drove. She was an extremely good driver, and didn't need to show off.

When she'd finished her shopping and a light snack, it was already evening. She made her way home along the coast, watching the sky fill with vibrant, rich colors as the dusk settled in. The sun dropped quickly behind the horizon, the sand of Miami Beach rippled into waves like the ocean behind. It was surreal, in a way, that she had come halfway around the world to live this life. By the time she arrived home the sun was gone, and there were only a few gulls left in the sky.

She drove through the villa's front gates and took the car around to the garage. In the garden, the exotic plants were now interspersed with tables set with crystal glassware and fine china. Pots of orchids stood in the middle of each table. Everything was perfect—Alejandro had done a good job, no doubt about it.

Julia crossed the terrace and went through the French doors into the living room. She set down her shopping bags and glanced out the window to see if Alejandro was outside. Through the expansive windows overlooking the garden, she saw the pool surrounded by palm trees and the palms lit by hidden lights. It was stunningly elegant. She saw catering staff setting out the last of the chairs, but not her fiancé.

She took her shopping bags upstairs to get ready for the party. She laid out the sophisticated emerald dress across the oversize bed, and went into the bathroom for a quick shower. By the time Alejandro came upstairs, Julia was dressed and ready for the party.

"You're finally home?" he said as he entered the room.

"Yes, shopping took longer than I thought," Julia replied.

"Well at least you got here in time for your party."

Clearly, Alejandro wasn't happy about her having spent the day out alone.

"I'm sorry," Julia said. She crossed to him and kissed his cheek. "The time just went so fast, and I didn't realize how late it was. Wasn't it worth it?" She stepped back and twirled to show him her new dress.

Alejandro watched her and his mouth curved into a smile. "That dress is absolutely stunning on you," he admitted.

"Do you like it?" Julia said, regarding herself in the mirror, turning to look at her body over her shoulder. The sleeveless emerald silk dress was ankle-length, with a deeply cut back that showed her beautiful spine to the lowest possible point.

"Mmm," said Alejandro, in appreciation of her naked back. "It is certainly a gorgeous summer party dress."

"Thank you. I'm happy you like it."

"I like your hairstyle, too," he said. He softly touched her long wavy hair and sensually slipped his finger along the smooth skin of her back.

Julia felt a shiver along her spine—she couldn't resist his touch. With a fast move, Alejandro turned her body toward him. Her hands felt the contours of his chest muscles as she looked up at him. His face was tanned from the Miami sun, and his deep blue eyes savored her. Alejandro ran his finger softly over her pink lips and moved forward to kiss her, but Julia pushed him back.

"I think you should get ready for the party," she said, with a wicked gleam in her eye.

"We still have time." He gazed romantically into her eyes. "So exotic."

"What?"

"Your emerald eyes and this green dress. I want to make love with you in this dress," he whispered in her ear. Slowly, his hands slid inside her dress.

Julia smile teasingly and grabbed his wrists. "You will have to wait for that. But after the party I have some surprises for you," she whispered back. She was planning a sensual private striptease with the sexy lingerie she'd bought that afternoon. "It'll be worth the wait, trust me," she said with a seductive smile.

Alejandro felt a stab of desire as he wondered what her surprise could be, but he wanted her now—and after the party, too. "I can't wait until after the party," he moaned.

"Yes, you will." She softly kissed his lips.

The party was exactly as Julia had imagined. It was a whirlwind of congratulations on her pregnancy and compliments to Alejandro for his beautiful partner. And of course, Alejandro was delighted. He'd made a point of inviting his most interesting and entertaining acquaintances, and Julia was making a very good impression.

In the garden, people were dancing. Waiters moved smoothly through the crowd, filling glasses with champagne and serving an exotic signature cocktail. At the bar, guests ordered their drinks of choice. Alejandro had taxis standing by for anyone who drank too much—he wanted to enjoy the party, not deal with out-of-control drinkers.

Julia noticed Jack Walker at a table by the pool, sipping what looked like a vodka tonic and playing with his phone. She headed in his direction.

"Thanks for coming, Jack. I'm happy you made it."

"I couldn't miss such an event," Jack replied, touching her arm. "Happy Birthday!"

"Thank you, Jack!" She lightly touched his shoulder. "I hope you enjoy my party."

"Of course he's enjoying the party," Alejandro said as he strolled over. He clapped Jack on the shoulder. "Have you seen Danny Lancash around?"

"Yeah, I spoke with him earlier," Jack said. "I didn't know he was still dating that girl—you know, the one we saw him with last Christmas?"

Jack gestured curiously toward Danny, who stood in the garden chatting with a girl who waved her hands wildly while she spoke. Alejandro looked at her and raised his eyebrows. He assumed she'd had more champagne than necessary. The fact that Danny was still with her surprised him as well—the girl had seemed like an alcoholic, and he felt Danny deserved better. But it wasn't his business to get involved in Danny's private life.

Alejandro turned to Jack. "Mind if we join you?" He held a chair for Julia, then sat next to her.

"Everyone seems to be having fun," Julia said.

"It looks like it," Alejandro replied.

Suddenly the lights in the garden went off.

"What's wrong with the lights?" Julia asked. Across the garden, four girls appeared on the terrace with flaming torches. Between them appeared two waiters bearing a large cake lit with candles, followed by more waiters with champagne. As the cake procession moved toward the pool, the waiters topped up every guest's champagne glass. The DJ faded out the dance music and played "Happy Birthday," and everyone stood to sing to Julia.

It was like a dream. Julia felt drugged by the firelight and champagne and the party atmosphere, and her skin flushed with emotion.

The waiters reached their table, and Julia stared at the three-tiered cake, iced with dark chocolate and decorated with miniature, live red roses. On the cake was written in white letters: Love You Forever.

"Happy Birthday, Amore!" Alejandro said, bending to kiss her. "Thank you for your gorgeous smile that wakes me every morning. I've been so lucky to meet the sweetest love I never dreamed I'd have. I can't imagine my life without you by my side."

"You're so romantic," Julia said.

"You need to make a wish and blow out the candles."

"Right, I almost forgot," Julia replied. She shut her eyes for a moment, and wished that this fairy tale would last forever. Then she opened her eyes and blew out all the candles. "What a beautiful cake."

"I chose the design myself."

"Don't forget I have a surprise for you, too, tonight," Julia whispered in his ear. Secretly, she couldn't wait to see his expression when she appeared in the sexy black lingerie.

"What is it?"

"I can't tell you."

"Mmm…I have a feeling it's going to be something very naughty," Alejandro said as he moved forward to kiss her.

"I can't say anything. You will have to wait until the party's over."

"You're so cheeky," Alejandro said.

"And you like it," Julia replied. She kissed him and playfully bit his lower lip.

"I don't want to interrupt the moment," Jack said

from across the table, "But I have to say you two are the most romantic couple I've ever seen."

Alejandro smiled, realizing he'd forgotten Jack's presence. "How are things going in New York, Jack?"

"Bit of a hassle with the new contracts," Jack replied, setting his glass on the table.

"Ah, that's right. I got your email with the new contracts."

"I meant to ask you," Jack said. "Did you read it yet?"

"Yes, I did, and there were some important points I didn't like. I made some modifications and sent it back to the lawyers."

"Well," Jack said. "I told them you'd never agree with articles eight and nine, and maybe you'd want some other changes, too."

"Indeed," Alejandro said. "Let's see what the lawyers say about the changes."

Julia listened in silence. Every day she'd heard variations of this conversation. Alejandro spent hours and hours over the phone in long business conversations. Couldn't he avoid talking about work tonight, and just enjoy her party? Alejandro shifted his chair closer to Jack and dropped his voice, giving a little nod toward a party guest—probably someone in the market for a yacht. He'd turned his back to Julia. She was decidedly unhappy at the idea of sitting here and watching the two men talk without her—and she didn't want to be included in a work meeting tonight!

Around the garden, some guests had departed after having their piece of cake, but the most hard-core partiers were still drinking and dancing. The DJ had pumped up the beat of the music, and bodies swayed on the dance floor in the light from the torches and the trees. Suddenly Julia felt tired. All she wanted to do was sleep. She stood up and spoke softly in Alejandro's ear.

"I'm going upstairs, feeling a bit tired."

"Okay," Alejandro said. "As soon I finish here with Jack, I'll be coming, too."

"I'll wait for you upstairs. Don't be late."

"I won't." Alejandro watched Julia walk away, the stunning open back of her dress drawing admiring glances from every guest she passed. He smiled with satisfaction. "She is wonderful."

"You're a lucky man," Jack said.

"I agree. Julia has changed my life. I'm a happy man." Alejandro nodded thoughtfully. "I want to marry her before she has our baby."

"Man, life is changing for you at a hundred miles an hour," Jack said.

"And I like that. Julia's a wonderful fiancée and she's going to be a brilliant wife." For a moment, a cloud passed over Alejandro's face. He loved her so much and she was such a special woman, it scared him that this was all too good to be true, that one day this life would vanish.

"I'm thinking," Jack said, going back to the business conversation, "Why you don't come to New York for a few days and we can have a meeting with the lawyers and define those contracts? It always goes faster when you're on the spot."

"I hate to say it, but maybe you're right," Alejandro said. "And the faster we wrap this up, the sooner I can put my focus on planning the wedding."

"I agree," Jack said.

"Can you give the airport a call and let them know I'll want my plane in the morning?" Alejandro asked. "Ditch your return ticket and ride with me. We can go through everything on the flight and sort out those contracts before the end of the week," he added. *It'll be so much better to have this matter off my desk, and then I can really think about my marriage,* he thought.

"I'll do that right now," Jack replied.

"Great! I'm going upstairs—I'll get a few hours' sleep and let Julia know I'm going to New York for a few days. I'll see you on the plane in the morning."

Alejandro disappeared into the garden and made his way into the villa.

Upstairs in the bedroom, he saw Julia lying on the bed, still wearing her party dress. *Hmm… No sexy surprises for me tonight.* He stood and watched her for a few minutes. She was so beautiful. He wanted to take her dress off and help her sleep more comfortably, but he didn't want to wake her. An expectant mother needed her sleep, and she'd been running herself ragged today. Gently he eased onto the bed and lay next to her. Sleep fell upon him as dust settled in stagnant water.

A few hours later he awoke, realizing it was time to get to the airport. Julia still slept deeply—it would be a shame to wake her just to tell her about a quick trip. He'd probably be in New York before she even woke up, and he could call her as soon as they landed. Surely she'd understand the urgency, how much he wanted to be done with business so that he could plan a wedding with her that would be fit for his queen. Anyway, it would only be a couple of days—Julia could have some more shopping time, get some rest after the party, relax by the pool. He knew for sure she wasn't ready to head back to New York.

Chapter Thirty-Six

Julia woke up in the late afternoon. She stretched and opened her eyes, then rolled over to see if Alejandro was behind her. To her surprise, the bed was empty. She got out of bed and went to the window. Outside, all the tables and people from the night before had disappeared and the garden had returned to normal. She opened the window and enjoyed the smell of the exotic flowers, staying there for a while, the soft ocean breezes caressing her face. Then she went downstairs to search for Alejandro, but he wasn't there. *Where is he hiding?* Perhaps he'd run out to pick up something for lunch? She tried calling, but his phone was switched off.

Julia shrugged. He'd turn up sooner or later. She thought she'd shower, put her swimsuit on and sunbathe by the pool. It was a beautiful day.

As she entered the bathroom, she gasped and held onto the doorframe. A strong pain ran through her stomach. Something warm ran down her legs, and she looked down to see red blood forming a pool around her feet. Her body burned and her head whirled with dizziness. She looked up into the mirror and saw a woman she barely recognized, her face contorted with pain. The image faded and she fell to the floor.

When Julia woke, she wondered for a moment where she was—the floor was hard and cold and she was in a puddle. The memory of pain crashed back into her mind. How long had she been lying here? The afternoon sun slanted through the windows—was it still the same day? She tried to stand, but her legs weakened beneath her and she couldn't feel her lower body. Logically, she knew there was nothing to prevent her from moving, but her body didn't want to cooperate.

Julia used the door frame and furniture to drag herself across the floor to the bed, where she'd dropped her phone. She hit redial, but Alejandro's phone was still off, so, weeping, she dialed 9-1-1. While she waited for the sound of sirens, she tried Alejandro again, but still nothing.

"Turn the damn phone on!" Julia screamed helplessly into her mobile phone, her eyes filling up with tears.

It was twenty-four long minutes later that the ambulance came, having fought their way through rush hour traffic. Julia still lay on the floor, holding her phone tightly in her hands and curled into a ball, another pool of blood around her on the bedroom carpet.

She faded in and out of consciousness as the ambulance slid through traffic. The stretcher jostled out of the ambulance and wheeled into the ER. Vaguely, she heard someone official-sounding, "Critical, she's lost a lot of blood, let's get her temperature down—"

"What's your name, miss?" another voice asked, but Julia couldn't speak and she was shivering with cold. A quick sting in her inner elbow, a cold feeling in her arm, and unconsciousness welcomed her. The blurred visions of a few hurrying beings faded away and darkness seeped in.

Julia woke, again disoriented. Surely this wasn't her bedroom. The light was all wrong. And shouldn't it be evening now?

"You're going to be just fine, dear," a woman's voice said.

Julia turned her head and realized that a woman was holding her wrist to check her pulse. The woman wore nurse's scrubs and her middle-aged face was kind and soft.

"You've had some painkillers. Are you feeling any pain now?"

Julia remembered something—she'd called an ambulance. But it was a blur after that. Her brain was empty. "How long have I been here?" she asked the nurse.

"You were admitted two days ago."

"You mean I slept for two days in row?" Julia opened her eyes even wider.

"You'd lost a lot of blood, and we kept you sedated. When you came here you were half-dead," the nurse said. "So you needed lots of rest to recover your energy.

"But now you will be fine, and soon you can have another baby," the nurse said, patting Julia's hand.

"What are you talking about?" Julia's hand flew to her abdomen, which felt somehow hollow. She ran her hand over her stomach and felt it flat and empty. "What have you done with my baby? Where is my baby?" Julia couldn't control herself, her voice seemed to be coming from another person. Her eyes filled with tears, sadness gripped her heart, and still she screamed, now wordless with heartache. She gulped and her voice caught in her throat. In the sudden silence she realized, *Where was Alejandro?*

Why hadn't Alejandro picked up the phone when she called? Why hadn't he come to the hospital? The ambulance crew had left a number for him—hadn't he come home to find her gone? Suddenly she hated Alejandro, she hated The Signature Quintana and Jack Walker and every bit of business that kept him away from her, that made him break his promise to take care of her. The more her mind ran through these thoughts, the more her heart ached. *This is his fault*, she thought. *If*

I hadn't been alone, if he had been there, I wouldn't have stayed on the floor so long, maybe we could have saved the baby.

The nurse smoothed Julia's forehead with a damp cloth and brought out a hypodermic. The nurse's mouth moved, but Julia couldn't hear anything she said. She could only see the movement of the nurse's mouth, her hands trying to keep Julia calm enough to give her another injection. The cold washed through her arm again, and unable to fight any longer, Julia closed her eyes and fell asleep again.

It was Wednesday evening and Alejandro still couldn't get in touch with Julia. He'd called her many times, leaving voicemails and texts telling her that after the party he'd had to fly urgently to New York, but Julia hadn't responded to any of them. Maybe she was upset that he'd left for New York without telling her? Maybe she didn't want to speak to him because of that? Julia was a stubborn woman sometimes, and he knew her very well. He could totally see her being upset and not speaking with him for days. A strange thought crossed his mind. *What if she met someone in Miami Beach while I've been gone, and she's falling for him?* Just as quickly, he dismissed it. *No, Julia is in love with me, she would never do that. She's just mad at me, that's all*. He imagined her beautiful face flushed with anger and missed her sharply. The business in New York had taken longer than he'd thought, but he'd be finished by Friday and able to fly back to Miami that night, or Saturday morning at the latest.

Alejandro checked his reflection in the office window, fixed his tie and buttoned his jacket. Jack Walker was entertaining the clients and their lawyers in the meeting room, and it was time for Alejandro to head in and kick-start the meeting.

Julia had been in the hospital long enough to start getting out of bed for short walks. Still, she couldn't understand why Alejandro had left, or where he was now. Her phone had terrible reception in the hospital; what if he'd left a message and she hadn't gotten it? *Then she realized, she didn't care.* It didn't matter if he'd left a hundred messages—what mattered was that he'd left her alone, without telling her where he was going or how long he'd be gone. How could she ever believe anything he said again? Hatred filled her, replacing the last remnants of love in her heart. She walked to the window and sat in a chair there. She'd try to call Samantha—if the phone would work.

"Hey sweetie," Samantha said. "How are you?"

"My baby is gone," Julia said. "I lost my baby." In her devastation, Julia couldn't stop crying. Samantha was shocked at the weakness in Julia's voice. She couldn't imagine what condition her best friend must be in to sound like this. How could it be true that her powerful, fascinating friend was so broken? "What are you saying? Where are you now?"

"I'm in the hospital, in Miami," Julia managed to get out through her tears.

Samantha tried to calm her. "Everything is going to be okay, sweetie. You will have another baby."

"I don't want another baby, I want this baby, I want my baby back. I hate Alejandro—this is his entire fault."

"What do you mean it's his fault? Has he done something to you?"

"He left me alone at home. If only I'd been able to get to the hospital faster, but I was alone with no-one to help me."

"He left you alone? What do you mean? Where is he?"

At that moment, a message beeped through.

I am in New York and very worried.

Where are you? What's going on?

"I guess he's in New York," Julia said grimly. "I guess his business is so much more important than his wife—or his baby!" Julia was gripped by a storm of sobs.

Samantha's calm voice reached through the phone.

"Please, I want you to calm down and tell me what happened?"

"I woke up in the morning and I was feeling bad and Alejandro wasn't there to help me and his phone was off."

"Okay, and where is he? Did he call you after?"

Julia squinted at her phone, which now had a badge for 17 messages. "Yes, he did call me, but it was too late. My baby is gone now and it's Alejandro's fault. I don't ever want to speak to him again."

"He knows that you are in the hospital?"

"No, and I'm not going to reply to his messages. I hate him." Julia felt an icy determination. Losing the baby had changed all her emotions; it had changed everything. She was no longer a passionate and willing woman. She felt as if her nerves were made of steel.

The nurse came in. "I hate to cut your conversation short, dear, but the doctor needs to see you now."

Julia said goodbye to Samantha and walked the short distance to the examination room. The doctor told her she'd made plenty of progress, she'd be fine.

That's what you think. Julia knew she'd never be the same again.

When she returned to her room, the phone began buzzing in her hand. She stared at the screen—it was Alejandro again. She switched it off and shoved the phone under her pillow.

During her stay at the hospital, Julia didn't answer a single one of Alejandro's calls or texts. Every day, her hatred for him grew inside her. She knew she could never stay with him after this, and began planning how to leave. Would he even miss her? Clearly, Alejandro loved his job more than he loved her. Why hadn't he told her he was flying to New York? What kind of man left his wife-to-be while she was sleeping?

She listened to one voicemail, the first one he'd left. Alejandro's voice, breezy and unconcerned, told her he was going to New York for some urgent business and would be back Friday. *He can stay there forever, Julia thought. I won't be here when he gets back.*

Thoughts whirled through her mind. How could she have given up her career to move in with Alejandro? That wasn't a "compromise", that was being the one who gave up everything for love! Where was Alejandro's compromise? Why didn't he give anything up? She needed to take her life back, and for that she needed to get away from Miami—from America—as far away from Alejandro as she could. And she knew exactly where to go—she would fly to Argentina and spend the winter holidays with *mamá*. Then she'd go back to Milan and start modeling again. It had been foolish to give up her dreams and her career for love. She could only hope her foolishness hadn't ruined the rest of her life.

Chapter Thirty-Seven

Julia left the hospital Saturday afternoon. She took a taxi to the house. After a long week of medicines and syringes her body felt heavy and weak.

At the villa she was surprised to discover things exactly as she'd left them—Alejandro wasn't back from New York. She went upstairs. At least the maids had been in and cleaned up the mess. The thought of what had happened a week ago sent a sharp sadness through her chest. She took a deep breath and stripped off the hospital scrubs they'd put her in when her own clothes were too blood-stained to clean. She threw the scrubs into the garbage and took a long shower. Thoughts flooded through her mind as she stood beneath the shower jet. She touched her abdomen, hoping for all of it to be a wicked nightmare. It wasn't.

She changed into a pair of comfortable jeans and a blouse. She pulled out her largest suitcase and began to fill it.

The bedroom door opened. Alejandro stopped in the doorway. *What was Julia doing?*

"Are we going somewhere?" he asked.

Julia startled at his voice—she hadn't heard him coming up the stairs. She turned her head.

"No, we are not." she said, giving him a sharp look. "I am."

"What do you mean?" Alejandro stared at her—something was different, Had she been eating properly? She looked skinnier than he remembered. "I know you're upset with me, Julia, but I can explain. I'm sorry I left so suddenly for New York, it was—"

She cut him off. "I don't need your explanation. It's too late now for that."

"You okay?" Alejandro asked. "What's happened? You seem so different." He came close to her and put his hands on her shoulders. "Could you please stop with this luggage and look at me?"

She wrenched her shoulders out of his hands, nearly falling over from her own force. He stretched out an arm to steady her and she stepped back, not wanting any contact with him.

Alejandro looked at her, shocked. Was this the same woman who only last week had made love to him so beautifully?

Julia started to cry. "Because of you I lost my baby." She pushed the last of her clothes into the suitcase and zipped it.

Alejandro put his hand over his face. Blood ran through his head like thunderbolts. It took him a while to register the reality into his mind. "Why you didn't tell me anything? Why didn't you answer any of my phone calls or my messages?" he asked, terrified. "I could have flown back to help you and be with you!"

"I was too busy trying to save myself." Julia shot him another look. "I tried to call you, when it first happened. I needed you to be here with me that morning. But your phone was off. Or maybe you were still on the plane you didn't tell me you were getting on."

"I didn't realize that my battery went dead…" Alejandro said. Guilt swept over him, and he wanted nothing more than to make her sorrow go away—her sorrow that he had caused. He came to her and tried to embrace her.

She pushed him back. "I don't need your comfort. Not anymore."

Alejandro had never seen her like this. Julia had completely changed. He was confused—she seemed to be a totally different person. "I know you're hurt," he said. "But please don't let this change your feelings for me."

"After what happened, everything has changed between us," Julia replied.

"Please don't say that. We can have another baby."

"It's too late now."

"You are so young!" Alejandro exclaimed. "Of course it's not too late."

"I am leaving you, Alejandro," she said between tears. "I will sleep in the guest room tonight, and tomorrow I will leave this house."

Alejandro shook his head. "Please don't do that, don't ruin this beautiful love story."

Julia ignored him. She pulled the suitcase handle out, thankful for wheeled baggage, and took it with her into the guest room. She stood for a moment inside the door, feeling a greater sorrow than she had ever known. Then she hardened her resolve, and locked the door.

Alone in what had been their bedroom, Alejandro ran his hand over his hair. *I never should have gone to New York that day,* he thought. But he had, and now it was too late. It was entirely his fault that Julia was so hurt and angry, and he could only admit the truth of that.

He didn't want to sleep alone, imagining her body next to him in the bed they had shared. That night he tossed and turned on the sofa—the thought that Julia wanted to leave him broke his heart. Thoughts were fighting in his head. Could she ever forgive him for his stupid error? What he could do to convince her from leaving? She was so angry… He still hadn't closed his eyes when the grey dawn crept into the living room. Was it already morning?

Upstairs in the guest room, Julia was awake, too. She needed to get to the airport for her ten a.m. flight to Buenos Aires. She looked at her image in the mirror over the bathroom sink. Her face was pale and drawn. She put on a pair of light jeans and a T-shirt, and added sunglasses to cover her eyes. When she was ready, she slowly bumped her luggage downstairs. The taxi she had called was waiting for her outside.

Alejandro heard her coming downstairs and jumped up from the leather sofa.

On the landing of the stairs, Julia looked down at him silently. Then she went straight to the door and waved to the taxi driver to come and take her luggage. As the driver heaved her bag into the trunk, she sat in the back seat. Alejandro had gotten himself together—he seemed to realize she was really going—and he started toward the taxi. Julia rolled down the window and asked the driver, "Hurry up, please—I don't want to miss my flight."

Before Alejandro could reach her, the taxi had taken off. He saw his happiness, his desire, the better half of his soul, drifting away in his wake. He stood helpless while his spirit crumbled from within. Julia looked back for a moment and saw Alejandro angrily kicking a palm tree, his face dark with anger.

"Your boyfriend seems pretty angry," the taxi driver acknowledged.

Julia didn't bother to answer. She certainly wasn't going to share her problem with a stranger. At the airport she tipped the driver generously, and checked in at the curb, where a skycap took her heavy suitcase.

Scarcely two hours later, Julia settled into the plane, on her way to Argentina. More than anything, she wanted her mother.

Chapter Thirty-Eight

When the plane touched down in Argentina, Julia's eyes were red and swollen. She'd cried throughout the flight, hiding behind her dark glasses. Outside the airport, she picked up a taxi and was soon at her mother's house. Mamá met her at the door with open arms and words of comfort. Julia set down her suitcase and threw herself into her mother's arms.

"I know it's easy to say, but soon you will be fine," her mother said, cuddling Julia's head on her shoulder.

"I feel so sad," Julia said. "When I first found out I was pregnant, I was so happy. I wanted to have kids and make a family with Alejandro, and now I have lost everything."

"It's all going to be okay. I know you're upset with the entire world now, but trust me, soon you will forget everything and you will start to live and love again," her mother tried to reassure her.

"It's not that easy," Julia said.

"I know. But you are strong and you can do it, and I am here to help you," her mother said.

"I am so happy I've got you," Julia replied, and after hugs and cuddles with her mother, she fell into bed and slept a deep sleep.

The next afternoon, Julia closeted herself in her room and called Samantha.

"I think you're making a mistake," Samantha said. "You shouldn't blame Alejandro—what happened wasn't his fault."

"Maybe not having a miscarriage, but it is his fault for not being by my side when I needed him," Julia pointed out. "And looking back, I made so many mistakes when I first met Alejandro. I should have had the courage to stand up for what I wanted. Now it's too late. I don't even know how I feel right now—whether I'm more angry with him or proud of my decision."

"I think you just need time to forget what happened. Give it a few weeks, and you'll be fine," Samantha said.

"I will never forget this pain," Julia replied. She felt wetness on her cheek and realized tears were again running down her face.

"If you want, I could come to Argentina and stay with you for few days?"

"There's no point in you coming here. I'll only be in

Argentina for a month. After Christmas, or January at the latest, I'm coming back to Milan."

"That's great! Are you thinking about going back to modeling?" Samantha asked.

"Yes. Going back to my career is the only thing that will help me get over this. I need to take my life back into my own hands again."

"That's wonderful," Samantha said. "I can't wait to see you back in Milan. We are going to have lots of fun again!"

"I think I will need time for that, but thank you. Thanks for encouraging me."

"Of course. You're my best friend, and I care about you," Samantha said. "Oh goodness! We've been talking for half an hour—I need to go back to the table, I'm having dinner with one of my clients. I hope he's still there after all this time I've been gone."

"Oh sorry, why you didn't tell me before that you were out for dinner with someone?" Julia said.

"Don't you worry, he'll wait. I'll ring you later. Take care."

"I'll try," Julia said. She hung up and looked in the mirror—she felt disgusted.

She realized how foolish she was. Living in a fairytale and believing it could last forever. Her life changed once, now it was about to change again. She immediately started thinking about everything and everyone, as if every aspect of her life was flashing before her eyes. Memories came flooding back. She couldn't wait to go back to Milan and start modeling again. She paced the small room and stared out the window at the sunlight reflecting from the buildings.

Her mother knocked on the door and Julia jumped to hug her.

Her mother hugged her back. Julia seemed a little more cheerful—hopefully talking to Samantha had helped.

"Tonight I am going to cook something special for you," her mother said.

"What is it?"

"It's something you were always asking me to cook for you when you were small." Her mother smiled and ruffled Julia's hair, trying to cheer her up.

"Can't wait to see what it is," Julia said. Suddenly she felt a bit hungry. She looked at her *mamá* and took her hand. "Thank you for being there when I need you."

"You don't have to say thanks, I'm your mother and I will always be present when you need me. But don't forget, you're a strong girl, and you can get over this."

"I wish I was as strong as I used to be," Julia replied.

"You are just as you were. But remember, in life nothing lasts forever, no matter how beautiful or perfect things seem."

Julia looked at her mother with thoughtful eyes. "I thought I could control everything, but I was wrong," she said sadly. She threw herself in her mother's arms again, and they hugged each other tenderly. Her mother understood her daughter's pain very well, and there were no words spoken, no formal discussion, just the natural and right connection between a mother and her daughter. Julia's mother comforted her heart.

"I need to go and collect the cakes I ordered earlier. When I come back I'll finish cooking dinner for us," her mother said.

"If you want, I can go to the pastry shop to pick up the cakes and you make dinner in the meantime," Julia suggested.

"Are you sure you can do that?"

"Of course I'm sure."

Her mother offered the car key and Julia took it. "I thought you got rid of this old car," she said, looking at the key.

"It's still a good car," her mother replied. "And the money that you gave me, I helped your sister buy a new car for herself."

"But that money was for you, to buy a good car so you can be safe when you drive."

"Don't you worry about me, this car is enough for my needs."

Julia touched her mother's hand. "This week I will buy you a new car."

"I don't need a new car, this car is still good enough for me."

"It's not very safe." Julia looked at her. "Anyway, it's better for me to go get the cakes before the bakery closes. Which shop has the order?"

"Ah! It's at la *pastelería* on the highway near the gas station, do you remember? The one we used to go to every Sunday morning when you were a kid."

"How could I forget? They used to do the best cakes in the city," Julia replied.

"And they still do the traditional confectionary," her mother said. "That pastry shop is the oldest shop in this city."

"I remember, you always say that." Julia smiled at her sweet mother. "I'm leaving now, do you need anything else?"

"No, I don't need anything. Come back soon."

"I will."

Julia jumped into the old car and pushed back the seat to make her long legs comfortable. It didn't sit well with her that her mother hadn't bought a new car. As she drove down the highway and looked around, she felt she was home. Her body relaxed, feeling suddenly like she was in a peaceful haven. Her childhood home, and here with her mamá, who cared for her so much. She was so thankful to spend Christmas together, and after New Year's she'd go back to Milan.

She parked the old car around the corner from the pastry shop, collected the cakes and carried the armload of white boxes back to the car. As she set them carefully on the back seat, she heard a familiar voice calling her name. It couldn't be—but she turned her head, and it was. Her father. She hastily shut the door and rushed around to the driver's seat.

"Julia! I want to talk to you, please don't run away!" her father shouted.

"We don't have anything to talk about!" Julia got into the car and slammed the door. She threw the car into gear and skidded out into the road. A cloud of dust surrounded the car, but in the rear-view mirror she could see her father standing, waving his arms. Pablo hadn't changed at all—his body was still young, and his face showed few signs of aging. *He should be in his fifties by now,* she thought.

At the age of fourteen, Julia had met her father for

the first time. She had bawled her eyes out and told him she would hate him for the rest of her life. What he had done to her mother was unfair—it wasn't right. She'd been a model wife and mother, and he'd abandoned her and his children for another woman. The woman had manipulated him, and he had come crawling back, penniless and trying for a second chance. Fortunately, her mother had been too proud to give in to him, and Julia and her sister had wanted nothing to do with the man who had walked away from them when they were babies.

Still, it had saddened Julia to be without a father, and many nights she found herself crying alone in her room. Eventually, she'd heard about the modeling scene in Milan, and thought perhaps she could make a career there. She'd done a few jobs in Buenos Aires, and everyone who photographed her had exclaimed over her potential. It had been time to take a big step, and her mother had supported her every step of the way. She hadn't bothered to tell her father when she left the country. In her new life in Milan, she'd known she would never return to live in Argentina, but she would support her mother as soon as she had money enough to send.

Julia started to cry as the memories came back into her head. She accelerated, trying to speed away from the past, from the man she'd never known or trusted. Thunder rolled and raindrops started to splash on the windshield, but Julia sped up and passed a slower car in front. As she pulled out, she was blinded by the high beams of an oncoming truck. She stomped on the brakes, and the pedal went to the floor without slowing the car. Frantically Julia pulled the handbrake, and the small car skidded into a spin. Before she could respond, the truck slammed into her, rolling the small car over the embankment.

Pablo had followed in his own car—he'd known Julia must be heading toward her mother's house, and had caught up easily on a straight stretch of roadway. He couldn't pass up the chance to speak to his daughter, to try to explain how wrong he had been all those years ago. As her car rolled, bits of fender and glass broke off and scattered across the road. He pulled over and jumped out, screaming after the truck driver, "Stop! You must stop! Why don't you stop!"

The truck kept going, and Pablo felt guilt flow through his body. *She wouldn't have been driving so fast if I hadn't called out to her. She was running away from me.*

He pulled out his phone and called for an ambulance, then rushed to the wreckage of Julia's vehicle. She lay cradled in the shattered metal, her body trapped between the steering wheel and the seat. Pieces of glass had made deep cuts on her face, and blood ran down her mouth and neck. Pablo touched her hand. A faint pulse beat in her wrist. He looked up to the heavens and expressed his deepest thanks. She was still alive. He had made her suffer when he abandoned his family, and now she was again in undeserved pain.

People gathered around the wreckage. Some of them took out their cell phones and called the emergency number. Pablo did the same, only he couldn't stop trembling and the responder barely understood a word he said. Fifteen minutes later, an ambulance rushed Julia towards a hospital, bleeding and broken. The sirens echoed through the streets as it paved its way through the rain drenched road. Pablo followed the van, broken into sweat, his hands drenched with Julia's blood. His heart was dedicated to constant prayers. *No God, no. Not today. Not like this. I am prepared for my punishment but not like this. Not her. Take me. Not her.* Tears flooded his eyes as he cut through the rainfall barely inches behind the van.

"Not her", he whispered.

Chapter Thirty-Nine

In Miami Beach, Alejandro was still fighting reality, refusing to accept that Julia had left him. He paced through the living room, and then went upstairs to the bedroom. The bed they'd slept in together, the bathroom where he'd lovingly soaped her body in the shower—everything reminded him of her.

He couldn't stay in the villa any longer. He needed to go back to New York today. Quickly he packed a bag, then went through the house, shutting doors and windows. The guest room door was open, and when he went to close it, he saw the bed Julia had slept in the previous night, the sheets still tangled, her fragrance still lingered. There was a piece of paper on the floor, near the bedside table. He rushed to pick it up, and read:

By the time you read this letter I will be far away from here. This has been a terrible week, and even if I could continue our relationship, I could never again give you that happiness we had once.

There were so many things I thought I could do and

be with you. But now I need to be alone, to heal my soul. Staying here would not help me—it would only confuse me more, and that's why I need this time alone.

Losing my baby is the worst experience I have ever had. Every room in this house is full of memories that sadden my heart. Maybe you will think I'm stupid for doing this, but right now all I can feel is that I need to go far, far away from here, from those memories, from you.

Being with you was an unforgettable experience. Thank you for everything you gave me and everything we did. Now things are different, though—I have a deep pain in my heart and I need to close the door on that hurt and stay away from everything that reminds me of the terrible feeling. This house is full of sadness, and I can't pretend that anything would ever be the same between us. I am exhausted. I am run down, and I need to find my own way back to who I used to be.

I wish our story could be different, but there's no way to ignore what happened. I suppose that's life, and life is about loving, losing, and lots of other things that we will never fully understand.

Drops of water splashed onto the letter in his hand, and Alejandro realized tears were rolling down his face and falling onto the letter. He was numb—his brain unable to wrap itself around the idea of losing Julia. Reading her letter, he realized he'd lost her forever. *But why couldn't she understand that she needs me now more than ever, that we should work through this together?* He knew, though. She wanted to hurt him because he hadn't been with her the day she'd miscarried. He hated himself, too, because of that. He felt guilty, guilty for not being with her when she needed him the most. Clutching the letter in his hand, he turned and slammed his hand into the wall. Julia was the only woman he'd ever loved that much. And now the woman who had changed his life was breaking up with him without even having a calm and normal conversation first. She couldn't forgive him for a stupid error.

They had belonged to each other, and now everything vanished like a beautiful dream. All that remained were a few fragments of memories. He knew he could never love another woman as much as he loved Julia. She was the woman he'd always wished to have, the partner who gave him strength and reasons for living. She completed him in every sense, and every time he saw her he felt butterflies in his stomach. She had stimulated him in every way, intellectually, physically and emotionally.

He didn't know if he could make it without her by his side.

Alejandro landed in New York after midnight and drove directly to the office. He'd called Jack earlier, and would meet him there to review some paperwork. *Was it true that all he cared about was business?* A song played through the radio—a song they'd danced to at the engagement party. He punched the button and got the pop song she'd walked down the catwalk to, that first night he'd seen her. Another button and it was a song she'd sung in his ear after making love.

He turned the radio off. I'll go crazy if I keep thinking like this. But how can I forget how happy I was with Julia? So many men never have a single perfect moment, and I lived so many with Julia….

Chapter Forty

As Julia lay motionless in a small bed, she could hear the monitors beeping in the dead silence. The bandage covering half of her face sent a shiver down her spine. *My face*. She was in so much pain that it had become a part of her feelings. Tilting her head slightly, she saw an elderly man sitting by her bed. His face moist with tears. And his eyes closed in prayers.

"What are you doing here?' She spoke softly. Pablo opened his eyes, startled.

"Oh my dear, How are you?" He said in his trembling voice, as the tears flooded his eyes. Where is my mum? "What are you doing here?" She repeated her unanswered question. Pablo lowered her head, too ashamed to meet her gaze.

"Julia, I know you're mad at me. I didn't tell your mother you are in the hospital because I wanted to spend time with you. I know you are upset with me for what have done in the past, but I want to explain everything to I you now."

"Is it too late for an explanation now?"

"I know, my sin is unforgivable." He said steadying his voice, "I was seduced by my desire. I learnt my mistake only too late. Never a day passes by when I don't wish to alter my past." He looked at her intently "I am sorry." And broke into a sob.

"Go ahead. Tell me your story." She said with a cold heart. "Be honest for once."

Pablo sat in silence for a while, as if trying to figure how to shape the story so as to make it look less ugly than it was.

"While I was married to your mother, I fell for another woman, Rosy. Your mother had just given birth to you." He commenced. "I cheated on her and I felt bad for that. I wanted to come back to her and be a good man a good father, but a few months into the relationship Rosy became pregnant with twins. Unfortunately she was not as strong as your mother is. She was ill, and she was dying. You were very little." He smiled remembering her reddish face. "I fell into a terrible dilemma. I had to choose between my family and my ailing love. I chose the latter. In a matter of a year, Rosy passed away. The twin babies died after few weeks too. I messed up my life. I missed you and your mother every second of my life when I was separated from you. And now I miss you so much. I feel I can't go on if I don't have you in my life." Tears emerged again, but this time it had found its place in Julia's eyes too.

"You abandoned me! You abandoned us." She said while the tears washed their way through the corner of her eyes. "I hate you. Go away! Go away!"

"Julia please." He pleaded, "You are the only one I have, your brothers and your sister they don't want to see me either. I don't wanna lose you too."

"You lost me the day you walked away from me." She closed her eyes, remembering the void he'd left on her life. The void of a fatherly love and tenderness. "If you leave me alone now, and never return to my life, I would understand that you had loved me all along."

Pablo felt astounded at the strange proposal. He wanted to protest but something told him that Julia won't move. He had done something for which he couldn't redeem himself no matter what he does. He slowly stood up and walked away. Just as he was about to exit the glass door, Julia opened her eyes and looked at him for one last time.

The hatred within her was alive like a stubborn inhabitant. Her hate was like a volcano, containing enough heat to melt even the mightiest of cities. Pablo doesn't deserves her forgiveness. He has never been there when she needed him. When she was sad, when she wanted to call him Dad, when she wanted to give him the goodnight kiss. No, he wasn't there and now she doesn't need him back, now is too late.

Four months after the accident, Julia was still in her mother's house. Although she'd had several plastic surgeries, she still had a network of fine scars, as well as a deeper mark on her left cheek that, the doctor had said, needed another six months before the next surgery.

She stared into the mirror in her room. No, she wouldn't be going back to modeling. Not for at least six months, or maybe even more. She didn't want to go back to Milan—she couldn't bear the thought of Ruben and her friends from the fashion world seeing her in this state. Six months—yes, she'd wait to see how her face looked after the next procedure. Maybe it was time to think of another job.

At least she'd saved her money, and by living in her mother's house she had next to no expenses. She'd picked up her old camera, just for fun, to take some shots of her sister and her mother together. Before she'd started modeling, she'd always thought maybe one day she'd be a fashion photographer.

Julia sat down and opened up her laptop. Searching for fashion photographer jobs, she saw several entry-level openings in London. Well, she'd always wanted to spend time in London. Riffling through the pile of photos of her sister, she selected the best ones—Lucila smiling in the sun, looking beautiful in some of Julia's couture clothes. Lucila with her hair whipping in the breeze, so like her older sister. Julia made an online portfolio and sent emails with the link to as many job openings as she could find.

A few hours later a magazine emailed her back. They wanted a new look for accessories spreads, and they'd like to meet her in person. Julia jumped around the room, hugging herself and smiling. She looked into the mirror again, thinking, *Nothing can keep me from starting again.* The ugly scar on her cheek seemed to mock her, but she was determined. *Nothing can stop me*—*not even you.* With a few quick strokes of the brush, she restyled her hair so that a soft curtain covered the left side of her face and hid the scar.

Downstairs, her mother was sitting on the living room sofa, reading a book.

"I want to begin a new life," announced Julia.

Her mother looked up. "What do you have in mind this time?" Her glasses slipped down her nose, and she took them off and lay them on top of the book, which she set on the table.

Julia took a deep breath. "I think I'm going to live in London for a while."

"Are you joking?" her mother asked.

"I'm serious," Julia replied.

Her mother watched her for a moment. "If you feel

that's what you want to do, and it will make you happy, then I am happy for you too."

"I knew you would be." Julia nodded. "I've been lucky to have many experiences in only a few years, and every single one, good or bad, enriches my life in some way, and helps me go to the next step in my life."

"Then London will be your next experience," her mother said. "I know you're strong, you have always been that way since you were a little girl. I'm glad you're going to take the chance to start over again in whatever you want to do."

"I've been thinking that in London I'm going to try to work in fashion photography. I'm in touch with a magazine—I sent them some of those pictures I took of Lucila—and they want to see me next week for an interview."

"But where will you live?" Her mother's mouth twisted.

"I'll rent a small flat at first, somewhere in the center. Then I'll see how things go."

For a moment her mother didn't know what to say. "I admit I'm a little confused—I didn't expect you to leave so soon." She picked up her glasses and set them down again. "London is a very expensive place to live."

"What better place to spend my money then?" Julia smiled. Maybe it wasn't her choice, but this would be her real life now. It hurt to have modeling taken away from her, but she needed to be strong. She'd already survived the accident that had devastated her body. At first she hadn't recognized her own face in the mirror—her eyes were swollen and bloodshot, every inch of her skin black and blue from the impact. She'd had casts on both arms and one leg, and bandages everywhere else. It had felt as though her whole world had crashed down. But she was alive. God had given her a second chance and she didn't want to waste even one minute of it. In six months she'd do the next surgery in London and maybe she'd have a new, normal life.

A thought of Alejandro streaked through her mind. She'd hated how he'd left her alone in Miami Beach, how he'd stayed in New York for a whole week for business while she was alone in the hospital, struggling with the pain and sadness of losing her baby. Why did it have to happen that way? Had she been blind? Could everyone else see something she couldn't; that Alejandro loved his business more than he could ever love a woman, that he would never have put her first?

I still don't understand—why didn't he tell me he was leaving for New York that morning?

Chapter Forty-One

Six months later

Julia was without doubt a courageous woman, and when she wanted something, nothing could make her change her mind. She had come to London to begin a new life, to do something that she was passionate about, something that could not only substitute the chasm of modeling, but that could fill the void of sadness in her heart. Photography had touched her soul since she was a little girt, and she had always loved watching the photographers work on her modeling shoots, sometimes even advising them, which the photographers often didn't like. *Let me do my job lady*, they thought. She'd studied photography in high school, thinking that she might go on to college. When instead she entered the modeling world, she'd made time for some short courses in studio photography between her many jobs. Many times it felt better to work and learn than to take a vacation. Her photographers in Milan had laughingly answered her questions, then, seeing her serious intent, showed her their lighting systems and how they set up shots. Julia found herself in London with a good basic knowledge of cameras and equipment, and more importantly, a natural eye for how to make women look beautiful and clothes look compelling.

At her first job, she'd loaded film and run errands without complaint, and the lead photographers had admired her work ethic and sometimes allowed her to take a few extra frames at the end of a shoot, giving her access to models and clothes that were normally beyond entry-level photographers. Soon she'd assembled a decent portfolio, and used her connections to make sure the best editors and top ad agencies saw her work. Sure, the doors had opened for Julia Belmonte, top model, but it was Julia Belmonte, up-and-coming photographer, who stepped into the offices of fashion directors and impressed them.

She became a regular photographer for Glamix, the London magazine at the forefront of style. Through them, she was invited to many events and met the movers and shakers of London fashion. Her work was becoming known for its strong artistic voice, and day by day her life was changing. She was surprised to find herself socializing even more as a photographer than she had as a model, though now, of course, it didn't matter how late she went out or what she ate.

Julia and Samantha phoned each other regularly to keep up with each other's news. Alejandro was rarely mentioned during those conversations, and whenever Samantha brought him into the conversation, Julia always made up an excuse to avoid speaking about him. She couldn't forgive him, and she had convinced herself that Alejandro was the wrong man for her, that she needed to move on and forget about him.

After the accident she had refused to feel sorry for herself. And she'd gotten used to brushing her long hair on the left side to conceal her scar. But today was the big day—six months since her last surgery. Now it was time to get rid of the ugly slash on her cheek. The thought of being beautiful again had dominated her thoughts the whole day. Being beautiful again was everything she desired, to never again be asked, "What happened to your face?" Or worse, have it whispered behind her back.

Life had always been a game to her—beauty had never been something to achieve, it was just something she had. But after the accident, as much as she hated to admit it, she wanted her face back desperately.

Sitting on the examination table, she asked, "Do you think after this surgery my face will be OK? I mean, I won't need another surgery after this?"

"I think this will be the last one," the surgeon said. "How about if you try to stay calm and try to relax now." He gestured to the nurse to bring the equipment tray.

"You make it sounds so simple," Julia said.

"I promise you, everything will be okay. Let me do this in my own way."

"Okay. I trust you."

The surgeon placed his hand on her shoulder and looked into her eyes. "After this surgery you will be even more beautiful than before," he assured her.

"Oh yes, that's what I want to hear." Julia replied, and gave him a dazzling smile.

The surgeon watched her intensely, feeling lost in her beautiful emerald eyes. Julia had been his most fascinating patient, and he longed to know her outside the examination room.

Julia held the doctor's gaze for a moment. He was an American, good-looking and tall, with an athletic body and an attractive face, perhaps thirty-five. She took a deep breath.

"Okay, let's do this."

Julia lay back on the examination table, feeling the fresh air against her skin that had been under bandages all week. The surgeon entered the room, carrying a mirror.

"Are you ready to see your new face?"

"I can't wait," Julia said, sitting up.

He held the mirror in front of her, and she turned her head slowly from side to side. Julia blushed—she looked much younger, not at all like a woman who would celebrate her twenty-sixth birthday in a month. The memory of her last birthday was so far away.

The doctor watched her reaction carefully. "After removing the scar, we passed the laser over your face to rejuvenate the skin. I hope you're good with sunscreen every day—some women find it a hassle."

Julia's eyes fixed him thoughtfully. "Not at all," she replied smoothly. She stared at her face again in the mirror. This was like a dream—better yet, like waking from a bad dream. Her skin was so fresh, smooth and soft. In the months after the accident, the first surgeries had left their own scars, and signs of the accident remained for Julia to cover with thick makeup. Now, she would be fine with sunscreen and moisturizer.

"Thank you," she said. "I feel so happy."

"I was hoping you would be happy," the surgeon said, smiling. He put one hand on her shoulder and with the other, gently held her chin, turning her face to inspect his work. His fingers brushed her neck, and Julia reached up and held his hand in place. She looked up at him and their eyes met.

In the breathless silence between them, Julia realized she was shaking. Her breath quickened, showing the state of her emotions. His eyes were watching hers, and she had no doubt what he was thinking. He leaned toward her then stopped himself. "I'm sorry—Miss Belmonte—my medical ethics—"

Julia shook her head. "It's not about ethics—you are a man, and I am a woman. And it has been so long since anyone has seen me as just a woman, not an accident victim."

He slowly pulled her into his arms, pressing his warm lips softly on her new skin, moving over the bridge of her nose and down her cheek until their lips met. She was weak beneath the force of his desire and any part of her that wanted to pull away was subdued by his passionate kiss. She had never expected something like this to happen with her doctor, but the testament to her overwhelming beauty could not be ignored.

After a moment, he pulled away. Julia fixed him with her gaze. His color rose, and he looked away for a moment.

"I am sorry," he said. "I was rude, I didn't mean to—"

"I believe that is the usual way for a doctor to say goodbye to his patients," Julia said lightly.

"I have no idea what came over me—usually I don't—" he replied, confused.

Julia smiled. She didn't believe a word, but that wasn't important. What mattered was the feeling of her compelling attraction, even stronger than before. She rose and came close to him, softly kissing him on the cheek. "Thank you. You've done a very good job."

The surgeon opened his mouth to say something, but Julia was already at the door.

Outside the clinic she walked a few blocks to find a cab. Heads turned to admire her—it felt good to be beautiful again. She didn't know why she'd responded to the doctor's kiss, why her blood raced again at the thought of a virile man's touch. But she had been reminded of how incredible it was to yield control, to feel as though she could not help her reactions. *I'd never understand that unless it had happened to me,* she thought. She didn't want to overthink it, though. She wanted to go home and admire her new look.

At home she examined herself in the mirror, with the natural light from the windows, and with the curtains drawn and the lamp on. Either way she looked incredible.

Julia felt she was going to explode from happiness.

Chapter Forty-Two

A few weeks after the surgery, Julia stood by the window of the departure gate, observing the planes coming and going on the runway while she awaited the boarding call for her flight to Tokyo. Glamix was sending her to Japan for the summer collections. Julia smiled wickedly as she thought about getting the assignment. Her colleague, Alice, had been furious.

"I've worked for this magazine more than two years, you know that?" Alice said to the photography director. "And you never sent me to Japan."

"I didn't send you because I needed you here in London," the beleaguered director said.

"That's rubbish," Alice replied. "Julia's been here less than a year, her backgrounds not even in photography, and she's getting all the good assignments."

Julia knew Alice was jealous of her talent, and at the

tremendous rate at which she'd risen through the ranks.

It was curious how she unwillingly dragged a bit of envy wherever she went. Julia also had a reputation for being aloof—she tried to stay professional, and didn't develop many relationships with colleagues. She knew people found her difficult to get close to, but that had only added to her allure.

Alice had continued to protest. "You can't send her to Japan; I have more experience than her at this magazine."

In the workroom next door, Julia overheard every word. She'd known that Alice hadn't liked her from the moment she'd arrived at Glamix, but she didn't care. Julia wasn't here to be liked. Anyway, she was tired of listening to Alice's whining, so she left the workroom and tapped on the photography director's door.

"I just wanted to say goodbye before I head out," Julia said sweetly. She ignored Alice, who rolled her eyes. The director wished her a safe trip, and Julia smiled at Alice on her way out. She felt relieved she wouldn't have to see Alice for a while. *After all, it's not my problem she didn't get the assignment,* Julia thought. *Time to focus on the trip.*

The pre-boarding call was announced, and Julia felt a little thrill. It wasn't the first time she'd been to Japan—she'd modeled in shows there many times. But this was a different story, a different role. Her life had changed so much. The gate agent continued with more information, but Julia barely heard over the many thoughts fighting in her mind. For a moment she wished she could go back in time and change the path her life had taken—but that couldn't happen. She had to admit, though, her life wasn't too bad now.

As she was combating her thoughts, a man wearing a classic dark suit appeared by her side. Julia gave him a quick look and looked away. But the man was so close to her that she could smell his aftershave. He placed his suitcase on the floor, almost touching her feet. Julia gave him a sharp look.

"Sorry about that," he said lazily.

"That's okay." Julia stepped away, and watched him run his hand casually over his hair. From his outfit, he was traveling for business. The man turned his head and smiled at her deliberately. Julia shook her head and looked away, feeling a hot blush rise into her cheeks—had he seen her checking him out? She abruptly picked up her bag, thinking she'd head to the ladies' room. *Damnit! Am I running because of him? Apparently, yes.* Then suddenly she stopped. She had forgotten for a moment that her face was normal now. Why should she run away? She didn't need to hide behind her hair anymore, either.

Relieved, Julia found herself laughing at the idea that she didn't know what she looked like any more. She looked around, hoping no one had seen her laughing at herself. It was a funny situation, she had to admit. She headed for the ladies' room, thinking to freshen her lipstick.

Once there, Julia stared at her image in the mirror for several minutes. From the day she'd come out of the bandages after surgery, she'd checked her face often, as if she couldn't have enough of it. She opened her bag and applied pink lipstick, then went back to the gate, supposing it was open by now.

Chapter Forty-Three

Julia's flight landed at Narita late at night. She grabbed a taxi to the hotel, where she unpacked and set out her camera and her clothes for the morning media event. She slept for a few hours, and was up early for the press conference. She was amazed to be surrounded by photographers and journalist from all over the world. Looking down at the press credentials hanging around her neck, she thought, *this is my new world.*

Waiting in the photographer's pen at the end of the runway that night, the start of the first show only a few minutes away, memories came flooding into Julia's head. Her modeling life—how she'd been number one on the list. Flashes began popping around her, and automatically she raised her camera and started shooting. Watching the girls on the catwalk, she couldn't believe she wasn't one of them anymore. Had she ever taken full advantage of that time? No, she'd been busy falling in love with the wrong man. Love is never like it seems to be. She felt a hot flash of anger at

Alejandro, and then caught herself wondering—*does he ever think of me?*

She turned her attention firmly back to the runway, where model after model strutted past, their hands going to their hips for poses at the end of the catwalk. Julia took shot after shot, and with each one shoved the old memories further away—Alejandro was part of the past, now. Leave him there.

After the show, she went for a late supper with the editorial staff from Glamix who were covering the shows, and some of their counterparts from other magazines. The after-dinner drinks were threatening to drag on all night as the fashion editors exchanged their thoughts on the hits and misses from the day's shows. Julia excused herself and went to get a taxi.

Twenty minutes later, she was still waiting. Millions of taxis in this city and none around when I need one.

A cab drew up to the curb. "Finally!" Julia exclaimed. She opened the back door, then stopped dead. "I'm sorry—are you getting out here?"

"You looked like you'd been waiting awhile," said a man with a British accent. "What hotel are you going to?"

Julia took a step back. "I'm fine, thank you."

The man saw her concern and smiled. "Don't be

scared, we're both from London—you're Julia Belmonte from Glamix, right?"

Julia shook her head and didn't answer, pretending to look for another taxi. But the man reached into his jacket pocket and handed her his business card.

"David Wexler. Veance."

Julia peered suspiciously into the backseat of the taxi. She'd heard Wexler's name—he'd founded the fashion magazine Veance, and this man looked like the newspaper pictures she'd seen of him.

"Come on, Julia!" he said. "I'm not a serial killer."

Julia threw him a look. "How do you know my name?"

"You work for Glamix. I always keep an eye on my competitors. I hear you're quite the rising star in editorial photography." He grinned. "I'm sure I'll be safe in your hands."

"Very funny," Julia said, but she got into the cab. It was already later than she wanted to be out, and god only knew when another cab would show up. Sitting next to David Wexler, she gave the taxi driver her hotel address. She saw Wexler looking at her curiously.

"Yes?" she inquired.

"It's good to see you in person—you look even better than your pictures."

"You too, David," Julia replied saucily.

David raised his eyebrows in surprise, then his mouth curved into a smile. "So you knew me, but you still hesitated to share a taxi?"

"Women need to be aware, even of people we already know."

David laughed. "I never knew you were so cynical."

"There is a lot about me you don't know."

Julia turned her head and looked at him frankly. She'd never liked blond men, but David's dark blond hair and brown eyes gave him a certain allure.

"I've been keeping up with your work," he said. "You're very good. I need new talent for my magazine, and I think you fit the bill."

"I have a good job at the moment," Julia pointed out. "But you know that already."

"I know. But whatever Glamix is paying you, Veance will beat."

Julia looked at him. He'd caught her attention. "I'll think about it," she said.

"I'll call you when we're both back in London."

"Well, you can do that, but as I said, I'm not looking for another job right now." Julia calculated that by seeming less-than-eager, Wexler would raise his offer even more. She'd evidently achieved a reputation that made her a good prospect for the competition, and being headhunted like this felt like a huge step toward success.

She was grateful to be successful again. After her accident it had been an uphill climb to build her life again. She was proving to herself how strong she was. In London she'd surrounded herself with important people, and worked hard to turn her life around and get it back into her hands again. Wexler's approach had proved that she was becoming well-known as a photographer, and the people who mattered were talking about her skills and her success.

And now David Wexler was asking her to work for him. How cool is that!

The taxi pulled up to Julia's hotel. Behind her, Wexler got out, too. Julia shook her head curiously as he paid the driver and let the taxi go.

He turned back to Julia and noticed her confusion. "Are you okay?"

"I'm fine," Julia said coolly.

"I'm staying in this hotel too. I forgot to tell you," David said and gave her a wink.

Julia smiled weakly.

"I was meant to go out for a few drinks with some friends," he said, "but I just realized it's too late."

"I see," Julia replied.

They walked into the hotel, where Julia collected her room key from reception. "Thank you for the lift, David. Goodnight."

David noticed as she rushed towards the elevator. "Julia—why don't we have dinner together tomorrow night and talk about the job?"

Julia held his gaze. She wasn't looking for a new emotional involvement, but the way David looked at her felt kind of good.

David spoke again. "So, the answer is yes?"

"What was the question again?" Julia teased.

"Dinner? Tomorrow night? Job?"

"Yes. I think we can do that," Julia replied casually. She gave him a slight smile.

"Great!" David found her smile irresistible sexy. Suddenly he felt that something special was going to take place between them. Although Julia seemed a bit full of herself, maybe it was just shyness with a new acquaintance. It didn't stop him from wanting to begin something between them.

David had a plan. First he'd convince Julia to work for him, and then he'd easily seduce her. When he'd first heard that the former top model was working as a photographer, he'd carefully followed the industry gossip and learned she was single. He'd never yet had the occasion to get close to her. When he'd found out she'd be going to Japan, he'd booked a room at the same hotel. He was pretty sure that once there, he could meet her through a coincidence—real or staged. And whether or not he managed to join Julia in her bed, he could certainly use a hot new photographer. *Founder of the Venace magazine, A stalker*.

Chapter Forty-Four

The Signature Quintana was about to sell another pair of massive yachts. Alejandro sat at the big boardroom table with Jack Walker and the Mohamed brothers, Qatari billionaires who wanted matching—but exclusive—yachts.

Alejandro met Jack's eyes with good humor. This Thursday morning had dragged into afternoon. They'd taken a break for lunch, and he was hoping to close the biggest deal he'd ever had before by the end of the day. The Mohamed's were the wealthiest of a long line of rich clients, but even billionaires wanted to negotiate prices before signing contracts. In fact, the billionaires were notorious negotiators.

"After all," the younger Mohamed had said, holding up his hands and smiling, "how else can we have the satisfaction of a good transaction?"

"These yachts will be built exactly to your specifications," Alejandro said. "And I can assure you that you won't see these designs around New York, or anywhere else."

"We are very pleased with the modern and unique design you have chosen," spoke the older brother, "but I still think we can go a little lower with the price."

Alejandro looked at him and smiled. "My friend, we have reached the bottom. These are the most luxurious yachts you will find anywhere in the world, and that is my best price." And as soon he said those words, the Mohamed brothers leaned close to each other and whispered something in their own mother tongue.

Alejandro sipped calmly from his coffee, as if this was merely one of many deals. He watched the two men's eyes flick over the pictures of the yachts rendered in three dimensions on the large wall screen. Alejandro was a good reader of people and had a practiced ability to seduce them with his product. He never failed to show his own immense passion for his yachts. He loved sharing the story of his ascent through the yacht-building world and the creation of The Signature Quintana. His personal bond with his clients often allowed him to turn hesitation into a successful deal.

Jack had to admire his boss as he watched Alejandro across the table, shaking his head at every price, gently pushing the buyers up until they'd arrived at the price Alejandro had wanted all along. Finally, the Mohamed's signed the contracts and wrote a large check for the deposit, then invited Alejandro out for dinner to celebrate the deal. They agreed to meet at the restaurant in a few hours.

After the Mohamed brothers were ushered out, Jack pushed his chair back and crossed a leg over his other knee. He glanced at Alejandro with admiration.

Alejandro winked at him. "It went more easily than I thought it would."

"I enjoyed watching you take control of the negotiation," Jack replied. "I don't think they knew what hit them."

"Today we've done a good deal," Alejandro said. "I hope the London meeting with the Russians will go as well."

"It'll be great," Jack said. "We've still got two weeks to work on it, but as far as I know, they're ready to buy. And after the board meeting we can hit the clubs. I have a couple of acquaintances who own some of the best."

Alejandro gave him a sharp look. "Would you mind concentrating on business first? You never change, do you?"

"Well it's a shame to go to London and not visit one of those clubs."

Here we go, Alejandro thought, *Jack and his party plans!*

He shook his head at Jack and then they both burst into laughter.

"Sounds like you're more excited for the clubs than the deal," Alejandro said.

"Oh, absolutely not, it was just an idea," Jack said, grinning. "But we can do both, business and fun."

"Business first, buddy."

Since Julia had left him, Alejandro had thrown himself into The Signature Quintana. He was more interested in doing business well than wasting his nights in clubs. He didn't want to meet any other women, and he still hoped that one day Julia could forgive him and come back. He stood up and crossed the room, where he stood staring out the window.

Jack watched Alejandro, and noticed his expression change. "You're still thinking about Julia?" Jack asked.

"It's difficult not to think of her." Alejandro continued staring out the window with his arms crossed. "Julia was that special woman that every man wishes to have by his side for the rest of his life. She made me feel happy in every sense. I can still feel her presence in the penthouse, and when I open the wardrobe and I look at her clothes I can't believe she's not with me anymore. I failed with her," he said, running his hand over his hair.

Jack walked to Alejandro and clapped his shoulder. "We all fail sometimes. But you have to keep living and enjoy your life."

Alejandro turned to Jack. "I refuse to fail. I need to find Julia and bring her back home." He lifted his chin with resolve. "After London, I'm flying to Milan. I'm going to convince Samantha to tell me everything she knows about Julia. I'll pay any price necessary for her information. The thoughts of Julia—of not having her in my life—are devouring me. It's been almost a year with no information about her. I've called her mother, I've called Samantha, I even called Ruben, and none of them wanted to tell me anything about Julia."

"You need to stop thinking about her, or you're going to go crazy."

"I can't stop thinking about her. She's in my mind every hour of every day."

Chapter Forty-Five

Back in London, Julia was seriously considering David's offer. When he'd taken her for dinner in Tokyo, David had given her a lot of career guidance. His tips made sense and he clearly knew the industry. Julia had been very pleased to hear it all—and he'd been nice company to spend time with, too.

Before turning in for the night, she'd gone through her data cards and downloaded all the photos from Japan, ready to work with. Up early the next morning, she grabbed her laptop and sunglasses and headed for the Glamix offices.

The break room was empty when she walked in at six-thirty, so she poured herself a cup of coffee and headed for the photo workroom. She almost bumped into Alice, standing in the doorway with her arms crossed and a cynical look.

"So how was Japan?" Alice asked, pushing her curly blond hair back from her face and trying to sound casual.

"Oh it was good, very good," Julia replied in the same casual tone.

"I'm sure you had fun and plenty of champagne over there?" Alice said.

Julia looked at her and didn't deign to reply. Instead, she smiled and said lightly, "I'll be in the photo workroom this morning, going through my film. I'm closing the door for some quiet, so let me know if you think you'll need anything."

Alice still stood in the doorway.

"Excuse me," Julia said pointedly, and Alice grudgingly stepped aside.

As soon as Julia was sure Alice was safely in her own office, she texted Samantha. She had to tell her best friend about Japan, about David Wexler and his job offer.

It's really appetizing and I know I could succeed there. But I'm not sure…and I think he wants more than just me working for him.

Samantha texted back right away.

Did you have fun with him in Japan?

Julia thought about her brief time with David. He was interesting-looking, and she liked his sense of humor, but, *I just can't imagine myself with a blond guy! Totally ridic!*

At that moment, her phone rang in her hand. "Samantha!"

"Hey, finally you're back. I couldn't resist calling you and hearing the whole story."

Julia smiled. Suddenly she missed her impetuous friend so much.

"So David Wexler wants me to work for Veance."

"Sounds like he wants more than that," Samantha pointed out.

"I think so," Julia replied. "But I'm not ready to start a relationship yet."

"Did he kiss you?" Samantha asked. "I'm dying to find out all the dirty details!"

"No!" Julia shook her head, laughing. "We just had dinner together. Oh, and we met for a few drinks before I flew out."

"C'mon Julia, you know, between me and you there's no secrets. Did he try to *kiss* you?"

"No, of course not! We only met twice! Well, three times if you count the taxi encounter."

"Are you going to see him again?"

"I suppose so, he lives in London and we work in the same industry."

"What's he like?"

"Well…" Julia said slowly, "He's smart, and he's funny, I would say very funny. In the last year I've never laughed so much as I did at dinner with David."

"Someone had a nice time!" Samantha teased.

"It's not what you think," Julia said. "At least not yet. And anyway, I sometimes think about Alejandro—I can't get him out of my mind."

"Have you ever thought about calling him?"

"No, of course not, I don't want to call him."

"Why not?" Samantha asked. "Alejandro still loves you. If he knew your number, he'd be calling you. You changed numbers, you blocked his email, you moved to another city, for heavens' sake, and he's still trying to reach you, even though he doesn't know anything about your life anymore!" Samantha paused, then said softly, "He never wanted to hurt you."

"And I hope you will never give him my number," Julia said.

"Well, if you think that's what you really want, then I'll keep telling him I don't know anything about your life. But—" Samantha took a deep breath "—he came to my office in Milan, and we had a long conversation about you. I didn't tell you before because you never wanted to talk about him. But I talked to him, and Julia, he is suffering so much without you."

Julia leaned back in her chair for a moment. She'd never thought Alejandro might be suffering. Suddenly she realized that for the past year, she'd only focused on her own hurt, on how much pain was in her heart after losing her baby.

"Are you still there?" Samantha asked.

"Yes."

Samantha's voice became more determined. "You need to stop blaming Alejandro for what happened. Don't forget, it was only a day or two before your miscarriage you fell on the yacht and slammed your stomach into that bench. Maybe that had something to do with it."

There was a brief silence. Julia remembered that day. She recalled the fear in Alejandro's eyes. She recalled his delicate touch. She recalled everything that bore witness to his caring nature towards her.

"He left me home alone without even telling me he was going away," Julia pointed out. "I can't believe you're taking his side."

"It's not about taking sides Julia. Don't be childish for God's sake. It's about remembering how much Alejandro loved you. He treated you like a queen. He introduced you to his family. He made a home for you. He still loves you, even though you hurt him so much when you left without even talking about it. You didn't even give him a chance to apologize! You have to think about this, Julia. Or you're going to be sorry the rest of your life that you gave up a good man for one mistake. Julia, he loves…"

"End of discussion, Samantha" Julia interrupted. She could hear the strength of Samantha's emotions, and she needed time to think about her friend's words. "I've got to go—I have a ton of work today. Speak to you soon."

"Think about it," Samantha said.

"I will, Samantha."

Julia hung up and her phone immediately beeped with a message.

Let's meet for lunch tomorrow, are you still considering my offer? x David.

Julia covered her face behind her hands and closed her eyes. What Samantha had said was ransacking her from the inside. Maybe her best friend was right—how could she leave a man who devoted himself to making her happy, who loved her and wanted to make a family with her? She picked up her phone again before realizing she'd deleted his private mobile number nearly a year ago. Instead, she threw herself into frame after frame of next summer's styles with grim determination.

After a long day she went straight home and drank a whole bottle of red wine without even pretending to make dinner. She lay in bed and tried to relax, but loneliness swept her like a wave. She remembered the sun shining on the water while she and Alejandro cruised on Biscayne Bay… Julia tried to focus her thoughts on London. She'd met great people, and in a short space of time was becoming known for her fashion photography. But at the same time, she had to admit she felt something was missing in her life. Now Alejandro had come back vividly into her mind. It was better, she realized, that she didn't have his number. The last thing she wanted was to call and show him her weakness.

Oh great, I'm the one who pushed him away, and now I want him back. What's wrong with me? I don't even want to think about my past now. She tossed and turned in her bed, remembering when she'd first met Alejandro, how she'd been deliriously in love and on top of the world. She'd felt she had found true love, LOVE with capital letters. Had she been right to run away? Well, yes—it was the only way she could have moved on. Breaking up with Alejandro had been hard, and she had suffered too, but there wasn't anything to be done about it now; it was too late. She needed to stay strong, even if it took her years to forget the past.

Unsurprisingly, Julia woke up with a bad headache the next morning, with Alejandro still playing on her mind. She was annoyed to realize that leaving him could have been the biggest mistake of her life.

What a way to start the day, she thought. After she had a bracing shower and a cup of strong coffee, she decided she'd meet David for lunch. Might as well explore the opportunity to work for the most famous fashion magazine in the world. And maybe a change of scene would help her get away from the constant reminders of Alejandro.

At lunchtime, Julia took a cab to meet David Wexler. David had booked a table at the Dewey, a chic French restaurant. Julia was amused by his choice—the restaurant was intimate and dimly lit, and David's choice showed he was obviously flirting with her.

David studied Julia from his table as she walked into Dewey. She wore a white pencil skirt, high heels, and a casual, electric-blue jacket. Her long hair was swept into a ponytail and silver earrings completed her outfit. She still possessed a model's seductive walk, and her emerald eyes flashed in the restaurant's flattering light.

David stood up to greet her. "Thanks for coming," he said, moving forward to kiss her cheek. Julia forestalled him with a brief, formal hug.

"How are you, David?" she asked as she sat down.

"I'm good, very busy with the next issue, but that's always the case. Have you given any thought to coming to Veance?" he asked.

"Yes, I've considered it. But it depends on how interesting your offer is," Julia replied. She'd decided she wanted this job, but it was still much smarter to play hard to get.

David looked at her thoughtfully. "I want you on my team, and I can pay you double whatever Glamix is paying you now. Do you find that interesting?"

"Interesting enough to think about it and let you know." It was an excellent offer—but for some reason she still didn't trust David a hundred percent. "Why don't you send me a copy of the contract?"

"Sure." David said. "You don't trust anyone, do you?"

Julia shrugged. "I need to see the contract first."

"What are you making at Glamix—entry-level plus twenty percent? We'll pay you what you're worth, and Veance is the biggest magazine in the industry. This is too important an offer for you to screw up," David pointed out.

"We will see," Julia replied. She disliked being pressured. Of course she didn't want to miss out on a terrific offer, but before she agreed she needed to see it all in writing. And of course she didn't want to seem desperate to grasp at the next job. Not to mention David was definitely flirting with her, which could make things awkward in the office. Julia had experienced that situation before and she wasn't eager to go back. But if he was set on flirting, that was his lookout. Because David was nothing more than a good business deal for her.

Chapter Forty-Six

David's contract came by courier the next day, and Julia locked the workroom door and looked it over. It was two and a half times what she was earning at Glamix. It would only be a terrible mistake not to accept the offer.

Julia made him wait a week before she agreed to the terms, and David sounded as though he was jumping out of his skin. His happiness was not so subtle when he almost yelled in excitement when she told her about her decision.

"Welcome aboard." He said, "We should have dinner to celebrate."

"Sure," Julia replied. She didn't care much if David fell for her or not. She was sure she could manage him. Since she'd arrived in London she'd been asked out many times. She had given them a cold heart, rejecting their proposal blatantly. David was more interesting, but she still suspected it would be more or less the same.

"I'll book a table for tonight," he said.

"Sounds good," Julia replied.

The rest of the day passed quickly. The good thing about being in London was that she was always busy doing something. By the time she made it home, David had texted to say he'd pick her up at eight. She glanced at the time—it was already six. She rushed through a shower, brushed her hair and polished her nails bright red. Outside, December was creeping in and winter lingered in the air. She chose a black cashmere above-the-knee dress, black patent heels, and a light jacket. At eight sharp, David called to say he was waiting downstairs.

Julia went down and joined David in the car. He'd booked an Italian restaurant, he told her. "I hope that was a good choice?"

"Doesn't everyone love Italian food?" Julia said, a little sarcastically. "Of course that's a good choice."

"I'm glad we're meeting tonight," he said. "I have good news for you already."

"Oh really?"

"We're flying to Milan Thursday morning."

Julia looked at him. "Why didn't you tell me this when we talked earlier today?"

David brushed off her concerns. "I just found out

this afternoon. Anyway, we needed a photographer there, it's a great assignment to get you into the swing of things at Veance, and the tickets are booked, so we're good to go."

"*We?*" Julia stared at him.

"I need you there. And who better than you? You're very familiar with how things work in Milan," he added.

Julia wouldn't have chosen to go back to Milan now—for Veance or for anything else. But it had been a year—it was time to be strong and manage her emotions. She smiled coolly. "Why not? Sure, I'll go."

"Great!" David said. "I'm looking forward to visiting Milan with someone who knows the places as well as you do."

Here we go, Julia thought. *Now he wants me to spent time with him over there instead of focusing on my work.* "I'll see what I can do about that," she said, not happy at the idea of having David around in Milan.

A few days later, Julia walked into the Glamix offices to pick up the last of her stuff. As she filled up a box, the photography director came into the workroom.

"I miss having you here already," he said, putting his hand on her box of papers. "You know, I'm not supposed to miss employees who leave the magazine, especially when they go to work for the competition, but I do miss your smile around the office."

Julia placed her hand on his arm. "I can't thank you enough for everything you've done for me."

"I haven't done anything special," he said. "All I did was to give you the opportunity—your hard work made the most of it, and you've got talent. I'm honored I got to work with you."

"It was a pleasure for me, too," Julia said. "I'll see you around," she added, and picked up her box. As she walked toward the door, she saw Alice at her desk, watching Julia leave.

Julia stopped for a second, then approached Alice. She put a hand on Alice's shoulder and looked her in the eye. "I've always admired you as a colleague, and I think your work is really important to Glamix."

Alice was astonished—she couldn't figure Julia out. She'd pegged the upstart photographer as a conniving bitch, trying to edge Alice out of her own position. Maybe she'd misjudged Julia—maybe she was just a smart, confident woman who knew what she wanted and was willing to take some risks to get it. Alice realized she'd envied Julia without really getting to know her story. Maybe that had been a mistake… She smiled at Julia, "Thanks. Good luck."

Minutes later Julia was in a cab, planning how she'd

surprise Samantha in Milan. She hadn't said a word to her friend about the trip—she wanted to see Samantha's face when she showed up! They had so much to talk about. And it had been awhile since she'd gone out with a good friend for some fun. Yes, that was exactly what she needed—her best friend and some fun.

Chapter Forty-Seven

Wednesday morning, Alejandro and Jack left the VIP area at Heathrow and settled into a car to head to the hotel.

"I think we could open a branch in the South of France this year. We're doing a lot of deals with people who want to dock there; why not take the business to them?" Jack suggested.

"We have two Mediterranean offices already and I think it's enough for now," Alejandro said, barely looking at him. "But maybe we can open one in Spain instead."

"Sounds good." Jack thought of the attractions of Ibiza…or Marbella…beautiful tanned girls…dance clubs.

Alejandro looked over and saw Jack with his eyes closed and a look of bliss on his face. He tapped Jack's shoulder. "Sorry to interrupt your fantasies, Jack, but we're at the hotel."

The car pulled up in front of a luxurious hotel.

"There's everything here," Alejandro said. "Spa, restaurants, pool, and an amazing sky bar."

"Great!" Jack said. He got out of the car with Alejandro and they looked at the beautiful building. Porters appeared to take their luggage, and the driver tipped his cap respectfully and drove off. Jack sighed. "I can get a massage before the afternoon meeting."

Alejandro smiled at him. "You can do whatever you want; there's plenty of time before the meeting." He'd come to this hotel many times, and he appreciated its elegance and luxury.

At two o'clock sharp the meeting with the Russian buyers took place. They had many questions, which Alejandro patiently answered with good humor and charm. Eventually, his explanations satisfied the oil magnate and his attorneys, and they were able to mutually approve and sign a contract. At the end of the meeting, all the men walked out happy—the Russian with his top-of-the-line The Signature Quintana yacht, the attorneys with their no-doubt hefty fees for the negotiations, Jack at the prospect of the sky bar, and Alejandro that the deal was closed and now he could take off to Milan to find Samantha, and through her, Julia.

He wondered, suddenly, *what if she was seeing someone else? What if she'd gotten married, even?* A year was a long time, anything could have happened...

Thoughts swirled in his brain. He didn't want to even imagine these things before going to Milan. Somehow, some way, he would make Samantha see how important it was that he be able to see Julia. He knew she didn't want to betray her friend, and that was an admirable quality. *But this time I will stay there until I convince her to tell me where she is.*

He would fly to Milan tomorrow morning. He paced the lobby, willing the time to move faster. Impatiently, he punched Samantha's number on his phone. There was no answer, whether she was busy or just wasn't taking his calls. He didn't leave a message. It didn't matter. Tomorrow he would talk to her in person.

Chapter Forty-Eight

As his cab pulled up at the airport, Alejandro was gripped with a strange feeling in his gut —something was about to happen. He'd felt this way the morning of his first big yacht sale, and the morning he'd decide he was ready to propose to Julia, but also on the day his grandfather had died. Something was going to happen—and there was no guarantee it would be good. Maybe Samantha would keep Julia's secret forever; maybe he'd never find his love again.

The car pulled up at the entrance to the private plane terminal, just as Alejandro realized he'd dressed so hurriedly this morning that he'd left his aftershave in the bathroom of his hotel room. Instinctively checking the time, his bare wrist showed he'd also left his watch by the sink.

"Driver, take me over to the main terminal—I need to visit the Duty Free." As the driver took him to the other side of the airport, Alejandro texted Jack to check with the reception about his watch. He smiled—Jack might still be sleeping; he'd stayed out late last night and planned to have another three nights in London to enjoy the clubs. Alejandro had no need to argue with him—he had other, more important things on his mind.

As he walked through the terminal, a voice over the loudspeaker announced that the next flight to Milan was delayed by an hour. Alejandro smiled. *Thank god I can decide to leave whenever I want.* His own jet was a regional, so he and Jack had flown first class to London, but he'd had the hotel arrange a private flight for the journey to Milan.

Julia knew she was keeping David waiting while she decided which one of the new winter fragrances to buy, but the man had invited himself along when he wasn't needed, so he could very well practice patience while she shopped.

Vaguely, she registered the loudspeaker saying something blurry about a flight delay.

"Dammit!" David said, "that's our flight."

Julia smiled calmly and went back to smelling perfumes.

David had evidently reached the end of his patience. "I'm going to check the monitors; I didn't catch how long it's been delayed."

"Mmm, okay," Julia replied, picking up another bottle of perfume.

Outside the Duty Free, David stood before the bank of monitors, scanning for their departure, when he heard a familiar voice.

"David Wexler! What a surprise!"

David turned to see who had called his name. "Alejandro Quintana! The surprise is all mine!"

The men shook hands. Neither of them realizing what a peculiar coincidence they just fell into. David and Alejandro had been acquaintance back when both of them were nobodies. Later as they dug deeper towards their spate goals, the contact broke and they barely met or spoke to each other.

David regarded Alejandro with content. "I can't believe it—after so many years you haven't changed a bit."

"Neither have you, my friend." Alejandro smiled.

"What were you doing in London?" David inquired.

"Oh, I'm still in the boat business," Alejandro replied. "What about you, what's new in your life? Remember the last time we saw each other? You were full of big plans for your new magazine."

"I was indeed." David clapped Alejandro's shoulder. "Now Veance is doing over a million copies a month."

"That's wonderful," Alejandro replied.

"Thank you," David said. "Next time you come to London, let me know, we'll get together."

"I will." Suddenly, Alejandro stared past David. His smile faded away and was replaced by a frown. He felt his hair stand at their end. His skin turned pale and cold. He looked at the distinctive apparition of someone with whom he had shared a beautiful life. A probable ghost was advancing towards them with an equal state of confusion. Julia emerged from the shadows, stealing the breath and the heat from his skin. Suddenly his defenses were just paper, paper that was soaked by the rapidly falling briny drops. He could feel her slender body and the heart that beats within.

David turned to see what had shocked Alejandro so much, and saw Julia emerging from the Duty Free. "That woman is a piece of work," he said, and winked at Alejandro. "Julia, come over here! I want to introduce you to one of my oldest friends. We haven't seen each other since college. This is Alejandro Quintana, and he's one of the richest men in New York."

Julia stopped dead and her face went white with shock. She felt as if she was struck by a thunderbolt. She stood numb beside David who had a wide smile on his face.

David put an arm around her waist. "Alejandro, let me introduce Julia Belmonte, the best fashion photographer in London."

Alejandro felt as if his heart had stopped. *How could this be possible?* His eyes were fixed on Julia, and he stammered, "I...I had the pleasure of meeting Julia some time ago."

"Oh?" David said curiously. "So you know each other?" He looked back and forth between Alejandro and Julia.

Julia was in shock, and now her face blushed pink. Finally she looked into Alejandro's deep blue eyes. She had forgotten how handsome he was. Her stomach fluttered and feelings rushed back into her mind. *My love for him has never changed. Maybe life is giving me a second chance.*

He looked disheveled. His eyes had sunken and his hairs were unkempt. The cheerful aura which he carried around him seemed to have abandoned him. Samantha was right. He was suffering. He looked at her with his placid eyes, as if telling her something which she had failed to realize all these time. *How could you forget that I lost a baby too*? In her rage and battle with her fate, she forgot that Alejandro lost someone too. The baby was as much his as it was hers. She recalled how he'd begged for her to stay back and make things work, but she paid no heeds to him. She ran away from the suffering, and left him behind. She left him in the same house in which they had created so many memories. He was the one who would have to wake every morning and expect her to be by his side on his bed. He was the one who would have mistakenly made two cups of coffee instead of one. She wondered if it really was him who she should have hated all these time, or if it was herself.

"Yes," she said. "We know each other. How are you, Alejandro?"

"I am well," Alejandro said, looking at her searchingly. She was even more beautiful than before. The immense love of his life was before his eyes, but now she belonged to David. He could do nothing to change this. It was too late. He willed his tongue to work again. "It was a pleasure to renew our acquaintance, but I should go now. My plane is waiting."

"It was good to see you again," David replied. "Let me know when you're back in London."

David was speaking, but Alejandro couldn't hear him. It was as if he was at the other end of a vast tunnel. Nothing in his entire life had been as painful as this moment. He had found Julia only to lose her again, to lose the most beautiful love he'd ever had. This past year, he had lost himself, too, many nights wandering sleepless through the empty house, no longer filled with Julia's laughter and their happiness together. He'd been unable to move on, to pass through the worst time of his life, and now he had seen a glimmer of hope—and it was too late. He was losing her forever.

Julia watched Alejandro walk away, so preoccupied he was nearly bumping into people. Meeting him again had brought everything back, all their time spent together. The way he made love to her, the way he stroked her hair before she went to sleep, their promises to each other of forever love. She had never stopped loving him. She didn't want to admit it, but it was the truth.

The loudspeaker broke into her thoughts.

"Julia," David said as he clapped his hand on her arm. "It's time to go."

"Seriously!?" Julia said. She'd hated the way he put his hand around her waist in front of Alejandro. Was David trying to mark her as his property?

"Yes, seriously, we have thirty minutes to get to the plane."

Julia looked at him and hesitated. Why was David holding her arm so tightly? And what was the deal with him acting like they were a couple when he introduced her to Alejandro? A flash of realization settled to her clouded mind. David was trying to buy her, trying to flatter and intimidate her into being with him. And Alejandro was running away because he thought she was with David. That was why he'd walked away, that was why he was upset.

"Let's go," David said.

Julia threw him a look. "You go."

"What are you saying?" David laughed ironically.

Suddenly Julia hated his laugh more than any sound on earth. She raised an eyebrow and looked steadily at him.

"I changed my plans," she said coolly. She picked up her bag and stepped back. "See you, David. Or not. I don't think I care either way."

Julia took two steps, then stopped and turned back. "Oh, and David? I quit."

"Wait a minute, where do you think…" Julia was gone before he could protest. He followed her through the crowd.

She ran, muttering hurried "excuse me's" as she desperately sought Alejandro. She caught a glimpse of a tall, dark man in an elegant suit at the bar, and she grabbed his arm. "Alejandro!"

The man turned in surprised, and she gasped and pulled back her hand. The man was indeed good looking, but he was not Alejandro. "I'm sorry, I thought…" She couldn't finish the sentence, but backed away, turning to walk back through the terminal in confusion and disappointment. She had lost him. David advanced towards her. She was utterly unaware of his, or anyone else's, presence. All she wanted to have was one man. Alejandro. She wanted him back.

Julia craned her neck, trying to see where he could be, her eyes filling with tears. Could she ask security to stop his plane? No, that was the sort of ridiculous thing that only happened in movies. With her luck, they'd think it was some kind of threat and she'd get arrested.

Julia sighed, her shoulders drooping. She realized she was a mess of tears and flushed from running. She didn't really care, but at least the ladies room would be a place to hide…

As she walked toward the restrooms, he stepped out of the men's room. *Alejandro.* He walked hastily towards the end of the terminal. Julia dropped her bag and broke into a run, calling his name. "Alejandro! Alejandro!"

He turned and joy lit his face. She fell into his arms, crying.

"Don't leave, please." Julia gasped between tears. "I need to talk to you."

Alejandro felt her arms around his body.

"Julia!" Yelled David from a distance. "You can't go with him. He is not the right man for you." He said approaching the embracing couple.

He tried to reach for her hand but Julia shook him off. Alejandro let go off her, barely understanding what was going on.

"Leave me alone." Julia protested, "You don't know

anything about me and Alejandro."

David turned his attention towards the puzzled looking man, "I am sorry Alejandro, but Julia was on my list from a very long time. Trust me; I am doing you a favor. Julia is not good for you. And after her 'good fame' in London, I don't think you'll want her back either. I've known about you all along Miss Julia Belmonte, or should I call you Miss. Quintana."

Julia eyes stretched wide in bewilderment, "Have you been stalking me?"

"I am a journalist Julia. A journalist has a habit of prying into private lives. In a way, I know more about you than my friend here know."

"What the hell are you saying!?" She yelled and then turned to Alejandro, "Don't believe in a word he is saying. He is just inventing stories to build a barrier between us. You know he is a liar."

Alejandro stood still as the two being fought in front of him. He stood still, devoid of words. Confusion clouded his mind. He could no longer think straight.

"Let's go Julia. Alejandro will never take you back anyway." David said looking at Alejandro. "We have a plane to catch."

Julia expected Alejandro to say something, but he maintained his composure.

"Alejandro please don't believe him." Julia protested, "Please. I need to explain about everything that happened in all these time I was away from you."

"There is nothing to explain." Alejandro broke his silence finally. The words shot at Julia's heart like a poisoned arrow. Her spirit shattered in a thousand pieces. Alejandro escaped her gaze in disappointment.

David grabbed her hand, pulling her towards him gently while Alejandro looked away. The ground beneath Julia's feet seemed to break apart, paving an imminent void that engulfed her hope, her sanity.

David whispered into her ears, "Let's go Julia. Alejandro is not worthy. Trust me. You don't know him. You'll never be the only woman in his life. Why do you think he let you go so easily? You have nothing to lose if you come with me."

Alejandro heard David's words and turned his gaze to Julia, he noticed the pain in her damp eyes. A strong thought crossed his mind. His senses resettled in their place. His mind started making sense. *How could he do what he just did? How could he ever doubt Julia's loyalty*? Trust is the foundation of any relationship. David was just making up stupid stories just to take her away from him. He knew in an instant, that he could never make such a huge error in judging Julia. She was his, and she will be his for eternity. How dare David do this to him. Alejandro headed towards David as he carried Julia away. His temples were filled with rage. Before David could realize, a pounding fist crashed at his head and he felt the daylights out of his senses. Alejandro freed Julia from his grasp and took her by his side. "Son of a bitch. Julia is my wife, you don't know anything about our story. You just invent your bullshit fantasy pretending to know everything. Get out of here before I call the police and let them know your real story."

"Julia is mine." Alejandro said. His intent eyes gazing at David. He tried to counteract, but his mind said otherwise. Alejandro stood before Julia like an impregnable wall. David watched as Julia tore apart her boarding pass into pieces.

He scoffed at them and walked away, dissolving among the random people.

Alejandro took Julia by hand and they walked towards the terminal where his private jet was awaiting for him.

"Are you okay?" he asked.

"Yes, I am fine." she replied in a soft voice.

Alejandro cupped her face and kissed her forehead. His eyes met hers, he hugged her, she felt his heart beating into his chest, he kissed her and suddenly the noise and bustle of the airport vanished and there was nothing in the world but their two bodies against each other. Alejandro's words filled her mind with a mesmerizing scent. *Julia is my wife.*

"I am sorry. I doubted our love," he said. "I thought I lost you forever."

"I thought I lost you too," she replied.

"This is incredible, I finally found you, and I was searching for you so much. Nobody wanted to tell me nothing about where you were. I was calling your mum so many times; I went to Italy to speak with Samantha in case she knew something about you. I even asked Ruben.... Nobody wanted to help me. I didn't know where to look for you." Alejandro said. He took her face in his hands. "Please—promise you won't leave me ever again."

"I promise, I promise," she said through her tears. "I love you. I thought I had stopped, but I couldn't—"

Alejandro wanted nothing more than to kiss her soft lips again and touch her sweet body. He gently wiped her tears. "I never stopped loving you. *Ti amo da impazzire amore mio.*" He kissed her tenderly, and then passionately, her tears running over their lips.

"I missed you so much," she said.

"I missed you, too." He held her close to his chest, and she felt the security she believed she had lost forever. She rested her head on his shoulder as they embraced. He gently took her hand. "I feel like I can be happy again," he said. "We've wasted all this time far away from each other, when we could be happy instead."

Julia looked deeply into his eyes. Alejandro was the man of her dreams, the love of her life. How wrong she was for leaving him. And if she hadn't left—there would have been no accident, no surgery, no changes in her life. And yet, she'd also left behind the girl she was to become the woman she was now, the woman ready to be with the man she loved, for better or for worse. No, she could never take back the lost time, but neither would she mourn it.

EPILOGUE

One year later

Julia stood backstage; nervous in a way she'd never been when she walked the catwalk herself. Her designs were about to be seen by the cream of society, not to mention the press. And while modeling in New York had been fun for a little while, she'd thrown herself into the challenge of her new career as a designer.

Beside her, Alejandro squeezed her hand. "It will be perfect, amore," he said into her ear.

She squeezed back, grateful for his comfort. He'd been incredibly supportive of her long hours and late nights putting this collection together. She looked at his face, half-shadowed in the backstage lights. *How could I ever have ended a relationship with this man?* Then again, she realized, maybe it took the two of them falling apart to realize how much they needed each other. She'd felt lost behind the shadow of her pain, and hadn't appreciated the person who loved her. Losing the love of her life, too, had been a regrettable mistake. But one she'd learned from, and he had, too—they'd sworn never to be parted again. Whatever problems they had, whatever arguments, any issue would be solved better with two and the pain would be lessened by sharing it. They'd never again abandon the one they loved, no matter what happens.

Julia watched the models step out onto the runway, where they were greeted with thunderous applause from the very first look. She gasped with astonishment.

"Are you surprised, my darling?" asked Alejandro. "I'm not—I knew it would be a triumph."

Julia laughed and kissed him. She had another surprise for him after the show. She ran her hand over her stomach, imagining she could already feel the baby boy kicking. Alejandro would get to design the baby's room, and she was glad to yield to him in that. Now her love story was truly a fairy tale.

Alejandro gave her a gentle push, and she realized it was time to walk the runway herself with the line of models. The crowd rose to their feet, blurring into a mass of noise and flashbulbs as Julia's thoughts flew back over the past year. She'd never imagined that during their break, she'd realize Alejandro's importance to her. *More than anything,* she thought, *I've learned I have to be strong enough to confront my problems instead of giving up and running away. I've learned that sometimes love feels wrong when it's right...*

At the end of the runway, Alejandro's face was filled with pride as she walked toward him and toward their life. They'd nearly missed their opportunity, and now she was filled with happiness that she hadn't missed the love of her life.

About the Author

Years ago Elena Marica left Italy and moved to London, a place that deeply influenced the writing of her first novel, The Truth Behind the Shadow.

Since she moved to London, she was writing and kept waiting for the perfect time in her life to publish her book, but then she realized that perfect time would never really present itself. It's never the perfect time to take the courage and put out your first novel. Now at the insistence of her friend, she decided to just go for it! She's currently working on her second book.

When she is not writing, you will find her enjoying doing sport, traveling across Europe and long walks by the sea.

To find out more about Elena follow her on Facebook: *Elena Marica - fiction author.*

Printed in Great Britain
by Amazon